The Fall of America

CALL SIGN COPPERHEAD

(RUSSIAN REVENGE)

Book 6

WR BENTON

LOOSE CANNON ENTERPRISES
Paradise, CA

Ingram Edition
ISBN 978-1-944476-70-0

Author Photo © Copyright 2017, by W. R. Benton, LLC
Cover layout and other images © Copyright 2017 by WR Benton, LLC
Edited by: Daniel Williams, Bobbie La Cour, and Kay King
Logo fonts [*Shortcut, Dirty Ego*] by Eduardo Recife,
misprintedtype.com
Rear cover snake image: Agkistrodon contortrix by Haplochromis

www.loose-cannon.com

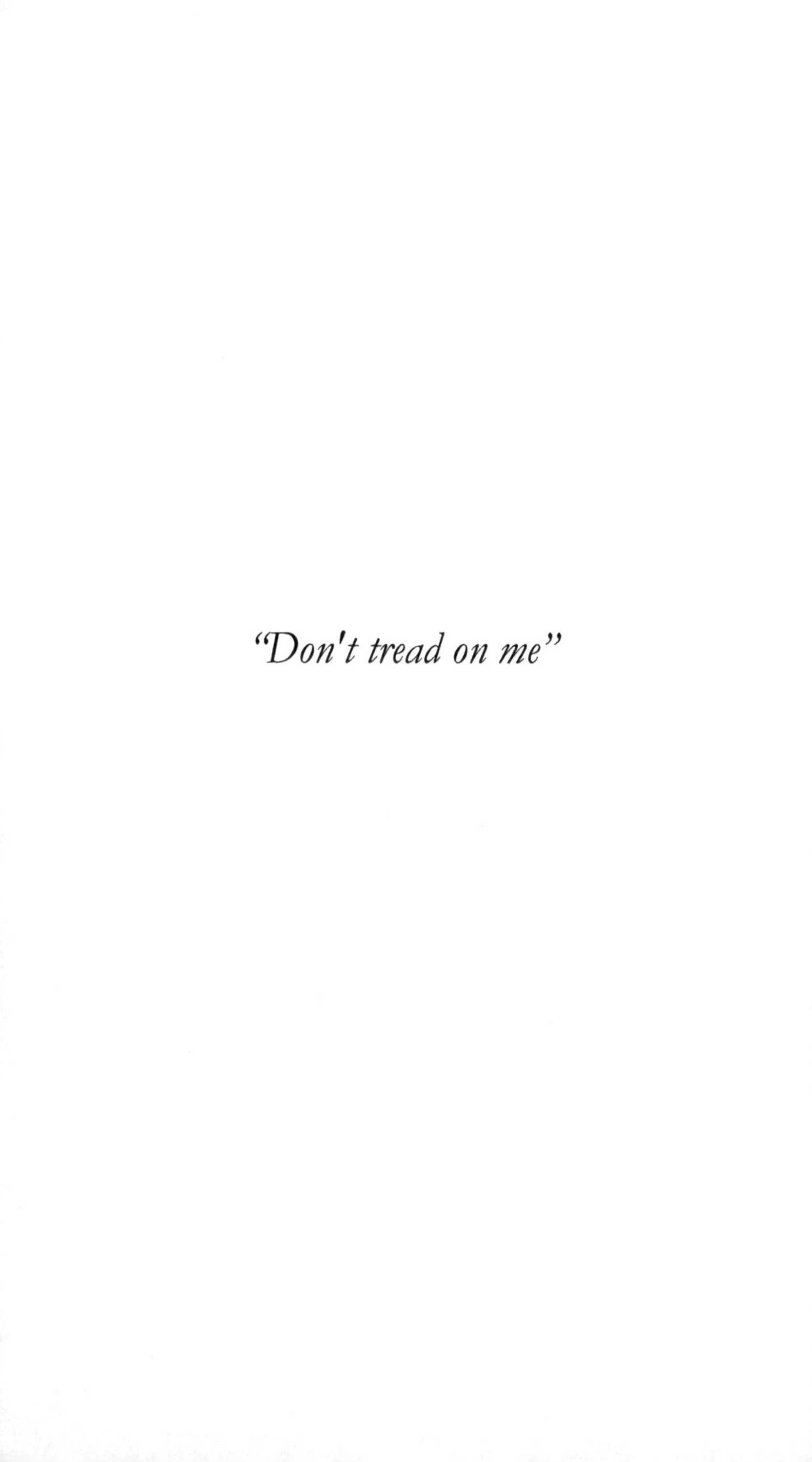

"Don't tread on me"

<u>Sci-Fi Books by W. R. Benton</u>

New World Order, California Invasion, Volume 2

New World Order, 666, Mark of the Beast, Volume 1

Eagle People, Snake People

Eagle People, The Year 2414

The Fall of America, Book 6, Call Sign Copperhead

The Fall of America, Book 5, Fallout

The Fall of America, Book 4, Winter Ops

The Fall of America, Book 3, Enemy Within — Also available as Audio Edition

The Fall of America, Book 2, Fatal Encounters — Also available as Audio Edition

The Fall of America: Book 1, Premonition of Death — Also available as Audio Edition

Visit http://www.amazon.com/author/wrbenton/
for more WR Benton titles.

DEDICATIONS

To all patriotic Americans, may we never have to fight in our streets for what we now have and few appreciate.

To all my fellow veterans; I salute you, and may God bless each of you.

What is the series "The Fall of America" about?

It started with the biggest stock market crash in history. Banks closed down under the weight of their bogus investments, and the financial sector failed. People looked to the government to make it all better. However, they couldn't. Hyper-inflation, mass unemployment and infrastructure started to breakdown. The food trucks didn't show up at the stores, and the shelves went empty.

Things turned ugly fast when there was no power for long parts of the day—then forever. Cops, doctors, and trash collectors just stopped showing up for work when the paychecks were delayed too often, or never came. Things started falling apart quickly after that. Whole regions declared a "State of Emergency" in an effort to maintain order and civility, but it wasn't always enough. Starvation, looting and murder became the norm. Then, our American civilization collapsed completely.

The Fall of America, Book 1: Premonition of Death is the beginning of a new series, about an average man whose life goes downhill fast once society breaks down. Set in the rural south, a scorched-earth showdown with some local thugs leaves John and his wife homeless and on the run. He encounters a member of a survivalist group, made up of former military personnel, and joining them may be his only hope. Just basic survival becomes vicious and resistance is at any cost, as the devastated country comes under a new siege—invading Russian troops.

The Fall of America, Book 2: Fatal Encounters is the continuing saga of the fall. John and his friends come face to face with Russian troops, but unlike the first book, this time they're ready and able to offer much more resistance. Russian invaders try to pacify the areas of the South under their control. The American resistance groups divide their forces into small cells to better operate effectively behind enemy lines. But as their efforts begin to gain ground, the Russians respond with harsh reprisals; mass executions become the norm and prison camps soon spring up in remote small towns. "Fear brings compliance," is their motto. The battle for control of Mississippi gets hot, and a violent world gets even more ugly.

The Fall of America, Book 3: Enemy Within. Things are turning more organized by the partisans and with this organization comes larger attacks on Russian targets, which results in more Americans killed in reprisals. As the partisans become better organized, the Russians become more sadistic. The Americans are now attacking gulags and air bases when the opportunity arises and Russian casualties mount, but there is at least one traitor or more within the partisans. Can the Americans discover the enemy within?

The Fall of America, Book 4: Winter Operations. The partisans turn mean after ambushing a Russian convoy and discovering cases of the 9K32 Strela-2M missiles, or as the Russians call them, arrows. The missiles soon change how the partisans operate; they are a portable, shoulder-fired, low-altitude surface-to-air missile system with a highly explosive warhead. They have an infrared guidance system. Soon the partisans are attacking Air Bases and shooting down random helicopters using the missiles and Moscow is not pleased. However, it is the discovery of two nuclear weapons, called suitcase bombs, by the Russians, that is about to change this war in ways that have never been considered. Which side will use the nuclear weapons first?

The Fall of America, Book 5: Fallout. First they used chemical weapons on the Americans, then the Russians set off a tactical nuclear bomb in an effort to destroy a suitcase nuke captured by the rebels. Deadly radioactive fallout now adds to the already fierce battle to reclaim the U.S.A. and the partisans have even less to lose. Now the rebels must decide whether to strike back in kind—an eye for an eye? In what may be a one-way mission, John's partisan team volunteers to pick up the gauntlet. Armed with a stolen suitcase nuke, the partisans try to carry the device deep inside enemy controlled land to reach their target. At first they don't realize that to strike the Russians they'll need to vaporize thousands of Americans too. Is this something he can do for the cause with a clear conscience, and then live with the consequences?

A Word from the Author

I am growing concerned with the number of police officers being intentionally gunned down on duty protecting us these days and in many ways, it's frightening. My father was a small town cop for a few years back in the late 1950's, and then moved on to other things. It's a hard job that requires split second life and death decisions, and there is no room for error. I've watched videos of police officers killing people in the news, and I see a couple of things in common in most of the situations; the victim either resisted arrest or in some cases physically attacked the officer. In almost every situation the victim verbally attacked the officer. Now, imagine you're a cop on a dark street and confront a possible killer or rapist. You are alone and your split second decision must determine if the man is a risk to society or not. If you make the wrong decision one of you may not go home that night.

Now, seems to me if you have any respect for the law, you will obey the officer when he stops you and do only as instructed. Additionally, that is not the time to be running your mouth, but to be following orders, and to the letter. I fear that one day our officers will have enough and walk off the job. I know I couldn't do the job, because I'd not last a day before I'd be in jail or fired. If you want to imagine America without law on the streets, read this series, because the only law in these books is what can be enforced with a gun.

This series is based on what I consider the political reasons America will one day fall. One of our biggest issues to date is finances; as a nation we continue to write checks without money in the bank, and we borrow, borrow and borrow. We send billions to our enemies, but why? Even kids know you can't buy friends. Don't believe me? Look at our national deficit, then. Even our nation's credit rating has fallen, which has never happened to this country before in history. Why are we trying to care for all peoples of the world? I'm a compassionate man, but there is a limit to our financial ability to assist others in the world, especially when we have our own people, Americans, who are poor and hungry. Help Americans first, then others if we can do so financially. I think we should pay our bills as a nation before we help any overseas charity or group, especially those who openly dislike us.

I'd just like to see the money paid to Iran over the last couple of years go to our veterans or elderly. All of them are more deserving of assistance than a nation that hates us and would love to see America fall flat on her butt. Some of the millions being spent on some really stupid research could be used to assist our first responders and police officers or their surviving families. Our men and women in blue were murdered in unheard of numbers last year alone, and it tells me a great deal about the decay of our society. It indicates a complete disregard by many younger Americans for any respect for authority. But, it's not just this generation, because each generation has their bad apples.

There have also been some negative comments from a few readers about God being in this series. I honestly don't think God comes up very often, but that's me. I suspect, like in a real war, when the shooting starts there are no atheists in foxholes. I could be wrong, but I do know that mankind is psychologically programmed to believe in a higher power whether He is God, Buddha, the Great Creator, or whatever you wish to call Him. When things turn to hell most Americans, I've seen, turn to God. You don't need to believe me; just watch how other people react when something bad happens to them. I've seen many folks who openly deny God, then when they end up in trouble, they cry out for His help.

Originally, I was going to title this book, *"Russian Revenge,"* but changed the name after I was about halfway through with the writing. Grab your favorite drink, find a comfortable chair, and open *"Fall of America, Call Sign Copperhead, Book 6."*

W. R. Benton
Jackson, Mississippi
26 January 2017

BOOK 6

CALL SIGN COPPERHEAD

CHAPTER 1

When I next opened my eyes I was in a bed, but the room was dark and I appeared to be alone. I heard no one, smelled nothing, and saw very little. I hurt all over and felt so tired, then my mind suddenly flooded with thoughts of my last mission. My heart gave a flutter as I thought of Carol and I tried to get out of bed, only to find myself wired to machines I'd not noticed, and an IV stuck in my arm. I flopped back down and called out, "Can anyone hear me?"

Silence.

I glanced at the machines I was plugged into and saw all the text was in Chinese. Then I remembered the Chinese crews had inserted and recovered us from the mission. I finally located the heart monitor, then traced the wires to my chest and pulled them off. The machine suddenly gave a loud warbling noise to indicate I had no heartbeat.

By God, if anyone is around, they'll be here soon, I thought just as a young woman ran in, and her eyes clearly showed she expected to find me dead.

"Are . . . are you okay, Colonel?" she asked.

Seconds later a smaller woman, Asian, entered the room and they began talking, but it was mostly in low whispers which made me more than just a bit concerned about my medical condition.

I placed the wires back on my chest, the machine grew quiet, and I asked, "What happened to the woman who was on the mission with me and returned injured? And, why all the whispering?"

"She's in the next room. She's recovering, just like you're to be doing and the doctor said she'll be fine, unless she gets an infection. She's weak and tired. Now, lay back down, because it's time for you to get morphine. The whispers were because we didn't want to wake the other patients." She moved toward my side and slipped a needle into the IV line.

"When you get the time, have someone get Top for me. Do you know him?"

She smiled and said, "Everyone knows Top. Sure, let me finish my rounds and I'll send for him."

As soon as they left, the morphine hit me, and hard, which made me sleep.

I have no idea if I'd been asleep for hours or just minutes when I heard a male voice ask, "You gonna sleep all day?"

It took effort just to open my eyes, but when I did, I was looking at Top.

"Feel a little sleepy this day, so I thought I'd catch a nap. Where am I?"

"Well," Top said, grinned, and then added, "You're not in Mississippi, but in Louisiana. You and Carol needed some medial treatment that we didn't have at home base."

"How is she?"

"She'll live and so will you. I thought both of you would die, to be honest, but the Chinese doctors are good, real good. I think you're lucky, because the bullet missed your spine and struck you high on the left side. Your main problem was all the blood you lost before getting the last injury."

"Uh, did the bomb detonate?"

"Yes, it did, and the cities of Jackson and Pearl as well as the airport and the school are in pretty sad shape. I won't give you the numbers now because you'll not remember them, but the cannibals that were there are no longer a threat. The Russians are either dead or they glow at night."

"I feel bad about the civilians," I said, and really did. I tried to rationalize my part in the raid as making their deaths faster and more painless. The Russians had thousands of captives in gulags around the city of Jackson, and the biggest was near the airport. I'm sure when the nuke suitcase bomb exploded, those near the airport were instantly erased. No one had time to scream or even run.

Top met my eyes and said, "Over time, most of the civilians that were killed would have been murdered by the Russians. We both know this, and I think most of them knew it too."

"When can I get out of here or check on Carol?"

"The doctor wanted to keep you two months and I said no way. So, you'll be out in two weeks. Carol died twice on them but they were able to bring her back, so you know her injury was serious. When you can get up and walk, you can visit her in her room."

I nodded in understanding and then asked, "How secure is this place?"

"It's ringed with surface-to-air missiles, part of an airport, and they have two squadrons of fighter jets assigned and on the ground. Last I heard was there were almost 5,000 Chinese troops assigned here. I've also seen anti-aircraft guns and dozens of attack helicopters here, so I'd say we're about as safe as it gets."

"That's good to hear, but have they had any attacks?"

"The day before you arrived, the Russians attacked with six of their old Bear bombers; five were shot down and one crashed when the pilot tried to land at Jackson. About once a week they make a try for this place, but nothing serious yet."

"The Bear tried to land?" I asked.

"Our eyes on the ground said the nose wheel collapsed and it slid down the runway, well, until it ran out of concrete and then struck a ditch. It then flipped over and exploded, killing all but two of the crew. I strongly suspect we got them the next day when the bomb exploded."

"Any idea of how many aircraft were at the airport the day the bomb went off?"

"Not really, but our last report from the area mentioned two attack helicopter squadrons, one squadron of heavy bombers, and three of fighters. I know they had some rescue and medical choppers there too, but we don't know how many. There were some international aircraft and crews there, so their governments are raising hell with the Russians, but shit happens."

I nodded.

"Now, most of the resistance are leaving the top half of the state and moving south. This is also happening in Alabama and Georgia, as the fallout continues to move in an east or northeast direction."

"What about us?"

"We're moving too, but not until you get out of the hospital."

"Do we know where to yet?"

"Missouri, is all I know, or maybe Texas. Both states are screaming for more assistance and while the Chinese will help us, they'll not put any traditional infantry troops on the ground. I have seen what an interpreter told me were "Snow Leopard" and "Falcon Commando" units. Both groups of special forces men looked lean and mean to me, each wearing face-paint and camouflage uniforms. But looking mean doesn't mean they have grit. I understand their special forces troops are established much differently than ours. Most, if what I read before the fall was correct, lack actual combat or hostile environment experience."

Suddenly a siren began to blow, and it was loud.

"Well, looks like the Chinese are under attack, so I need to get to my assigned position. Here, I brought you a gift. Some of the boys here from Kentucky attacked a Russian truck that was loaded down with whiskey. I paid good money for that pint, so make 'er last ya. Got to run, sir." Top gave me a quick salute, tossed me a bottle of good whiskey, and ran from my room.

I stuck the pint bottle in my housecoat pocket and wrapped it tightly around me, so it'd not be seen or fall out. I tied it in place with the strap on my housecoat.

The building shook hard, some dust fell from the ceiling, and a window shattered as bombs fell, and some must have been pretty damned close. Laying in bed wired to all the machines gave me one hell of a hopeless feeling, and I wanted to find a hole. The nurses came in at a rush and slipped something into my IV INT site, and I was out quickly. My world faded in a matter of seconds.

I came to hearing voices and when I opened my eyes, my room was a mess. Part of the roof had fallen in and the west wall was missing. The whole right side of my room had fallen when the wall gave way. My windows were blown out and smoke or dust filled the air. I prayed it wasn't smoke or I would soon be dead. Two small men entered wearing masks and one walked to me and started disconnecting me from the machines. He picked me up over his shoulder using his right hand to hold me down and carrying my IV bag in the other hand and carried me outside. He moved me to other patients from the bombed hospital. He held my IV until his buddy found a stick long enough to push into the soft loam. Once the stick was in place, he placed my IV at the top and they left me.

Soon a Chinese doctor was looking us over. I noticed his English was terrible, but he looked me over, shouted something in Chinese and two Asian women, who looked alike to me, ran to his side. He pointed at me, said something and then left.

"We are to wash you. Your hair and face are dirty from the bombs." one of the twins said.

Out of the blue a Russian fighter, a MiG of some kind, lined up on us and began firing his Gatling gun. Chunks of concrete, dirt, and rocks flew ten or more feet into the air and then rounds entered patients. I heard screams of the wounded and dying and closed my eyes, expecting death at any second. Within less than a minute he was gone. I glanced at the nurses and one was dead, the other dying. Blood now covered their pretty white uniforms. The wounded one kept saying something over and over, but I have no idea what, and a few seconds later she grew quiet. When I looked at her again, she was dead. Hopefully it was a prayer.

I must have passed out then, because I woke up in a tent, wired to machines again, with my IV over my head once more. I raised my head, looked around, and saw I was in a large tent. Medical personnel were hurrying all around me, and I had no inclination of what was taking place.

I looked to my left and smiled. In the bed next to mine was Carol and while she was sleeping, she looked good to me. I'd been so busy worrying about me that I'd almost forgotten her, plus drugs and exhaustion had my thinking all messed up. I needed about half the pint bottle of whiskey and two days of rest and sleep. I felt fine, overall, except my shoulder was sore again.

I finally flagged down an American doctor and said, "I'm in pain, Doc, can you see I get something?"

The man yelled something in Chinese and a minute later a young Chinese nurse added something to my IV. I found out later it was morphine and my pain went away, but I grew sleepy once more.

I woke to Carol talking to a nurse and when she noticed me moving, she glanced at me and smiled. Once the nurse left, she asked, "Are you okay? I saw you fall in the school so I knew you were hit, and hard too. I was so worried about you."

"The wound in the school was light compared to a round I took to the back boarding the Chinese chopper. According to the doctors here we were both messes when we arrived, and you died on them a couple of times."

"Weren't we in a building of some sort before?"

"Uh-huh, a hospital, but the Russians bombed it, either on purpose or by accident. Then they put us in this tent."

"Where are we? I know we don't have tents to use for a hospital."

"Louisiana, but I have no idea where in the state."

She nodded and said, "They just gave me a painkiller, so I'm getting sleepy. I love you . . . and glad we were . . . able to talk."

"I love you too, and I've been worried about you." I said, but she was already asleep.

I had a big hole in my chest where the bullet had exited, but it was up high near my shoulder. Each day when they bandaged the nasty looking thing, I'd take a good look, making sure I had no infection. Time passed, but slowly.

At the end of two weeks, I was up walking around and the doctors released me for light duty, meaning paperwork, and only for four hours a day. I'd do my work and then return to the hospital to visit Carol the remainder of my day.

I'd been given a private tent due to my rank of Full Colonel, but I was rarely there except to sleep. I expected the food to be Chinese but it was American, usually meat of some kind, beans, and potatoes. It was bland and the same day after day, so I enjoyed it when the Chinese cooks began to serve their foods as well.

I'm a big hot pepper fan and love hot foods, so I enjoyed anything spicy I could get in the chow line.

Two months after being wounded, Carol was released from the hospital and, while still weak, she'd had to leave to make room for more seriously wounded coming into the hospital. She was strong enough to walk slowly, and ate well.

My biggest problem was controlling my bladder after my hospital stay. The tube they had inserted into my bladder did the job of peeing for me so once the tube was removed, I had little or no control over my urine. It took me some time until I could control it most of the time. The first couple of weeks I felt so helpless as I'd be standing in my tent and suddenly feel my urine running down my leg. But, as time passed, I slowly gained almost normal control. I did learn that lack of bladder control can humble a hard man fairly damn fast.

One morning about a month after I left the hospital I entered my work tent, which was divided in half. The first portion was for Sergeant Warren and the other half held my office. The Sergeant looked up from some papers he was working on and said, "There are six officers in your office, sir, with the lowest rank a Full Colonel and the highest a Major General."

"Did you offer them coffee?"

"Yes, sir, and I moved the pot to your desk so they could have easy access to more."

I nodded, entered my office, and saw a lot of gold and brass in that small portion of the tent. I snapped to attention.

"Relax, John, and take a seat. Colonel Porter is here to brief you on the results of your last mission, which appears to have a been a great success. Our intelligence section claims the Russians are up to their necks in official protests from around the world. Colonel, please start your briefing." Major General Weaver said as he sat on the corner of my old wooden desk.

"Colonel, it is estimated that your mission has completely taken Jackson and the surrounding area well out of anti-partisan operations for the remainder of the conflict, while inflicting the maximum number of casualties on them as well. Our estimates are nearly 50,000 Russians were killed outright and we know the upper northeast of the state is still getting fallout from the blast. The number of Russians with radiation sickness is guessed at another 10,000 plus in this country alone."

"What of civilian casualties?" I asked.

"We have no real idea because many people in Jackson and surrounding small cities had been rounded up by the Russians, fled, or have died over the years from starvation. My numbers, this is a wild guess, oh, maybe 250,000 deaths, and twice that number in sicknesses following the detonation." Porter said and then smiled.

"My God!" I said, and know I turned pale. I hated the man's smile and said as much, but the General told me that I'd only followed orders. The mission would have been completed even if I had not been the trigger man.

"The Russians cannot admit that we did this or the whole world will know we have access to their nuclear bombs. That we possess their weapons of mass destruction would make them look weak. So, they've publicly announced that there was a mishap moving one of their bombs and it exploded."

I was still numbed by the number of civilian deaths, but knew most of those folks would likely have died before the war was over anyway. My mind rushed to find a dozen reasons it was good to have detonated the bomb.

All my reasons were lame excuses until the General said, "The Russian people grow tired of this war and today, for the first time, there were thousands of protesters in Moscow."

"I'm surprised the Russians allowed a protest march." I said.

"They don't like it, but there are too many news people from around the world in Moscow. Since the bomb blew, the place has been crawling with reporters." the General said.

"What of the United Nations?" I asked, knowing they'd never defend or assist us.

"Formal protest to Russia about using the bomb twice, but we didn't expect anything else. It pisses me off that we spent billions over the years as a member of that organization and all they are now is a loud mouth. We need help, but they ignore us."

"I agree, sir. What now for me and my troops?"

Colonel Porter, who'd grown very quiet after I confronted him, said, "You and your troops will be transported to the Missouri theater and you'll continue your fight there. Mississippi is in total chaos at this time and we're moving most of our troops out of the state."

I smiled because I knew the state very well, especially the Ozark Mountains. I thought for a moment and then asked, "Where in Missouri?"

"Your records show you know the southern portion of the state very well, so you'll be running partisan operations in the Ozarks, Colonel." General Weaver said, and than added, "Unless you'd rather have a different part of the state."

"Oh, no, I'm very comfortable in the Ozarks. I grew up there and have or had family in the area."

"Good, now one last thing. Colonel Porter, tell our Colonel the good news about our free state."

"As of noon two days ago, the Russians left Alaska and stated they were gone for good. It seems our activity in Mississippi caused the Russian bear to move his troops to the mainland. I also have reliable information that they'd never gotten out of Anchorage, and the partisans were tearing them apart during attacks. I think they really moved to cut their losses and to relocate to the continental United States, where most of the serious partisan threat is located. We know they didn't move because of the weather; hell, it's just like Siberia there."

"No, the weather didn't faze them," I said and then asked, "When do we leave, and what is our method of travel?"

"You'll fly there on a Chinese aircraft that is similar to our C-130. Their aircraft is a Shaanxi Y-9, which is their work horse for general transportation. It has 106 troop seats in the troop compartment and can carry 25 tons of material. Now, we have no safe area in the state of Missouri where we can land an aircraft, and right now we're looking for large fields that will allow us to place you there. If we cannot find enough open spots, we'll either position you north of the Ozarks and let you move into the region, or we may drop you by parachute."

"I understand, sir, but not all my troops are jump qualified."

"They soon will be, if we have to drop you. This is an emergency situation and if need be, I'll drop them with no training at all. The Russians have been coming up the Mississippi River to supply the state and also flying into the Saint Louis International Airport. Remember, Lambert Field is an international airport, so planes of all sizes can land there. The Russians have every kind of aircraft you can imagine on that field right this minute, and most are bringing in much needed supplies and materials to their troops."

"I understand, sir." I replied, but thought *I'll need to give my troops some rushed parachute training or we'll take some injuries during a jump.*

"Any questions?"

"How many troops will jump or go with me?"

"Right now it looks like a little over 200 people, but they'll leave the aircraft in different locations. Your administration folks will number 20 and out of that, one squad is combat reserves. Once we have more men and women, you'll get more from us. I plan to increase your numbers slowly until you have about 500 people. I also plan to resupply you with the Shaanxi Y-9's and on a regular basis. Any other questions?" the General asked.

"When do we leave and what time do we load on the aircraft?"

Smiling, Colonel Porter said, "You're scheduled to leave at 0500 in the morning. Good luck to you, Colonel."

"Oh, before I forget, the weather over the state of Missouri tomorrow will be clear with a temperature of about 70 and with no winds, so if you are forced to jump the weather will be ideal." Colonel Porter quickly added.

I nodded and replied, "Yes, sir."

I stood at attention as they left my office.

"Sergeant Warren, I want all officers and senior NCOs going with us in my office in an hour. See it gets done."

"Yes, sir." he replied, grabbed his hat and left the tent.

CHAPTER 2

I discovered a Shaanxi Y-9 was about as uncomfortable as a C-130. About a fourth of my officers and senior NCOs were jump qualified, meaning they'd jumped out of an aircraft before, and it also meant they'd spent a busy evening the night before teaching others how to do a parachute landing fall, and covering emergency procedures. I realized they were poorly trained and for some, their first jump could very well be their last. Some of my people had never been on a plane before and this would be their first flight. And, those that were "jump qualified" may not have jumped in ten years or more. But the orders given by Major General Weaver were legal, and off we went.

I had a headset to communicate with the crew, but their language was difficult to me and I had no idea what was being said. Dolly, my German shepherd, was attached to my parachute harness and when I jumped, if I did, she'd go with me. I sat and scratched her ears. I love the way she smiles when I give her just a little attention.

"Colonel, this is the Captain speaking, sir. You will not be using parachutes on this trip, or so it seems. Base has stated there is a field eight miles South of the town of Rolla, Missouri where we will land."

"Copy, and thanks for the information." I replied, and said nothing of his excellent command of the English language.

"Now, that's not written in stone, sir, so it could change at the last minute."

"I understand, Captain. Thank you."

About three hours later, the Captain spoke over the aircraft communications system. "This is your Captain speaking, and we're ten minutes out from our landing. Please fasten your seat-belts and prepare for a combat assault landing. We will be on the ground for approximately five minutes. Once you are off the aircraft, two pallets of gear and supplies will be unloaded. I suggest you break the pallets down quickly and then disappear. There are a number of radios in each pallet, along with spare batteries. On the behalf of myself and my crew, good luck."

I knew a combat assault landing would be a sharp angled landing, and the aircraft would not stop running engines once on the ground. The ramp would be lowered, we'd leave, and then the supplies would be pushed down the rolling rails in the middle of the aircraft to the ground.

Suddenly the aircraft pitched nose down, and I knew the landing was near. The aircraft leveled a few seconds later, the ramp went down, and I felt the wheels touch down. The ride was bumpy as hell, and small things bounced into the air. I saw one troop lose an ink pen and another a Styrofoam cup of water. I was thrown in all directions as the engines reversed and flaps came up to assist in slowing the aircraft down.

Once at almost a stop, the Captain told me to unload and prepare for the pallets. I was also to meet two members of the Missouri partisans at the rear of the aircraft once off the plane.

Within three or four minutes we were off the 'bird' and I watched as two pallets rolled toward us. The aircraft had never come to a full stop and was slowly creeping along the field. I moved to the rear of the Shaanxi Y-9 and met two partisans. Dolly growled as the two men neared.

I shook hands with a thin man, but both were closer to six feet tall than five. His eyes were cold gun metal gray, salt and pepper hair, and he looked to be totally professional. His hair was long and his beard trimmed.

"Colonel, I'm Major Joe Eller and my partner in crime is Captain Thomas 'Tom' Hensley. Tom is my chief of intelligence. Are we glad to see all of you! Looks like your dog doesn't like us much." He then turned toward a wooded area and waved. I spotted a team of partisans moving toward us.

"We'll help you unload the pallets. What we needed most were some replacement folks and supplies." Hensley said.

I heard the aircraft engines increase power, so I turned and watched the Shaanxi Y-9 taxi to the end of the field. Minutes later the aircraft flew into the air, banked sharply to the left and began to climb for altitude with the nose pointing high. I knew for this day the crew had survived their mission.

"Dolly is not trusting until she knows you a while. Sergeant Warren!"

"Yo!"

"Get the pallets broken down and move everything to the woods. Help is coming, so let them assist you in unpacking and moving the loads. Let's do things quickly, folks, others may have seen or heard our aircraft this morning."

The first pallet was soon stripped clean and we were halfway done with the second pallet, when one of the partisans opened fire. Across the field, opposite where the partisans were taking our supplies, I quickly spotted a couple of squads of Russian troops moving toward us.

Bullets began to impact the pallet, so I sent two squads to confront the threat as our Missouri partisans moved to flank the Russians. The gunfire grew louder and I knew the battle was in close, because I heard grenades exploding and the screams of the injured and dying.

"Break contact, break contact! Move out of the field and now!" Major Eller screamed into the radio.

"Copy." came an instant reply.

I gave the Major a questioning look and he said, "Russian Black Sharks are around and will immediately respond to any attacks on their infantry troops. They work together well."

The gunfire died down as we broke contact, so I moved to the pallet and removed a Russian 9K32 *Strela-2*. It carried a high explosive warhead and infrared homing guidance system, and I'd used them before. I'd compare it in overall performance to the US Army FIM-43 Redeye or pretty damned close.

Just then a Black Shark moved over the horizon and headed toward their squads. I aimed the iron sights on the aircraft and followed it until it hovered over the troops, and I saw the pilot obviously trying to find us visually. I squeezed the trigger slightly, and got a light buzzing sound. I then pulled the trigger harder and felt, as well as heard, the missile leave the launch tube.

The missile struck the aircraft in the engine and while the explosion was less than I expected, it was enough to severely damage the aircraft. I saw panels fly from the engine housing and the chopper wobbled uncontrollably for a few minutes. Dense black smoke started coming from the engine exhaust and I knew then we'd hurt them. The aircraft nosed down, began to spin counter clockwise and then fell to the field—landing hard.

There came no explosion, but by now the gear on the remaining pallet was gone and Major Eller yelled to be heard over the noise. "Let's move into the trees and now, sir! We need to get out of here before they bring in some fast movers with napalm."

We'd no sooner started running than I heard an explosion and, looking over my shoulder, I saw a huge dull red and black fire ball rolling into itself. I heard the screams of those still alive in the chopper, but it didn't bother me at all. I was fully aware they were burning to death. I'd grown hard during my years with the resistance and felt nothing. The Russians needed to leave my country, or I'd continue to kill all of them I could find.

Once in the trees, I saw no one. My people and the Missouri partisans were long gone.

"I sent my troops and yours ahead, sir. We need to make tracks, because I think these woods will soon turn hot."

As we moved, I heard a jet pass low over us, and knew the trees we'd just left were about to be worked over hard. There sounded two explosions and I heard the jet pull up and move around for another attack. Soon I heard the muffled explosion of napalm and knew the woods were now in flames. I felt no heat, but it was only due to the dense woods we were moving through. Dolly seemed to take it all in stride and stayed by my side.

An hour later, we walked to a cave and a guard said, "Dog and Pony."

"Show."

"Pass."

The inside of the cave was filled with supplies and my administration troops. I turned to Major Eller and said, "I want all officers and NCO's in here tomorrow morning, if possible, so I can get a situation brief and meet my new people."

"Captain Hensley can give you the situation brief, but I'll put the word out about the morning meeting over the radio. It'll be sent in code, of course."

"Let's do the briefing, then. I need to know what's going on, and the sooner the better."

"Sir, if you'll move further back into the cave, I have a map I can show you." Captain Hensley said.

"Sure, but Major, I want you to attend as well. You may be able to expand on some issues." I said.

"No problem, sir."

An hour later, I could understand their demand for more troops. The Russians had taken over Fort Leonard Wood, but not before our partisans had struck it hard, removing most weapons and ammo from storage. They'd pretty much cleaned the place of chemical warfare suits, munitions, clothing, and anything that they felt might be needed. Thousands of cases of MREs were taken, along with canned foods for the mess hall. Of course, over the last three years the canned foods were used.

The Russians were in control of Saint Louis, Jefferson City, Rolla, and the Fort. Most small towns between Rolla and Saint Louis were also under their thumb. The biggest concentration of Russians, besides Saint Louis, was Fort Leonard Wood.

We were located about 10 miles south of Rolla, Missouri, and then maybe the same distance west. We were south and east of Fort Leonard Wood.

I knew the Fort was about thirty miles from us, so I asked, "What sort of changes have the Russians made to Fort Leonard Wood?"

"They immediately doubled the length of the runway on the Fort so they could take deliveries from large aircraft. The main gate is very strong now, with concrete bunkers and thousands of sandbags. Some of our people work inside the Fort doing jobs the Russians don't like or want to do." The Captain handed me a photo of the gate taken, so he said, by a partisan.

"Gulags there?"

"There are three gulags, but two are very large with oh, maybe 5,000 people in each. The smaller one has maybe a thousand people. We've never attacked the Fort before."

"That will soon change. I want you to draw up an attack plan on one of the larger gulags. We need to show our people, the prisoners there, that we know they are captive and we'll try to free them when we can."

"Colonel, our loss rate will be high." the Captain said.

"It's worth the cost. I realize our losses could be as high as 70% and I'm willing to pay that, so we can show the Russians we can attack what we wish. It will not only scare the enemy, but show our folks we'll make an effort to save them, thus improving their morale. I believe the morale alone will aid in saving some lives of those held captive."

"Sir, no disrespect intended, but with 70% losses, most of our people will say you're playing with their lives. After all, you will be safely out of the way while they do the dying."

"I don't work like that, Captain. I will be part of the first wave to hit the gulag and so will you. I'll leave the Major here in case I'm killed or seriously injured. I lead by example, Captain, and so will all our leaders in the resistance. Now, I suggest you go work on the attack plan, because I want to hit the Fort by the end of the week. It's Wednesday, so you have a few days to prepare a night attack on the place. Now, at the same time we strike the gulag, I want the Fort airfield hit by teams of sappers, teams sent in only prepared to destroy aircraft, so they'll need plenty of explosives."

"I understand, sir." The Captain snapped to attention.

"Can I speak with you privately, sir?" Major Eller asked.

"Captain you're dismissed. Step outside with me a minute, Major, and unload your mind."

As we left the cave, the troops were opening boxes and removing all sort of things the Chinese had given us. I saw a case of their grenades and winced. Sometimes they worked and sometimes they didn't. The damned fuses were set for five seconds but due to manufacturing errors, they often exploded much earlier than that. I always pulled the pin and tossed 'em, not counting on any delay.

Once outside, the Major said, "Our previous commander was relieved of duty for two reasons. The first reason is he came down with prostate cancer, but the primary reason was he'd not get off his ass and attack the Russians. Now, Colonel Haynes was a good man, in many ways, but I feel he'd been promoted beyond his abilities. He'd strike an outpost or an isolated tank, but never any big targets. We have Russian convoys moving all the time from Saint Louis to Rolla and he'd not attack them."

"Why?"

"He was worried about the loss of American lives, which I can sort of understand, but this is a war and people are expected to die. I feel the only way the Russians will ever leave is by making them pay the price of invading us in blood and bodies. The cost must get so high the folks back home will force the war to end."

"I can spend lives if it serves a worthwhile purpose, even yours and mine. However, we will be part of any major attack because the troops must know that you and I will go into harms way, too. Now, since there is a supply convoy route, I want you to line up an attack for us and do the job quickly. We need to show our troops that we'll no longer sit on our asses and do nothing. I want the railroads attacked as well. There are many places between here and Saint Louis that are ideal for us to ambush a train."

"I have a lot of respect for you, sir. I felt like my hands were tied with Colonel Haynes, and he just would not take any risks. You'll discover in the morning some of the lower ranking leaders lack the guts to do much, as well. They want to wait and kill a lone Russian here and there."

"No need to give me their names, because I'll spot them quickly enough. And if they won't do the jobs assigned to them, we'll replace them. However, if they are fired they'll be demoted and added back to the rank and file as privates or corporals. We are all here to do just one thing—kill Russians."

"I totally agree, sir."

"Now, Major, if you'll excuse me, I have some work to do with my Administrative NCO. We are going to start fingerprinting our people so we can reclaim bodies after a battle or this war. In many cases, we'll not be able to recover the dead, so they'll have to wait until we can do DNA on them. In all cases, we need a list of their next of kin. Some may not be identified until years after the war."

"Is it true that you're to receive the Medal of Honor for a classified mission done recently?"

I know I blushed and then said, "I have no idea and this is the first I've heard of it, so you know more than I do. I don't see how they can award me the medal when we're not in a declared war. Besides, all I did was complete my assigned mission."

"Rumor has it you were wounded a number of times and still completed your task, whatever that may have been, deep behind enemy lines."

I gave a loud chuckle and once sober said, "I think more is being made out of the mission than what really happened. It was far less exciting than what you just stated. I suffered a serious knife wound to my neck and suffered two gunshot wounds. Write it all off as wishful thinking from someone's active mind. I don't rate the medal."

Our field rations didn't improve by moving to Missouri, except as a full bird I could have had a better menu, but I meant what I said before about my officers setting the example. We would eat, drink and sleep the same as our troops did. I did raise some eyebrows at the morning meeting when I said, "All of us in this room will actively engage the enemy where you find them. If you can only kill one or two Russians, do the job. However, I fully expect each Officer in Charge (OIC) to be aggressive and take the fight to our enemies or I'll replace you. Armor is to be taken out when at all possible. I expect you to eat the same food, and amount, as your troops do. In the field, all of us will pull guard, even officers.

Following your engagements with the enemy I expect an after engagement intelligence report filed with my office. You can see Sergeant Warren on the way out if you have no idea how to do one. I want the report within 24 hours of your fight or sooner, if at all possible."

"What about prisoners?" someone in the back of the room asked.

"I want all enemy personnel who are injured to be cared for by our medics and left in place, as long as they are permanently disabled. I have no POW camp, so we have no place to keep them. If you capture a Russian that is not injured, you will make him disabled by an injury to his or her knee or arm. Our days of killing all prisoners is over, but I don't want them to recover and then be assigned back here to fight us again. Permanently disable them, by shots to the arms or legs. Any other questions?"

"What is your role in this whole mess, Colonel?" a smart ass asked from the back.

"My job is to see you all do your jobs with the least number of casualties we can have and yet hurt the Russians. I will be going out with my own team at times and at other times, I will join one of you. Once in the woods, you will be in charge, not me, and as far as you're concerned, I'm just an additional man."

The man grinned and then nodded.

"We have three targets that will soon be hit, and hard. We have an attack plan being drawn up for these attacks and you'll learn much more about them once you have the need to know. Right now, none of you have any reason to know anymore than what I just told you. If any of you have the urge to hit a train or the highway as a convoy passes, I'll support you in all ways I can.

Any more questions?"

Silence.

As I turned to walk from the cave, Staff Sergeant Warren yelled, "Teeennn – huuuttt!"

I made my way outside and moved toward a creek at the bottom of the hill. I wanted to do some thinking. Some of the platoon leaders and OICs seemed shocked, well, at least by their faces, that I wanted to take the fight to the Russians. I could tell some of them liked the idea and some didn't. I needed to find those who dislike leading their men and get rid of them. I only had room for aggressive combat leaders and those who could think as the bullets were fired at them. Those that didn't measure up to my expectations I'd remove and move on.

I'd just sat on a big rock as the released officers began to walk back to their units. I was deep in thought about Carol when Sergeant Warren stuck his head from the cave and said, "Sir, one of our units is in heavy contact with a Russian Platoon."

I jumped to my feet and made my way to the radio. I didn't notice Dolly following in my foot steps.

CHAPTER 3

M aster Sergeant Romanovich had the Americans right where he wanted them, and they were dying as his men laid down a heavy field of fire. He had two Black Sharks above, ready to take the battle to the enemy if they disengaged and pulled back. So far, they'd stood toe to toe with the Russians and were trading bloody punches. The helicopters couldn't be used now because the enemy was too close. There came a noise above the sounds of battle and when he turned his head to look, a missile was moving toward a Black Shark, which immediately threw chaff and hot flares in all directions.

The colored aluminum and burning flares falling from the helicopter are almost pretty, he thought.

The chopper took the missile dead center of the engine; panels flew off and it began to smoke.

"Bear One, this is Bear Two. I have taken a missile and have most of my console lights lit up, so I am returning home." the stricken aircraft pilot radioed.

"Roger, and I will follow you home. Badger One, you are on your own. Looks to me like you have a good handle on your ambush. Good luck. I am returning to base escorting Bear Two. There are two fast burners that will be here in about ten minutes so hold on, and they will clear the partisans for you."

"Copy, Bear One. Out."

Knowing he needed to end this battle and now, Romanovich yelled, "Fix bayonets."

The long knives were heard clicking into position on all rifles.

"Prepare to charge the Americans!"

A few men were heard to pray, a couple cursed, but most tried to work up enough guts to move forward when the order was given.

Rising to his feet, Master Sergeant Romanovich screamed, "Charge!"

A purloined Russian machine-gun began it's *rat-tat-tat* as the men jumped to their feet, and some fell right back down with massive holes pushed through their bodies by the heavy gun. There was an explosion followed by screams, and the men moved forward once more. The Americans rose from the long stem grasses and yelled as they rushed the Russians.

Rifles banged and pistols barked as men on both sides died. Some screamed when a long knife blade entered their stomachs or when they were knocked back by the hard swing of a weapon butt. The fight was brutal but as fast as it started, it was over. Three Russians, besides the Master Sergeant, were still alive or uninjured and all the Americans were down.

Pulling his pistol, the Sergeant moved to every American and placed a bullet in each head. One man was still praying, his hands together, so he bypassed him temporarily and killed him after the others were shot. Picking up his radio handset, he discovered it was useless, having taken hits from the machine-gun.

"What now, Master Sergeant?" Private Yakovic, the radioman asked.

"We move toward base on foot. If we see a helicopter we may be able to signal it, but expect them to handcuff us and take us prisoner first. They have no idea who we are."

"I understand."

"Private Igorevich, take a compass heading of 0120 degrees and lead the way. It is time you three earn some medals to show off at home. All those farm girls will make big heroes out of each of you. Private Vasilievna, you are my drag, but stay maybe 20 meters from me. Let us move, but keep an eye out for mines."

They moved quickly the first hour, until the Sergeant said, "Igorevich, slow down some. This is not a race. If we enter an area with mines, we will send what is left of you home in an aluminum shoe box."

"Yes sir, but I have seen nothing to indicate the Americans are near."

"They have been through this area and you can bet your ass on it, so slow down."

The gray clouds overhead began a light sprinkling of rain that was more of a fine mist than rain drops. They donned their ponchos and continued moving.

Less than an hour after the warning, Private Igorevich suddenly screamed and stopped walking.

Everyone waited for the noise of an explosion, but nothing was heard.

Cautiously moving forward, all his senses on edge, the Sergeant asked, "Why did you scream?"

"I . . . I pulled a fishing line and . . . a grenade landed beside me. Do you see it, it's beside my right foot."

"I see it, and it is Chinese so I think this is your lucky day. If that was made in the United States, you would be dead right now. Move forward and wait for us near the huge oak tree dead ahead." the Sergeant said, then motioned his folks around the explosive, and then he walked by it last.

Once at the tree, he said, "Slow down and if you believe in God, he just warned you, son."

"I . . . I hear you."

Over the remainder of the day, the Private kept the speed slow and the Sergeant figured they'd walked a good fifteen miles. After looking at his map and triangulating his position, he saw they were just over half way back to Fort Leonard Wood. It was slightly before dusk so they moved into some thick brush where they'd sit back to back the whole night. Since there were four of them, they'd sit at the four main compass headings.

Once seated in the grasses, they pulled their rations and began to eat as Private Vasilievna pulled guard. She'd pull it for two hours and then the next person would take it for two hours. The task of guarding would be pulled more than once overnight by each of them.

"Damn me, Sergeant, but— I have a long and fat snake on my legs." Private Yakovic said, his voice quivering, just as the last sliver of light was on the western horizon. He gave a hard shiver, because he was scared to death of snakes.

"What is the color of your snake?"

"Looks like two shades or brown, almost copper in color. Do something, please."

"First, do not move, and quit talking. It is a copperhead, and a most dangerous snake. I will try to kill it." Master Sergeant Romanovich said as he drew a small caliber pistol that had a silencer.

Two minutes later, the pistol in hand, the Sergeant leaned over Yakovic and fired twice, poot, poot, and the snake began to curl and wiggle. When the Private looked down, the head of the snake was missing. He quickly brushed the dead body from his legs.

"You watch where you put your hands, because that snake's head can still inject venom in you, even without a body. If you can find it, push it away with your boots."

"I see it, Master Sergeant, and I am moving it now."

"It is dark, so time for all of us to don our NVGs for the night. Keep them on, even when you sleep. If we are attacked, you will be glad they are on and ready to use. It is good the rain has stopped."

Once his Night Vision Goggles were on, Master Sergeant Romanovich saw the world in various shades of green. He'd get the least sleep overnight, because he didn't trust his young and tired troops to stay awake. While he knew the thought had never entered their minds, he was concerned about Russian helicopters with Infrared (IR) monitoring systems on-board. He knew without a radio or way to contact the aircraft, they'd be attacked. He whispered to all his Privates to have their ponchos beside them. Covering with a poncho would hide the IR image on the screen for a minute or so.

The night passed slowly, and a little after midnight he saw a group of Americans moving near them on the same trail they'd been using. They were close enough he saw they were wearing NVGs, but he didn't worry much about being discovered. All four Russians were dressed in camouflage uniforms, wearing camouflage face paint, and not a one dared to move. After about five minutes, the Americans had moved down the trail and were out of sight followed minutes later by their drag person, who was extremely alert.

Near 0300, according to the Sergeant's watch, a flight of helicopters were heard passing overhead and he suspected they may have been looking for him and other survivors of the fight. He had no way to signal them, so he remained in place.

An hour before dawn, he had each of them eat a ration and prepare to leave. He walked off to do his morning toilet and hadn't been gone three minutes when he heard weapons fired on automatic. He heard yells in both English and Russian. There were three loud explosions and then silence. The Sergeant made his way very slowly on his hands and knees to where he'd left his troops. Two were clearly seen moving and the last one looked injured. He moved toward them, only to have two guns pointed at him.

"Oh, it is you, Sergeant."

"W . . . what happened?"

"We were eating when I looked up right into the eyes of an American. He was on the trail scanning the area. The main body of men was there, so we fired our weapons and threw three grenades. I think we killed all of them, but Private Yakovic has taken a wound to his shoulder."

"All of you remain here, but watch for their point or drag man to near. If you see one of them, kill them, but try not to shoot me. I have enough scars as it is."

He moved slowly to the trail, saw a good ten men down and he began to check for wounded with his pistol in hand, the same one he'd killed the snake with. All were dead, so he checked their pockets and took their gear. He found nothing of interest for intelligence, so he stripped the weapons and threw the parts all over the forest into the high weeds and grasses.

"Yakovic, you lean on me as we move. Vasilievna, you take the point and Private Igorevich, you pull drag. Now, keep our pace slow, because we have a wounded man walking with us. Remember to always keep your pace as fast as the slowest man with you."

The injury slowed them down a great deal, and finally the Sergeant cut two limbs and taking a poncho, made a litter. He took the point and had the two Privates carry the injured man. Since Private Yakovic was no longer able to walk, he was given an injection of morphine to kill his pain. They were just a few miles shy of the base when dusk found them still moving. Not wanting to be caught out in the open by a Russian helicopter, they moved into some thick brush and sat back to back.

It was quiet most of the night and while they'd seen no Americans since their fight, they were nervous now. All expected something to go wrong at the last minute and injure or kill them.

Whispering, Private Vasilievna asked, "How will we gain access to the base?"

"We will walk to the main gate. They will make some calls and verify who we are."

"I see."

"Our biggest concern tonight is hoping no IR capable helicopter flies over us. We have no way to signal them."

"I understand. All we can do is cover with a poncho and hope they move on before long."

"You are correct; now no more talking."

Just as dawn was breaking the two privates were in the woods doing their morning toilet when a Russian Ka-60 Helicopter flew overhead, circled and then made another pass and the guns mounted on wing pods began spitting bullets. As the lead struck the ground, clods of dirt and rock were thrown six feet into the air. The bullets began to walk toward the two Privates.

There came screams from both Privates, especially Private Igorevich, who was stitched down the middle by the Russian machine-gun. He fell to the ground where he jerked and twitched as his central nervous system shut down.

Vasilievna raised both hands over her head as a sign of surrender and the helicopter began to lower to the ground. Romanovich thought the pilot a fool, but maybe he'd noticed the Russian uniforms. The Master Sergeant stood and raised both hands over his head, then slowly moved to the Private. As he stood beside her, he noticed the door gunner had them covered well.

A crew member ran from the chopper and asked, "Who are you?"

"I am Master Sergeant Romanovich, returning from a mission. My radio was damaged and failed to work properly. I have a wounded man behind me, maybe 40 feet, and one dead that was just killed by your aircraft, you stupid sons of bitches."

"I am just a gunner, so do not blame me. I must ask the two of you to place your hands in front of you so I can handcuff you. This is only until we get to the base and confirm who you are."

Ten minutes later, they were airborne with all but Igorevich handcuffed. His body was thrown on the floor, and he was torn to hell and back by the big guns.

As they flew, the door gunners checked them for injuries and discovered all had some sort of damage done to them. The Senior Sergeant had a long shallow cut on his left hand he did not remember receiving. The Private had a deep scrape on her right shin, to the bone, that she knew she had, but at the time she was injured she had just let it go. Others were dead or seriously injured and her scrape seemed minor.

Suddenly, there were two loud *thunk-ping* sounds, and two holes instantly appeared in the floor. One of the door gunners fell with blood spurting from his thigh and, since his hands were in front of him, the Senior Sergeant removed his belt and then tried to use it as a tourniquet on the man.

The other door gunner was using duct tape to keep a fluid from leaking from overhead pipes into the compartment. He finished his task, which did not work well, and moved to the injured man. He pulled the tourniquet as tightly as he could and then slipped the leather tip under the belt. He gave the man a shot of morphine and could be seen talking to someone with his microphone.

There was an explosion just outside the right door, and bright red blood began to fly back from the cockpit into the crew compartment. From where he sat in the middle of the troop compartment, Romanovich could see a mangled helmet leaning to the left, and most of the blood appeared to be coming from that man, the co-pilot.

Dark gray smoke began to fly past the doors, but both had been removed for the gunners. Glancing forward once more, he saw all the console lights looked to be in the red. Then looking out the doors again, he saw they were near 2,000 meters in the air. There sounded a loud bang, and a large piece of sheet metal flew pass the right door.

The aircraft made a straight in approach, landing hard on the closest empty spot on the flight line, and the engines were quickly cut along with all electrical power. A couple of minutes later the aircraft was surrounded by the Main Directorate of the Military Police. As they left the aircraft, two ambulances arrived and all were taken to the hospital. The Master Sergeant noticed a Military Police officer rode in each ambulance, his pistol loaded, safety off, cocked, and in his hand.

As each person was looked over closely, the identifications of the recovered Russian Army members were verified. As a doctor was looking him over, a Private entered and removed the handcuffs from the Sergeant.

"Sorry, Master Sergeant, but the handcuffs were required."

"I understand, Private, now get to where you are to be."

The doctor grinned as the young woman left and asked, "Any pain or injuries, other than your hand, that you feel right now?"

"Uh, no sir. I feel well, except the hand hurts."

"I will have a nurse sew it closed in a few minutes, and I suggest you have some vodka in your room later today. Or, if you wish, I can give you pain pills."

"Vodka; painkillers mess my head up too much. Doctor, how are my troops?"

"Well, as you know, Igorevich is dead, Vasilievna will be released today and Yakovic will be our guest for about a week. Once he is released he will be on light duty for at least a month."

"I see. Did the gunner from the helicopter survive his injuries?"

"Yes, he will live, thanks to your quick thinking. Your belt saved his life. The bone was shattered and the femoral artery cut. Without the tourniquet, he would have bled to death in a few short minutes. Now, I am going to give you some antibiotics to help your hand heal. It is hard to say where the hand has been the last few days. It will be cleaned well here, but I will give you the pills just to be safe. Any other questions?"

"No, sir."

His prefab quarters had not changed at all while he was gone. Master Sergeant Romanovich entered, walked to his table and took a snort of vodka right from the bottle. The local painkiller they'd used to clean, stitch, and wrap his hand was wearing off. He was suddenly very tired and knew the adrenaline from the mission was wearing off. He placed the bottle back on the table.

There was a knock on the door.

"Just a minute." he called out.

He opened the door to find Senior Sergeant Georgiy standing at the entrance, so he said, "Come on in, Ilik, and have a drink or two."

Smiling, the Senior Sergeant said, "I can do that."

"So, what brings you to my humble quarters?"

"Mainly checking on you to see if you have everything you need."

"I am fine, and have four more quarts of vodka in this place, so I will feel little pain."

"Rough mission, eh?"

"Rough enough, and have a seat, if you have the time. I just walked in the door." he said as he poured a drink in a water glass for Ilik and then handed it to the man. He poured a drink for himself and joined his friend on the sofa. The bottle went on the coffee table.

Romanovich said, "Your promotion to Master Sergeant came in this morning, and you are scheduled to put the promotion on in four months. I spoke with our commander at the hospital for a minute giving him my restricted to quarters letter from the doctor. Along with your promotion was a reassignment to Moscow, to work with Spetsnaz. You are to leave this base two days before your promotion and return to Russia."

"By God, that is good news; so what is the bad news?"

"Intelligence thinks more partisans have moved into our area of operations (AO). They suspect the men and women are from Mississippi, where two nuclear bombs have exploded. I have no idea what the Russian Army may have found so frightening that they needed to use A-Bombs, but they did. Now the whole state glows at night."

"Fools are what they are. I think both were accidents, or so say the rumors I heard."

"I have no idea, but if not heads rolled, and you can be sure of it. No force of that strength was needed, well, unless there is more to it than we know." Senior Sergeant Georgiy said.

The Fort's sirens went off with a warbling tone, letting everyone on base know they were under attack and it was not a drill. Explosions were heard in different areas of the huge base. Opening the door, they saw men and women running in all directions.

"I need to get to my troops!" Senior Sergeant Georgiy yelled to be heard.

"Go! I will move to the perimeter here and help out where I can."

"Good luck!" Ilik said as he took off running.

There was a huge explosion and fireball from the direction of the aircraft hangers, so the Master Sergeant suspected a plane or helicopter just exploded.

Tracers, green and red, filled the air over his head, and at times one would hit the concrete or a rock and zing off at a different angle. *If not so deadly, the tracer bullets would be pretty*, he thought and then chuckled.

He neared a deep ditch, jumped in, and spotted a good dozen soldiers with him. Glancing over the edge, he said, "Here they come and, my God, there must be a thousand of them!"

CHAPTER 4

I was leading the attack on Fort Leonard Wood and fell after I tripped over something; then I saw a line of tracers pass low over my head. Dolly, angered by the closeness of the tracers, tried to bite others in flight. I had to pull her down beside me. If I hadn't just fallen, I would have been killed by the bullets. I shivered, climbed to my feet, and noticed we had men and women in the wire. Explosives were being placed in the wire and I watched an injured man stay behind to set off the explosion. He'd just given his life to clear that stretch of wire. The opening was about 20 meters wide, but onto the base we ran, all one thousand of us. While we were greatly outnumbered, we had surprise and determination on our side.

I was unable to keep up with the younger men and women because a middle-aged man with a heavy pack can't compete with an eighteen or nineteen year old soldier. I slowed and moved to Top, who I was surprised to see in the attack. He gave me a big smile once he recognized me.

"Top, come with me! You and I need to try and find their command post." I screamed to be heard.

He nodded and ran after me.

The whole base vibrated under foot from explosions. Looking to the west, a huge fireball was moving skyward, rolling inside itself as it moved.

"POL storage!" Top yelled.

I nodded and began to run again.

"Look for a flagpole, Colonel!" Top said.

That made sense. They'd for sure have a flagpole outside their headquarters, and usually the command post was in a Russian Headquarters. I finally saw it on my left.

As I moved toward the building, two machine-guns opened fire on us and down went Top, screaming. An unknown number of troops had followed him or me, and now I started giving orders.

"Try to flank those guns and take them out with grenades, Sergeant!"

A squad sized group moved away from us.

"Fire at the sandbags so they have to keep their heads down. If they know they're being flanked, they'll murder our squad."

Our rifles began to cough and I made my way to Top. I grabbed his left ankle and pulled him behind a concrete wall. He'd taken the rifle bullet to the side of his chest and after listening to him labor to breathe, I used the plastic in his first aid kit to seal both holes and then wrapped him tightly. Dolly was alert, scanning the countryside as I doctored my Top Sergeant.

"W . . . Willy would . . . be proud . . . of you." he said, and then smiled faintly.

"Save your strength, Top, I'm sending you out of here, now. You, soldier, bring the man beside you to me, and now!"

Two young men neared, both ducking and dodging the flying bullets.

"Return to base with this man and remain there. See he gets medical treatment as soon as you can. He has a sucking chest wound. Understand my orders?"

"Yes sir." the oldest looking one said.

They picked Top up and quickly disappeared into the hazy fog of battle.

There came three explosions and the machine-guns quit firing. I got to my feet and screamed, "Follow me!"

Some of my troops were in front of me, and I saw them make fast work of the Russian soldiers cowering behind the sandbags. One of my Sergeants kicked the door to the building open and was met with automatic rifle fire. He dropped dead. We tossed three grenades in and once they exploded, we entered with guns firing. A huge Russian officer ran toward us, his Bison sub-machine gun throwing bullets. Men fell around me, so I aimed at his chest and pulled the trigger.

My Bison took the man down almost the center of his body, after the first rounds struck him in the chest. The big man fell unnaturally, and I watched one of my women lean over and cut his throat. Blood spurted into the air and the man kicked and jerked violently.

That was as far as we got into the command post, and the fighting soon grew so intense I pulled my troops back and moved toward the flight-line, wondering what kind of damage we could do there. I wasn't willing to pay the price in blood and lives to take the command post.

Tracers were flying all over the place and I couldn't depend on the colors to indicate the enemy from friends. We used any weapons and ammo we could find, so we were likely to be shooting red or green. I watched tracers hit the concrete of the flight line and then bounce into the air, to zing off and finally strike a huge transport aircraft in the tail.

We were huddled behind a burning truck as a machine-gun crew tried hard to keep us at bay.

"Get a flamethrower up and lets get this gun out of our way!" one of my Sergeants yelled.

A chopper flew overhead, the door gunner lining up on us, when a surface-to-air missile was fired and the left side of the aircraft exploded into flames. The pilot, fighting hard to regain control of his helicopter, began a horizontal spin and soon crashed on a taxiway about 100 meters from our position. The aircraft instantly exploded, sending flames and smoke high into the air.

The flamethrower arrived; it was operated by a Corporal, and she knew her business. I watched her aim high into the air, squeeze the trigger, and watched the sticky jell-like flames spurt from the nozzle. The flames landed just in front of the Russians and I saw a handful of men turn and run, not wanting to fight the nasty weapon. The Corporal adjusted a little, squeezed the trigger, and I saw the flames land on the gunner and his assistant. Dolly had moved behind me when the flamethrower was used, not liking the weapon at all.

"Move forward, and now!" the Sergeant yelled as he stood and ran toward the flaming sandbags.

Two Russians moved toward us, both in flames, but in seconds our gunfire killed them. The smell of burning flesh joined the smells of human waste, blood, burning oil, and gore. One Russian rushed me, his left arm in flames. I fired twice, saw the bullets strike his chest and down he went. When I neared, he looked as if he was twelve years old to me. His eyes were open but unseeing, and his body jerked as it shut down.

I watched something strike a fuel truck, probably an RPG, and it exploded into flames instantly. The noise was loud and my folks fell to the ground, not sure what was happening. I saw the driver jump from the cab, but he was immediately shot down. The truck, still moving, struck a huge transport aircraft dead center and I knew in just a few minutes the fuel on the aircraft would explode. I was right, and about five minutes later another explosion rocked the flight line. I heard a loud plop and looking to my right, I saw a glob of burning fuel land beside me. I moved forward quickly.

Some of my troops, sappers, were seen placing explosives on different aircraft and as I watched, my radio came alive. "Bacon One, be advised, our friends have stated an unknown number of aircraft are nearing the Fort. It is advised that you pull out now."

I knew our friends were the Chinese so I blew my whistle to indicate to withdraw. As my troops broke contact, I replied on my radio, "Roger that, base. We are disengaging the enemy at this time. What is the estimated time of arrival (ETA) of the aircraft?"

"Wait one."

"Roger."

"Fifteen minutes is the estimation. They are inbound from Saint Louis. Radar indicates most are choppers, but some fast movers have been noted."

"Copy and out." I said on the radio and then yelled, "Pull back and return to base!"

Most of us were gone by the time the aircraft arrived, but we soon lost over 100 people to helicopters with infrared radar. I'm sure their screens were jumping with red images because most of my folks had been running and fighting for almost an hour. Their body heat was high and we surely provided the Russians with plenty of clear targets. As usual, following an attack, we broke into our small squad-like units and tried to disappear. There was no way we were all going to return to our base camp, because the flow of personnel would have been like a pointer to our exact location. We scattered into the winds.

When my squad exited the Fort, we'd moved south by east and then, near the Big Piney River, we moved north. Just a few miles south of Interstate 44 we ran into the old Route 66 signs and we then moved due east. It was still dark, so we crossed the river using the bridge on the old Route 66 highway. The road overall was in sad shape, with buckled concrete, potholes, and just falling apart. In some areas it suddenly ended and there was grass for a few yards, then it started again. It was hard to believe that a few years ago Route 66 was a famous highway, and movies had even been made about it. Now, it was dead and disjointed in some spots.

Once across the bridge, I said, "Move off to our right and into those oak trees. Take ten minutes of rest and then we move again." We were all wearing stolen Russian NVGs so we saw everything in a light pea soup green.

"Choppers." someone whispered, but the tone indicated fear to me.

I heard the *whop-whop-whop* of the blades and suddenly a bright spotlight lit up the bridge. It was a Black Shark and for some reason, perhaps maintenance problems, his thermal gear on board wasn't working or not turned on, thank God. Everyone with me fell to the grasses or moved into the woods to hide behind the trunks of the big trees. The chopper scanned the bridge and then backed up and began using the flood light in the grasses and trees. I realized we were fairly safe from the naked eye unless we moved. My folks had been trained to lay still and not move at all, but that's hard to do. Especially when you've seen the damage these big choppers can do to a human body.

I watched Sergeant Parsons remove a 9K32 Strela-2 hand held and shoulder-fired surface-to-air missile from her backpack. The model she carried was much improved over the older Strela-1, with much better range, improved sighting, smaller size, and lighter in weight. While an old weapon, it did its job very well, and was hard on aircraft who flew into its limited range.

The chopper threw the light in all directions and I think the goal of the pilot was to scare someone, if anyone was below him, into running. I spotted two Gatling guns mounted on the external pods of the aircraft and knew they'd grind a man or woman into hamburger and in just seconds, too. Only a fool would attempt to run from this beast.

Parsons gave me a questioning look and for right now, I shook my head. She removed the missile from the ready to fire position on her shoulder and lowered it to her lap. I suspected if we fired other choppers would come to this spot, and we'd have a difficult time moving and avoiding detection. My primary goal now was to escape and return to base. Dolly was laying over the tops of my boots, her tongue out, panting, and wearing a grin. I rubbed her head slowly.

The helicopter suddenly moved his light into the trees and his Gatling guns began to throw bullets at an astonishing rate. I heard screams, looked into the trees and saw three troops being turned into ground meat. I glanced at Sergeant Parsons and noticed she was ready to fire the SAM.

As soon as the guns on the aircraft grew quiet, I yelled, "Now Sergeant, fire!"

The missile left the tube and struck the helicopter right in the hottest part of the engine. There was a loud explosion and the aircraft began to wobble. The nose came down, the speed was increased and then the helicopter nosed over and the rotor blades struck the last span on the bridge. The blades disintegrated, and quickly too. There was a huge fireball, lighting the area for hundreds of yards.

"Move, and east!" I yelled as I gained my feet and tried to lead the way.

Of our downed troops, Sergeant Parsons told me later they were dead and torn to pieces by the meat grinders on that chopper. I hate napalm and Gatling guns, both of which are, in my opinion, nasty and vicious.

After about a quarter mile, I gathered everyone around me and said, "I know of a cave near here, and we can spend the night or a day or two there. We'll be safe there, unless Russians are in the place."

"How far, and do you have a compass heading?" Parsons asked.

"No, but if you'll look to your right above the river, you'll see a dark hole in the side of the bluff. That is it and it has running water, too. Let's move. I want Private Davis on point, and Smith, you bring up the rear. Let's go, and near the river we'll find a small wooden foot bridge over the water. We'll cross there."

When we neared the bridge, I sent Davis over to check the area alone, and then we went over as a group. I had Smith booby trap the ground around both sides of the bridge and then in the middle. If anyone tried to cross, unless they were really good we'd hear them coming.

The cave took some time to reach because the slope in front of it was steep and high. Footing was mainly shale and sandstone, so it was dangerous at times. Finally, about two hours after I'd first pointed it out to Parsons, we were at the cave. I kept everyone at the mouth until I, Dolly, and Corporal Ledford checked for booby traps. We found none.

"This is home for a day or two. Sergeant Parsons, set up a guard detail and include me in it as well. We'll guard 24 hours a day until we leave here."

"Will do, sir." she said, and I noticed her hands twitching and trembling, and realized the battle with the helicopter might have been rough for her. I made a mental note to discuss it with her later.

Choppers were in the air all night long, but I felt safe in the cave. At one point, a chopper neared the entrance to our cave, turned on spotlights and scanned the inside. Most of us had run back past a bend in the cave, so we were unseen. Two people remained in front, but they were laying behind stalagmites and stalactites. I'd kept an eye on the side door gunner, barely seen behind the bright lights, and I was ready to kill, if needed. The helicopter looked for a couple of minutes and then flew off.

I now sent people around the bend in the cave at the back if they wanted to sleep. That would keep them from prying eyes and they'd not have to get up again, hopefully. While half slept the other half pulled guard duty. I sent one woman, Private Dobins, to the very top of the cliff to watch over all of us. I had to point out a trail that led to the top before she'd attempt the move.

Just after dawn, Dobins returned, pointed west and said, "Troops moving, and they look to be Russian."

Looking from the hole, I spotted a good company size group following our tracks. I saw a dog team out front, so I sent Corporal Ledford, our sniper, to remove the threat. I knew it would take the Corporal time to get in position because I didn't want him to fire from or around the cave. I sat in the mouth of the cave, Dolly at my side, and watched the Russians with binoculars. They were an efficient group, led by a Master Sergeant.

About thirty minutes after Ledford left, I heard a single shot and saw the dog collapse. A few second later, there was a second shot and the Master Sergeant fell. As the Russians moved for cover, the dog handler dropped as well. The shots echoed in the long valley.

I watched a young medic attempt to reach the Master Sergeant, and Ledford dropped the man with a shot to the head. Two more men rushed toward the Senior NCO, and both fell, fatally injured. I knew about now my sniper would move out of the area and then make his way back to me. I thought I could hear the screams and cries of the Russian wounded, but it was my imagination. They were too far away for me to hear anything, except gun-shots.

I sat watching the group with Dolly's head in my lap, and then heard Russian helicopters approaching. I moved deeper into the cave and kept my glasses on the Russian troops. One of the aircraft was obviously a medical aircraft and the other two were Black Sharks. I watched the attack helicopters work the woods over that Ledford had used. They hit the trees with everything they had and I wondered about the expense of what I was watching. After a couple of minutes, I realized they'd just spent thousands and thousands of dollars to try to kill a single man—who was long gone.

I watched the Russian dead and wounded placed on board the medical chopper. The Master Sergeant was the last man on the aircraft and he moved pretty much under his own power, with only a medic guiding him. I saw a pea green bandage wrapped around the man's chest and knew he'd been hit hard. He was setting an example for his troops and I had to respect the man, even if he was my enemy.

Two nights after we arrived in the cave, we left in the middle of the night moving south by east. The weather was warmer than usual, no rain or precipitation at all. It was late morning before we arrived at the perimeter of my base camp. The last few miles were rough, with Russian aircraft heard overhead, and it made me wonder if they were looking for our headquarters.

As we sat in the grasses watching my camp, something was odd about the movements of the troops. Dolly growled and lunged forward, and that did it for me. I pulled everyone back about a mile and said, "I think our base camp is under new management."

"I saw no one I knew." Sergeant Parsons said.

"People were moving, but they didn't have the tired eyes and slow gait of most partisans." Ledford said.

"What now? I mean we have a lot of gear and supplies at our base camp." Parsons asked, and met my eyes.

I smiled, pulled Dolly's head to my lap and as I scratched her ears, I said, "We are going to hit the place hard and do all the damage we can, but only after we confirm it's not us in control. So, Ledford, take Private Dobins with you and see what you can discover about who's in control of our base camp. Try not to be seen."

"Sure, boss. I'll nose around and see what I can find."

"Once you start looking, see if where we stored the munitions is the same or if anything major has been changed since we left. Also, look for any partisans that may have been captured."

"Come to think of it," Parsons said, "I didn't see a single person with a cloth tied around their left arm."

"Neither did I, but it's not like the Russians to miss that detail. Now, Ledford, take no chances but find out what we need to know. If any of our people are being kept there, we need to plan to rescue as many as we can when we hit the place."

"Will do, sir. Come on, Dobins, we have a date with the Russians." The two left and I prayed they were successful.

Two hours later, my two partisans returned and Ledford was smiling. He moved to me and said, "The munitions and other storage areas have not changed. I did see about forty of our people being held in a weak half-ass corral of some sort, using barbed wire. They had four guards, and it'd not take much to rescue them. I suspect the guards can be taken out with knives and then we can arm our people."

"How many Russians there?" I asked.

"Maybe, oh, 50 troops that we saw total. It's hard to tell because they're milling around all over the place. They still don't have the armbands on their left arms, either. I'm positive they're in control, besides the prisoners they have, because I watched a Russian senior NCO in uniform chew some ass. He was a Senior Sergeant. While I don't speak a word of the language, an ass chewing is an ass chewing in any man's army." Ledford said, and then chuckled.

"Where are the prisoners being kept?"

"Just outside the old headquarters tent, maybe fifty feet to the north."

"Paxton, you and I will silence the guards."

"Colonel, I have a crossbow." Private Taylor said.

"Can you put a man down quietly with one? And, don't bull-shit me, because lives depend on your answer." I asked.

"I can take 'em out without a sound."

"Okay, then you do the job. Once the guards are down, we hit them, rescue as many of our folks as we can, and destroy all we see. I want to hurt the Russians during this attack."

"We'll need someone to lead the prisoners away from the camp."

"I want you, Brown, and Paxton to do that job. Now, saddle up, folks, and let's move."

CHAPTER 5

Newly promoted Master Sergeant Georgiy was hurting as the chopper left the ground and made it's way back to Fort Leonard Wood. He'd taken the sniper's bullet to his left shoulder, and right now the medic was treating the other troops first. He knew the flat bone in his back was struck too, because he'd seen fragments of bone when the medic on the ground worked him over. He'd refused morphine when first hit so he'd be able to still give orders as they waited for their ride home. The medic moved to him now, slipped a needle into his arm, and started an IV. He knew instantly it was morphine.

As his pain began to leave, he asked, "How many did we lose?"

"We do not have a clear number yet, Master Sergeant. I will let you know when I have the figures. I do know all your troops are being taken out by helicopter, so once back at base we will know for sure. How is your pain level now?"

"I feel no pain, but I am sleepy. I am starting to wish my orders to Moscow were not canceled."

Working on the Master Sergeant's bandage, the medic said, "Then sleep, because you have done all for your troops that a man can be expected to do alone, and then some."

The Master Sergeant's world faded into darkness.

Sergeant Georgiy awoke in a huge hospital in Fort Leonard Wood, and it took him a few minutes to remember the sniper and his injury. He was hurting now, his shoulder throbbing in pain, but he saw no one near.

"Nurse!" he called out in a loud voice.

Minutes later a young female Lieutenant entered and asked, "Do you need something, Master Sergeant? There is a call button beside your pillow, so the next time do not wake the whole ward."

"My pain is getting bad and I need something." he said, and he was sitting up now which seemed to lessen the throbbing. "As for my yelling, Lieutenant, I suggest you be a little faster at your job. I had better not discover any of my troops are laying in the beds in pain or I will come and talk to you about it—ma'am."

"I can give you morphine, so lay back, and I will end your pain for now."

"How many of my troops were killed, or do you know?" His tone softened.

"I do not have that information, but the doctor is due in to visit in maybe two hours, so I am sure he can help you."

"If you can, since I may be asleep, see if you can get the answer for me."

"I will try to find out for you. Now, lay back, relax, and get some additional sleep. Oh, a Master Sergeant came to visit you and said your gift was under your pillow. I suspect it is vodka, knowing you senior Sergeants."

Reaching under his pillow, Georgiy pulled out a pint of top shelf vodka and smiled.

"I know you will drink it, but I must warn you, alcohol and painkillers can kill you."

Breaking the seal and taking a long pull, the Sergeant said, "Yes, ma'am, uh, you have warned me. Thank you for not being a prude, Lieutenant. I have found many junior medical officers to be a pain in the ass, but you are different. Please, when you get a chance, look in on my troops."

"I figure you have been in the Army longer than I have been alive. It is kind of hard to pull rank on a man that is old enough to be my father, has years of experience, and is so good looking."

Georgiy broke out laughing and asked, "Good looking? I think you have been in my drink before me. No, I am not handsome, not in the least. The only person in my life that ever called me handsome was my mother, and I think she was lying."

"I disagree." Handing him a business card, she said, "Once you are out of here, give me a call one evening or visit my humble quarters. Just let me know beforehand, and I will try to get us a meal put together."

"I am a married man, Lieutenant."

"I am a married woman, Master Sergeant, and I am simply having you over for supper." She gave him a wink.

"I see, should I bring dessert?"

"No, just show up, because you are dessert; now get some rest." She broke into a big smile.

Georgiy closed his eyes. The lieutenant was a very attractive blonde, short, maybe 1.524 meters tall and close to 49.89 kilograms. She had a nice bust, showed enough cleavage for a man to notice her firm breasts, narrow waist, and wide hips. She had a nice curve to her rear that the Master Sergeant found sensuous. It was her long hair, wrapped on the back of her head, that caught his attention. He loved women with long hair. He'd joked about being married, because his Olga had died almost ten years ago.

She'd left the room, so he picked up her card and read, "Elena (Lena) Vadimovna, Junior Lieutenant, Russian Federation, Moscow." A phone number was on the card, crossed out in black ink and a local Fort Leonard Wood four digit number written in.

Seconds later, he fell asleep with the card in his hand.

The Master Sergeant had no idea how long he'd been asleep, but he heard a voice say, "Wake up, Sergeant, we need to discuss your condition. I am your doctor."

Lifting his heavy eye lids, he glanced up and saw a middle-aged Major with a clipboard in his left hand. He sat up, rubbed the sleep from his eyes and yawned.

"Sir, how did my troops do after I was shot?"

"I have no idea, but the last two helicopters picking them up came under intense ground fire and were lost. We lost ten men in the two aircraft, not counting the crews. Both were taken down by SAM missiles. Of the wounded brought here, we have not lost a man or woman yet. So, out of the company you led, fifteen were killed and twenty injured. We also lost a dog handler and the dog. Most of the injured were treated and released to light duty. I believe there are four of you still in the hospital."

"When will I be released?"

"That depends on your pain level, so I will speak with your nurse, uh, Lieutenant Vadimovna, and see how you have been doing. We can give you pills for the pain, but no drinking."

Laughing, the Sergeant said, "Why don't you keep the pills, and let me drink?"

The doctor laughed and said, "Just do not mix them or you may die. I will release you in two days if the Lieutenant agrees, and then place you on no duty status for seven days and then limited duty for a month."

"Sounds good to me."

"Good, now get some sleep, and from what I heard at my Stand Up meeting with the Colonel, you are a big hero and you have a couple of medals coming. They discussed a promotion, but I think he will talk to you about that first. I think it would be a great loss of prestige to go from a Master Sergeant to a Lieutenant."

Georgiy laughed and said, "That is true sir, but the pay would be better."

"Sleep and I will talk with you later."

Closing his eyes, the Master Sergeant was asleep in no time.

Three days later the Master Sergeant was standing at attention in front of a group of officers in a staff meeting. He had no idea what was going on, other than he'd been told to appear in his dress uniform. He was about half drunk, fighting the pain in his shoulder, and hoped he'd not pass out before this dog and pony show was over. Off and on, since his release from the hospital, he'd fought dizzy spells.

Master Sergeant Romanovich yelled from the pit of his stomach, "Teeen-hooouuut!"

Everyone in the room stood.

The commander of Fort Leonard Wood, Colonel Elkin Yanovich, walked to the center of the room with three medals on a blue velvet pillow. He faced the audience and said, "I will now present the Medal of the Cross of St. George, first class, Medal of Suvorova, and the Medal 'For Courage' to Master Sergeant Georgiy. All three are awarded to you, Sergeant, for your bravery and courage. In addition, you are immediately promoted to the rank of Captain. Once your tour here is complete, you will be placed on show in the Fatherland and visit our people. To them and to us, your comrades, you are a true hero. Once I hang the medals on you, please wait as I and Colonel Leonidovich change your rank."

A brief citation was read and the medals were placed on the Master Sergeant's jacket. Then, a Captain read, "Effective immediately, Master Sergeant Ilik Georgiy is promoted to the rank of Captain, by order of General Yakovich, Marshal of the Army, Russian Federation."

Georgiy bent forward and the two Colonels changed his rank.

"Due to the new Captain's injuries, his promotion party will take place one month from today. Captain, come by my office three days from now and we will discuss your new assignment. Let us have a hand for our newest officer, Captain Ilik Georgiy."

Captain Georgiy called Lieutenant Lena Vadimovna once back in his room and after he'd had a couple drinks for his pain. She said she'd be right over, so he removed his service coat. She didn't think he was up to walking to her place, not drinking like he was. The Captain had stopped at the commissary on the way back and picked up enough food for their supper. He'd also moved into his new quarters and it was very nice, compared to his enlisted prefab single room.

His new quarters were painted American quarters and they were excellent. He lived on the second level of a three story building, and he had a kitchen and a private bathroom with shower. He'd placed what little he owned in the room, looked the place over and loved the stove and fridge. He also had a clock radio, television, and a number of lamps. It was as good or better than his apartment in Moscow.

He moved to the stove and began to prepare a simple meal of roasted lamb meat on skewers. It was called *Shashlyik* by his people. This dish was a form of Russian *shish kebab*, with juicy chunks of lamb served with an unleavened bread, Russian pickles, and a spicy tomato sauce. It was a meal unto itself, was fast and easy, and most Russians loved to eat it as an evening meal. He put the meat in the oven under the broiler, and opened a top shelf bottle of vodka. He poured a drink and then placed the drink in the freezer of his fridge, one of the advantages of being an officer.

Once the meal was done, he placed it in the oven to keep warm and took a quick shower. He liked the idea of not sharing his shower, and having one to himself was a great change. He could learn to love being an officer.

Since they were not authorized to wear civilian clothes he owned none, but he wore a pair of his camouflage battle dress pants and an olive drab tee shirt. He wore only shower shoes on his feet. The room was clean and he'd found a broom, mop, and vacuum cleaner in the closets. He'd come a long way from a tent with a dirt floor. In some ways it overwhelmed him, because he was used to living a spartan life.

There was a knock on his door.

He walked to the door, opened it, and found Lena standing with a big smile on her face. She was looking beautiful with her camouflage battle dress pants and a black tee shirt. Her breasts stretched the tee to the point his eyes were drawn to them.

"Hello, Ilik." she said in a shy voice.

"Welcome to my quarters. Come on in, while I pour you a drink."

"Oh, this is nice. So, this is how they treat heroes."

He laughed loudly, handed her a vodka and said, "I am no hero. I was a Sergeant doing what I had been trained to do, take care of my men."

"That is not what I heard. I was told you refused medical treatment until all of your men were cared for first, and you continued to run the company even though you were seriously injured. From what little I know of you, it sounds like something you would do. You must have impressed Moscow because they promoted you, as well. To think, when you woke up today, I outranked you and by supper time, you outranked me." She gave a light laugh.

"Are you hungry?"

"Some, what is that delicious smell?"

"Shashlyik, with lamb, and I have some wild rice too, if you want some. I also picked up the pickles, and a spicy tomato sauce to eat with it, because I love anything spicy. I eat a lot of rice, but you might not like it. I guess I should have asked."

"Come, lets sit on the sofa." she said, and then laughed.

"What is so funny?"

"You have a television. I only have a radio." she said as she sat.

He turned it on and they found a documentary in Russian about Siberia, which she liked, so he sat next to her. The vodka bottle was on the coffee table, so if they wanted a drink, it was there. Both sipped their drinks slowly.

Minutes later, he stood, removed the food from the oven and prepared both of them a plate. They made small talk and ate as they watched television. Soon, half empty plates were on the coffee table and Ilik had his arm over her shoulder.

Finally, he asked, "Do you want to take a walk?"

"Not really. I was joking when I said I was married." she said.

"I was too. My wife died years ago."

"I am sorry, but that happens."

Looking into her blue eyes he asked, "So what now?"

She smiled and said, "I told you at the hospital you would be dessert, remember."

"I remember."

She stood, sat in his lap and said, "I am ready for dessert."

When he looked at her, she kissed him deeply, her tongue igniting the passion in both of them. She moaned loudly and then breaking the kiss, she pulled her tee shirt off. She was wearing no bra.

It was two hours before dawn when the noise started. Lena and Ilik were both in his bed sleeping when the sirens on the base came on, and they were loud. He turned on the TV and there was a message that read, "Hospital has sustained a number of hits from missiles or rockets. Large number of casualties. All medical personnel are to report to their duty sections immediately. This is not an exercise. All medical personnel report immediately to your duty sections."

Explosions were heard around the base, and Ilik went to his closet, pulled out his Bison and made the weapon ready. He placed the weapon on his coffee table beside the bottle of vodka.

"You stay here," she said, "and be a good little boy. You are still on medical hold, so have a couple of drinks and return to bed. I will come by to check on you after work today. I will be fine."

"You be careful. Sometimes the resistance follows their initial attacks with ground troops. They know they cannot take the whole base, but they just want us to feel their might and know they can attack when and where they want."

Ten minutes later, over a cup of green tea, the new Captain was alone and then noticed on the television that the gulag was being attacked and it was about to fall. He shrugged his shoulders, took a sip of his drink, and then heard a huge explosion. He turned to the television to see what would be reported next. He worried about Lena.

Five minutes later he read, "The base hospital has taken a direct hit and all personnel from the facility are being evacuated to the base gymnasium and local school buildings. All troops not assigned combat duties report to the hospital to assist in moving our injured. There are numerous dead and injured. I repeat, the base hospital has just taken a direct hit from a missile and has sustained great damage. There are unconfirmed reports of Chinese attack helicopters being part of this attack. It is suggested that all non-combat personnel seek cover immediately."

Georgiy wanted to help, but he wasn't assigned a new job yet and had no idea where to go. So, since he was still under a doctors care, he popped the vodka bottle open and took a long pull. Then he began to worry about Lena again, because she was assigned to the hospital. A fourth of a bottle later, the all clear sirens were heard and he dressed.

He left his quarters and made his way to the hospital, which was in flames. Smoke, dense and black, rose to the sky. People, including rescue crews, were coming and going. A number of men saluted Georgiy, but he'd never been saluted as an officer before and had no idea who they were saluting. He made his way to the on-scene commander to learn what was going on with the hospital and hoping to learn something of Lena.

"What do you need Captain?" the Lieutenant Colonel asked.

"What caused all this damage, sir?"

"Chinese attack helicopters, and we have photographs of them in flight. I have an unknown number of dead and injured."

"Were the injured taken to the base gymnasium, too?"

"That is correct."

"Thank you, sir."

He moved to the gymnasium and found the place a mad house with doctors yelling orders, nurses running to and fro as patients screamed and some cried in pain. One young soldier, missing three limbs, was calling for his momma and the Captain was sure he'd never see her again.

"Captain Georgiy!" a female voice called out.

"Lena, are you well?" he asked as he neared her.

"I am fine. I have small cut on my chest, but I will let you doctor it up later. Right now, you need to leave. There is too much going on here for someone to stand by and watch. Besides, you are under a doctor's care, so return to your quarters. I will come by later for a drink."

As he returned to his building he looked at the damage done around the base and knew it wasn't done by partisans alone. He had years of fighting the resistance and in too many countries, so he knew. This damage was done by aircraft, either helicopters or fixed wing. Complete buildings were blown apart or a huge number of structures were leveled for a whole block. No resistance in the world could do this.

Once in his room, he poured a drink of green tea, sat on his sofa and turned the television on.

". . . gulag was breached and over 3,500 prisoners were released. Our heroic guards managed to kill almost a third of them before coming under attack by Chinese aircraft. The remaining prisoners escaped, so be on your guard today and tonight as you move around. Some of the escapees are considered very dangerous, so do not venture out alone. All escaped prisoners are to be shot on sight. Now, here is our weather for today and the remainder of the week."

"Shit, not good." he said aloud, and he didn't mean the weather.

CHAPTER 6

"**S**ir, I have Headquarters on the line and they want to speak with you." Parsons said as she neared me. I was sitting on a log, sharing my evening meal with Dolly. My dog was a valuable asset to the unit; she'd been made a Sergeant and was entitled to an MRE of her own. She'd already eaten her meal and was helping me with mine. I can tell you one thing about German Shepherds, they do love to eat.

I took the handset from her and said, "Go, this is Copperhead One." His call sign changed because he no longer had a base camp.

"Do not attack your old base. Repeat, do not attack your base camp. Headquarters One," who I knew was the General, "has a much higher priority target for you. Do you copy?"

"I copy, but they have about four zero, uh, Poppa Oscar Whiskey."

"Uh, Copperhead, our friends will deal with your old base, copy?"

"Uh, copy." I said but wondered, *What in the hell is going on? If the Chinese deal with the base, they'll attack the place from the air and kill everything that moves, including the captives. I don't like this, not at all.*

"Copperhead One, return me to your radio operator. I have a mission for you that I will send in code. If you have any questions pertaining to your new mission, contact us after you read our message, but in code only. Copy?"

"Copy." I replied, and handed the handset to Parsons.

Ten minutes later, Parsons neared and handed me a written decoded message.

"Do not attack your home base, but relocate, and continue business as usual. You are needed for a much bigger mission now in the early planning stages. This mission is still classified and you have no need to know more at this time. The Chinese will attempt to rescue our POWs and will level your old base with air attacks.

Signed, Major General Weaver, Commander, United States Partisans, Missouri."

"Well, damn me." I said, and handed the message back to Parsons so she could burn it in a few minutes. *What a mess. I thought the Chinese didn't want to put any boots on the ground here.*

Our attack on the Fort Leonard Wood gulags had gone much smoother than we'd expected. Our loss rate was just a little over ten percent and while high, it wasn't even close to the percentage I'd been willing to pay. I wanted the Russians to know they were not safe no matter where they were in my country. I wanted them to live in fear that we'd come for them.

"Sergeant Parsons, check with the doctors and see how Top is doing. I've wondered about him since I sent him back for treatment."

"Will do, sir." she said as she stood from her desk made of wooden ammo crates.

She was filling in since Sergeant Warren was injured in the gulag attack. He'd taken a bullet fragment to his right arm and it would be weeks or maybe months before he'd be able to write again. Right now he was in a Chinese hospital dealing with a severe infection in the wound.

Major Eller entered, gave me a smile and said, "We have the Russians pissed off, and I mean as mad as a hive of hornets in a tow sack being shaken."

"Over our attacks?"

"That's partly it. The fact the Chinese assisted with aircraft has them fit to be tied. They've lodged an official complaint with the United Nations."

I laughed and once sober said, "Boy, that'll teach the Chinese, huh? The U.N. is useless and, by agreement, they should have come to our assistance years ago but they haven't done a damned thing, except make statements. They're inutile and have been from the very start. The Russians have some big balls, too. They use nuke weapons on us, then complain about the Chinese assisting us with air support!"

"They have threatened the Chinese with war, but Beijing simply laughed at them, I suspect. They're potentially the largest military force in the world and have an unlimited number of bodies to use in combat. For the U.N. to threaten them is like a bee threatening a grizzly bear." the Major said, and then added, "I have some plans drawn up I want to show you. It's a proposed attack on the highway to Saint Louis and a convoy that comes through three times a week, but always in the day time. Also, I have a proposal for blowing up Bagnell Dam at the Lake of the Ozarks."

"Why hit the dam?" I asked.

"It provides hydro electric power to the Russians."

"I know of the lake, of course, and have been there, but it's been years. What do you know about the place?"

"The lake is about 55,000 square acres in size, has close to 1200 miles of shoreline, The base of the dam is about 45 meters tall, and is close to a half a mile wide. It has eight generators that keep the Russians well lit at night. I propose we blow all twelve flood gates at the same time."

"What of civilian casualties downstream from the dam?"

"We'll warn them of course, but it will make our mission harder. We have no idea who is on the Russian payroll, but I can't see killing people without some warning."

Like I just did with the suitcase bomb? But, warning them is out, I thought, but said, "No, no warning at all. It would compromise the mission and lead to too many deaths on our side."

Eller grew serious and said, "I can't do this. To not warn them is—it's murder in my eyes."

"Murder? I think not, but I can understand your view, completely. Look Joe, the Russians are killing Americans by the thousands everyday and they have no guilt at all, not a bit. By hitting the dam, we'll shut their power off for a long spell, I believe, and it's worth the cost in military and civilian lives."

"I disagree, Colonel, and want to go on record that I disagree."

"Good, I'll make note of your comments. You need to start thinking on a larger scale, Major, and see how anything we do will hurt the Russians. Then weigh the cost, even in human lives, and decide if it's worth the expense. Tonight, you and I will scout the area out. What kind of arrival times for the water have you figured for some of the towns downstream from the dam?"

"I estimate it'll take about 11 hours to reach Tuscumbia, and it'll probably wipe out highway 63 and the Highway 50 bridge. Also, at about the same time, water would strike the Bonnots Mill area. Then Chamois at close to 19 hours after our detonation. Now, that doesn't include private homes, fishing camps, or farms in the flood path, sir. A number of counties would suffer from this mission."

"By morning, I want the latest census status on how many people live below the dam, with the amount of time these towns have before the water reaches them. Eleven hours is a substantial warning, and all could be evacuated in that time. Get the numbers and then you and I will make a decision."

The Major saluted and left. I could understand his concern, but at times civilian lives are just as expendable as our lives. The key to the decision is how much disruption will any mission cause the Russians, and is it worth the price?

Sergeant Parsons entered and said, "Top isn't doing well; I spoke to his doctor. Seems the injury has taken a turn for the worse because Top is a heavy smoker. They had to remove half of one lung and so far he's not responding to treatment well. I saw the man, sir, and if you want to see Top alive, I suggest you get to the hospital today. I don't expect him to be alive in the morning."

"Thanks, Sergeant, I'll walk over and visit with him in a while. He and I go way back, and he's a good man."

"Good people are being killed in this war too, sir, or so you told me once."

I had to chuckle, because my conversation with her when the Russians executed her parents must have been remembered well. I met her eyes and replied, "I hope we're keeping a list of all who have and will give their lives in the name of freedom. We need a grand memorial erected to list all the people who've died, and not just resistance personnel."

"I'd not start building your memorial yet, sir, because I think we have years of fighting left."

I nodded but didn't speak.

After a few minutes she asked, "Can I ask you a personal question, sir?"

"I guess, as long as it's not sexual."

"I don't mean this in a negative way, but don't you think Carol is a little young for you?"

I grinned and replied, "First, Sergeant Parsons, my personal life is none of your business, but I will answer your question since it's not sexual. Neither the Captain or I chose to fall in love, it just happened. Age is more than just a number and while I'm many years older than her, I don't see it as a problem. She likes older men, always has, and I'm the kind of man who needs a woman in my life. Right now, the way we live, I don't feel age is a serious factor. I don't think I'll live long enough to ever become impotent anyway." I said, and then laughed.

I watched her nod and knew she didn't like my answer. I think she may have had a crush on me. If so, I had no idea why, because with the troops under my command I was all business and at all times. I'm not good looking either, so if she had a crush, it was like some young boy who loved his 3rd grade teacher. Then again, it's more likely she was simply warning me of our age differences. In a normal society like we had before the war, Carol and I would have little in common, but with the war on we shared loneliness.

"Best of luck to the both of you. If you're going to see Top, sir, you'd better move."

"Thanks, Sergeant Parsons, you're a wonderful woman and an even better NCO."

She laughed and said, "We'll see if you and Carol ever break up, because I'll be knocking on your tent door. That night, you'll really find out how wonderful I am as a woman, *sir.*"

I blushed and replied, "I'm going to see Top."

As I walked to the hospital I gave Parsons a lot of thought. *There was no doubt she was all woman and would make a man a good mate for life. But, I don't love her and I do Carol. If something were to happened to Carol it would destroy me, only I'd have to put the grieving behind me at some point. Then, I'd not be taken advantage of by any woman, because I'd still be in the grieving process, and it's too easy to fall in love when you hurt. I need to stop thinking about love and women. Hell, I might be dead in an hour,* I thought.

I noticed guards at the hospital, but I wasn't sure if they were there to keep Russians out or the patients in their beds. Most folks hated the hospital, unless in some serious pain. They quickly grew bored and the staff sent as many as they could back to work or on limited work. It was not uncommon for a patient to bust out of the place and return to their unit.

I saluted the two guards and entered the tent.

A doctor quickly moved to my side and asked, "What can I do for you, sir?"

"I'm looking for a patient called Top."

"Follow me, but I can't give you much time with him. I'm afraid his time is limited and he'll not recover from his wound."

"So, how long does he have?"

"I think from twelve to twenty-four hours; after that, each breath will be a gift from God. His respiratory system is very frail, mainly due to years of smoking."

I nodded and followed the man around a tent full of sick and wounded people. Some had hideous injuries and others looked as healthy as me. I knew, however, they were seriously impaired or they'd not be in the tent.

When we neared Top he looked terrible, with countless hoses and wires running all over his body. He was plugged into an IV and I saw a heart monitor. Other than that I had no idea what all the machines did or monitored. He looked pale and very tired.

"Sergeant Major, you have a guest."

Top's eyes slowly opened, he saw me and gave a faint smile.

"I see you took the day off." I said, and then smiled at him.

"I'm . . . under the . . . weather, sir."

"Are you going to make it? The doctors say you'll not survive this wound."

"I'll make it . . . and just to show . . . them how much . . . control a Sergeant . . . Major has."

"You rest. Do you want some whiskey?"

"No . . . I . . . sleep too much . . . now."

"Wow, you must really be in bad shape to turn down whiskey." I said, and then laughed.

Top laughed and a minute later said, "I will . . . survive this."

The doctor neared and said, "That's enough, sir. He tires easily."

"Top, I have to leave now, but I'll be back to see you in the morning." I grabbed his hand, met his eyes, and noticed his smile. His eyes met mine, and we both knew I'd not see him alive again. He gave my hand a gentle sqeeze.

"I'm . . . proud of . . . you, son. I will be . . . okay." he said and closed his eyes.

He then gave my hand a hard squeeze and I left the hospital. Emotionally, I was busted up inside, but I knew it could have been any of us in Top's bed instead of him, including me. My eyes watered so badly I used an old rag in my pocket to wipe them dry.

By 2200 the Major and I were scouting below the dam. It was his people so he called the shots, but we'd been out for over two hours and I'd not seen a single house yet. We had seen a few old fishing shacks along the Osage River, but that was it. Every member of the team wore night vision goggles (NVGs).

I heard nothing, but our man on point suddenly dropped and began to scream. I tapped the medic on the arm and we moved to the downed man. He'd stepped in an open pit filled with long iron stakes with barbed ends. Looking down with my NVGs, I could see two stakes through his foot and ankle. He was bleeding hard, too. I was able to pull the two stakes from the dirt in the bottom of the hole and, once his foot was out of the hole, I pulled them through his foot by grasping the barbs.

I noticed the tips were discolored a dark brown, so I said, "Give him something for pain and also antibiotics, because the tips have been treated with human waste. I know this is one of our traps, so keep your eyes open for toe poppers."

We made a wide detour around the punji stake pit and all went well. But we had almost half his squad, four people, carrying the injured man. There was no way to avoid the litter, so we did what was required and accepted it. It did, nonetheless, slow us down.

Four hours later we'd seen only one home, so we turned back to return to camp. The injured man was completely out of it, un-conscious, and an IV was stuck on a stick so each person took turns carrying it and the litter. Most took to pinning the IV bag to a shirt pocket and that left one hand free.

When we were about half way back, I heard a chopper, but so did the whole squad and everyone dropped to the ground. I watched men and women frantically pulling ponchos out to cover with if the choppers flew too close to us. I knew when the flood lights came on by the door gunners this bird was not equipped with infrared detection gear. I hoped it would find nothing and leave, but as I waited, that little animal called fear began chewing on my belly.

I glanced at the Major and his eyes told me fear was alive in his belly, too.

After hovering near us for about ten minutes the aircraft flew away and I know everyone there said a quick prayer. We'd not been spotted, but even when an aircraft is looking where you know someone is, in the darkness, it's not as easy to do as it sounds. I'm sure the crew wore NVGs too, but we'd survived and that was all that mattered.

Soon we were all on our feet and Eller had us returning to base again. Suddenly, our woman on point signaled to get in the brush; she'd spotted the enemy. We were all camouflaged and would be very hard to spot. My fear became alive once more when the woman on point neared us and whispered one word, "Dog." She then moved to beside me in the brush.

As they neared, I saw it was a Russian squad using a dog handler, and they're tough if you can't take them out. I decided to use my silencer equipped .22 to kill the dog and then we'd start the fight. I wanted the dog out of the way and the handler too, and as quickly as possible. I held up my pistol and then a grenade, so they all understood that we'd throw the explosives *after* I fired the pistol.

When the Russians neared, I heard the dog handler talking in low reassuring tones to the animal. The dog was a big beautiful German Shepherd, just like my Dolly, and I dreaded killing the animal, but this was war and I'd done many things I wasn't proud of. I was also glad I'd left Dolly with Carol for this mission. The wind was blowing the direction the Russians were moving and that was in our favor. By them being upwind of us, they'd not see the dog alert until the animal was almost on top of us.

A few seconds later, the dog alerted and leaped at me with only the leash keeping the animal from tearing me apart. I raised the pistol and placed a round in his chest and another in his head. The big dog dropped instantly. I then raised my weapon and fired two rounds into the dog handler's chest and then I heard grenades exploding. Rifle fire was heard, as well as pistol shots, and when I glanced around there were tracers flying all over. Many resistance fighters used tracers for the last three cartridges, so they'd know they would need a fresh magazine. Seconds later, it grew deathly quiet.

"Wait as I check them." I said.

I stood and moved to each man, placing a round in each head. The last man was a Russian Full Colonel and I was surprised. I was even more surprised when I found him alive, but wounded. His legs were both struck and he was in sad shape. Him, I wanted to return home with so we could milk him for all the information he might know.

I motioned our medic to me and had her work on the Colonel. I stood at the ready with my pistol on the man. He seemed to be unconscious, but I didn't trust Russians any more than my mentor, Willy Williams, had years ago. I'd done a lot of growing up since Willy died. I'd started with him as a Sergeant and due to deaths, including Willy's, and injuries, I was now a Full Colonel. Stepping on the bodies of dead friends is a hard way to be promoted, and I remember every single one of them.

Eller neared me and whispered, "What now? If we take him with us, we'll have to pack him."

"Then I suggest we make another stretcher because this man has information we need. I honestly think intelligence will be tickled to get their hands on him. I value his life more than any of ours, because debriefing him will save lives in the future, maybe."

The Major nodded and then moved to his troops and they started making another stretcher using the Russian ponchos each dead man had. As they took the ponchos, they also took all the gear from the men that we needed and could use. Of course, grenades, ammo and food was at the top of the list of needed items.

Eller showed a few minutes later holding a Russian map in his hand.

"Old map and outdated, but I think they were looking for our headquarters. The map has three areas circled in red grease pencil and if my Russian is correct, they think any one of these places is our headquarters. If you'll look, they're a good five miles off and not even close."

"Good, bring all the papers and maps with us."

"This is pretty much it, because they don't even have unit patches on their uniforms. I know they're not Spetsnaz or we'd have experienced a much harder fight and they'd be dressed differently."

"Get your people to moving, and bring their radio. I'm sure our radio shop can change the frequency and we need more ways to communicate. Also, contact base and let them know we're bringing in a 'Big Bug.' That way they'll have a security team, along with an intelligence officer, in place when we arrive."

"Will do. Now, with two stretchers, all but four of us will be used to carry the two men."

"That won't work. Put two people to a stretcher, not four, and we'll have more folks to fight with if the brown stuff hits the fence. Hurry, because we've been here too long already."

"Thomas, you on point and Johns, you bring up the rear. Let's move, people, and keep the noise to a minimum."

I watched our medic give the Russian a shot of morphine so he'd be out of it on the trip. I wasn't sure if she gave it out of compassion for his pain or to keep the man quiet as we moved. I was to learn later it was for both reasons. Just a few years back we were killing every Russian we found alive, but we'd started treating their injured if they were permanently disabled, and if not, we made them that way. Cold? Perhaps, but I didn't want to face the same soldiers two or three times down the road.

The trip back was a slow one because of the two men we were packing, plus the fact the point man or woman started picking up booby traps; most were ours, and signs of antipersonnel mines, which could have belonged to either side. In all cases we cautiously moved around the danger and continued on our way.

When we were about two miles from our camp, Johns, who was now on point, screamed and began to do an almost comical dance on the trail. As his screams grew louder I moved forward and right off saw three metal barbs sticking from his back, each dripping blood.

"Medic!" I said in a low tone, but with a sense of urgency. I wanted to keep the noise down.

She neared, along with Eller, looked him over and then she met my eyes as she shook her head.

"Give him morphine for his pain and to end his suffering." Eller ordered.

The man had struck a thin line across the trail, usually thin fishing line was used, and triggered a limb that was about chest high and had five sharp barbs mounted on it. It was held back so when he pulled the line, it released the trigger and struck him full in the chest. There was nothing we could do for him except give him enough morphine he'd overdose and die in no pain. I didn't say anything, but the trap was one of ours.

Eller moved to the young man as the medic gave him the powerful painkiller, and he held the dying man's hand and spoke softly to him as he passed. The Major moved up a number of notches in my view because of his compassion. I'd changed over the years and while still cold at times, it was due to the nature of my work.

Minutes later the man shivered, gave a loud sigh, and fell limply. He remained standing because the limb was holding him up.

"We'll return for his body this afternoon. Thomas, you take point and Carol, you're on drag." the Major ordered.

Once back in camp, the wounded were turned over to the medical folks and a security team was assigned to guard the Russian Colonel.

As I walked to my office, Eller asked, "I hated to lose Johns; he was an experienced explosives man and an all around good troop and man."

"What makes it even worse is our side killed him. The Russians may plant mines and booby traps, but the resistance placed that one there. The Bear doesn't make homemade traps like that. All it takes is one second of being inattentive and you're a dead man. Or, he may have been tired, who knows why he didn't see the line, and it doesn't matter now."

"I hear you and agree. I'll get intelligence on the Colonel as soon as he wakes. After they milk him for all they can get, what then?"

"Let's find out what we can about the man before we make any rash decisions. The bullet wounds are to his legs, so lets see what his prognosis is, too. If he's permanently disabled, once we learn all we can we'll release him, unless he's a war criminal. If he runs a gulag or is a known killer of Americans, well, he'll die. I'll personally put the noose around his neck."

"I think that's understandable, sir. Now, I need see to my troops." He snapped to attention and gave me a crisp salute, so I did the same.

As he walked away from me, I wondered, *How many of us will still be alive a year from now?*

CHAPTER 7

Captain Georgiy was tired, but Lena was totally exhausted when she came to his quarters. He'd been sleeping when her gentle knock woke him. He'd been very pleased to see her, pulled her into his room and kissed her madly. Later, after she'd had a glass of vodka and some cheese, he'd cleaned her breast with rubbing alcohol, and found it was just a little more than a scratch. Then, still topless, she'd fallen asleep with her head in his lap, and stretched out on the sofa. Minutes later, he joined her in sleep.

He had no idea when he awoke what time it was, but glancing at the clock it was 2200 hours, so he moved carefully and placed her head on a pillow. He showered and decided to serve supper. He'd had a pot of borscht with meat simmering all day and the smell reminded him of his deep hunger. He moved to the stove, lifted the lid and smiled at the red beet soup. He found the smell tantalizing and couldn't resist a quick sip of the broth. He smiled again. *That's so good*, he thought.

He prepared places for two, placed the pot of soup on the ceramic tile on the table, and pulled out a long loaf of uncut fresh bread. He then moved to Lena.

"My sweetheart, you need to eat. Wake up long enough to eat, and then you can go back to sleep."

"I am tired, so let me sleep."

He kissed her forehead and then her chin before he replied, "I have borscht with meat, so eat a little and then you may sleep more. I think you would be better to spend the night here."

"Must I eat?"

"Yes, and that is an order, if that will get you to the table. Come on, eat with me, and then we will both go to bed if you wish. I promise to hold you close as you sleep."

"Ummm, okay, I will eat then. I know I need food, but I am just beat. Even my scalp tingles from fatigue."

"I have been that way many times. I know how you feel. Come." He took her right hand and pulled her up.

Once on her feet, she pulled him to her, and kissed him deeply as his arms went around her. His hands squeezed her butt cheeks, which caused her to moan, and she said, "I may not have supper."

"No, you will eat first. Then we will shower together and the rest of the night is ours. Come, please, and eat. You have worked well over twelve hours and you need the energy and vitamins from a good meal." He tossed her one of his clean uniform tees.

They walked into the kitchen, hand in hand, and he pulled her chair out for her.

She sat, slipped the tee over her head and then took a quick spoonful of the soup and said, "Now, this is so good. You are a wonderful cook, Ilik, and will be a good prize for a lucky woman one day."

He sat, shrugged and said, "I am no prize, just a normal man."

"Oh, I disagree with you. You are ruggedly handsome, intelligent, brave, passionate and a great lover. Not to mention, you can cook too. What more could a woman need in a man?"

"My only skill is killing, and not much call for that in the civilian world."

"You sir, are no killer, but a warrior. You can get a police or other related job after you retire. When they read you were decorated and promoted to Captain because of your bravery, you will get hired quickly. People with your training and background often work for the government in one capacity or another."

"I am confused about you, Lena, and my feelings. I was scared you had been hurt or killed today and I do not know why. I just met you last night."

"That is the compassionate side of you, do you not see?"

"No, this was more than compassion. It was not as if I had only lost a lover, but I was actually scared I had lost you, *you*, the woman you are. I find this hard to talk about because I am old enough to be your father. It is all moving too quickly too, which scares me."

"Well, I am attracted to you too, and believe me, I do not think of you as my father." She laughed, sobered, and said, "Let us finish this meal and jump in the shower. I cannot wait to help you wash. Let us let what will happen, happen, between us. I think we are both mature enough to take the risk of love, but right now, we can just enjoy each other's bodies."

She winked, and he shivered.

The following weeks passed quickly, with Lena spending most nights with Ilik unless she had night shift. She was a demanding lover who never pushed him away and often came to him. Their time together was enjoyed by both, and neither was aware they were in love. He often daydreamed of having her as a wife, and she dreamed of him being her perfect husband. Both knew the realities of their jobs, and either or both could be dead in a heartbeat. However, the concern of an early death was pushed to the very backs of their minds as their love grew stronger than their fears.

Finally, back at work, Ilik discovered they had him commanding a company of men and women, which he enjoyed. The troops respected him greatly for his enlisted time, his high enlisted rank, and the fact he'd been promoted for bravery. They knew their commander was no normal man, and they were proud to serve under him.

"Sergeant, I want all the troops assembled in fifteen minutes. I think it is time I meet them. I want everyone assigned and accounted for in formation. The exception will be any confined to quarters by the police or medical staff. Of those, I want to know their status."

"Sir, fifteen minutes is not much time."

"I disagree and you only have fourteen minutes now, so move!"

Fifteen minutes later, all but ten of the one hundred were in formation, standing at attention. Georgiy called the Sergeant forward and asked, "Where are the rest?"

"Sir, one is on medical confinement with a broken leg, one is in the guardhouse for being unruly, and the others just cannot be found."

"I want the man in jail out today. At least I know for sure I have one fighter in this bunch. From now on, our folks arrested for fighting will be released as soon as we can arrange it. I want fighters, not a bunch of nuns, understood?"

"Uh, yes, sir."

The Captain moved to the front center of his company and said, "I am Captain Ilik Georgiy and I am your new commander. You will find I demand a lot from you, but I will not ask anything of you that I will not be able to do, or that I have not done myself in the past. I rose from the ranks and was promoted to Master Sergeant. Then, I was promoted to my current rank. Why I was promoted is not your business, but I know the lives you live. I have been in your shoes, so I know the little games and ways to avoid attention like some of you use. I only ask you to obey my orders, keep yourself looking sharp and clean, and do your jobs to the best of your ability."

He slowly walked to the far left side of the formation, with the Sergeant at his side, and began moving down the ranks slowly. No one had expected an inspection, so some grew concerned.

As he moved, he spoke again, "This one needs her hair up higher, get it off the collar, or get it cut. This man needs a haircut, and this one looks like he slept in his uniform."

Half way through his inspection, he said, "From now on, unless you have a written pass, the Senior Sergeant will know exactly where you are at all times. You will sign in and out of the orderly room. I do not care where you go or what you do, as long as we can find you in the event we go into the field. It does me little use to have a hundred men and women if I can only recall fifty of them. If any of you have any serious bitches or gripes take them to the Senior Sergeant initially, and if he can't help you, see if I will see you to discuss your problem."

"Remember, I am not your mother or father, so I do not love you. I will, however, treat you like the adult soldiers you are. I may not love you like they do, but I will treat you with respect and dignity, and I expect the same from all of you. Look around you and take care of each other. Each man and woman standing here is your comrade." He looked the last soldier over and added, "This last man looks overweight, so have the clinic measure his body fat and let us know."

He walked to the front of the formation and yelled, "At ease, but remain in place. Starting tomorrow morning, we will be running every single day, rain, snow or shine. Our first run will be half a kilometer and it will slowly extend until we are running five kilometers a morning in our boots, and be sure to bring your backpacks and weapons. Our run will start at 0500 and not a minute later. Your only excuse to miss morning formation is you are dead, in the hospital, or in jail. Dismissed."

Turning to his Senior Sergeant, Georgiy said, "In one hour I want a meeting with all squad leaders. There are going to be some changes around here, but they will be implemented slowly. I think we have some good looking troops, but they have turned lazy since they got here, and I do not want to lead them into combat as they are. I cry each time I have to write a soldier's mom and dad that they are dead. Our jobs are to train them, keep them in shape, and prepare them to be the best damned troops in the Russian Army and I will do that, with your help."

Snapping to attention, the Senior Sergeant said, "Yes, sir."

"Good, now let us cut the bullshit, Sergeant, and go have a few glasses of vodka as you tell me all about our people. I know who runs the Russian Army, and it is the Senior Sergeants and Master Sergeants, not the officers. You do a good job for me and I can assure you will make Master Sergeant when you leave here, if not before."

"Yes, sir."

In his quarters two evenings later he explained to Lena why he'd fired two squad leaders, due to lack of motivation, but she'd not really understood. One had shown up reeking of alcohol and another had presented a poor appearance. The one that smelled went to jail and the other to the barber shop. He'd fired both on the spot, demoted them and made the next two ranking persons squad leader. He'd put off his meeting with the formation until tomorrow after their run.

"Hospitals are not known for their compliance with grooming standards and our hair is longer and our mustaches wider than the field troops." she said.

"I have to enforce all regulations, because it is my job. What most troops in the world need is discipline and respect."

"Respect?"

"Respect from me and each other. By the time I am done with these folks, they will think they are the best trained sonsof-bitches in the world. They will obey an order in combat without a second thought, and that will make a difference at times. I do not want my people to walk proud like the average soldier, but to strut like roosters. I want them proud of our unit, each other, me, and themselves. I really want them to be as good as they think they are —the best trained men and women in any army of the world."

"I think you will be a bad ass commander then." She laughed and then kissed his ear.

"I am personally responsible, baby, for how many go home sitting upright in that airplane and how many go home in an aluminum box. I take my responsibilities seriously." He put his arm around her and pulled her close.

"I can see how you would want them well trained."

"I had my first big problem come up today."

"Oh? And, what was that?" she asked as she started unbuttoning his shirt.

"Young girl, eighteen years old, is suddenly pregnant. At first she claimed she had no idea how it happened, but finally she admitted it was by the Sergeant I had sent to jail for drinking. Both of them were depressed, which explained his drinking, and she had been trying to hide her belly. To make a very long story short, I have her leaving in the morning for Moscow."

"Do they love each other?"

"She said no, but I could see the hurt in her eyes when she answered the question. I suspect she loves him, only he is using her as many men do. Well, their situation reminded me of us."

"I am on the pill, so relax, and neither of us are using the other."

"So was she, or so she claimed. She said the two of them have been drinking a great deal and she may have missed a day or more. She asked about him, and I said he would be facing disciplinary action for showing up to work intoxicated. I will not put him in prison, but I will do what it takes to scare the hell out of him. I placed the man in jail for fighting in charge of the drunk's squad. I know now at least three out of the four squads will fight."

Lena stood, stepped over his legs and then sat in his lap. She leaned forward, kissed him deeply and wrapped her arms around his neck. When the kiss broke, she moved to his ear and whispered, "I love you."

She was surprised to hear him reply, "I love you too, baby. Never change and no matter what the future holds, continue to love me as I will you."

"I promise to love you no matter what."

They would both discover that words so easily spoken can be hard to adhere to at times.

One month later, Georgiy was taking his troops into the field, and he wanted to break them in easy. They'd spend three nights and four days in the field. Along with him he'd have two tanks. They'd leave Fort Leonard Wood, walk down down old route 66, and then circle the area, more or less giving his people some field experience.

He was relaxed and didn't expect to run into any partisans, but if they did they'd engage them. When live ammo and grenades were passed out, his troops suddenly became quiet. Their previous commander hadn't taken them to the field often or in any way placed them, or him, in danger. The fort had used these troops as extra workers around the base. They'd augment the police, stand guard duty, pull kitchen police, or pull all the shit details. The other units loved having them on the Fort, because they were doing many of the details everyone hated. They'd started calling them 'KP' Company, because they were usually found in the kitchen, helping the cooks and bakers.

Captain Georgiy was about to change all of that, along with the company's reputation.

The second they walked out the gate, the Captain yelled, "Pugin, you are on point and Senya, you pull drag. Move, people, and get into position. Since we left the main gate, we are now in the food chain!"

The two women moved into position. They were all trained well, but lacked the fine tuning a few missions would give them. He'd spent every hour he had since he took command sharpening their skills. He'd spent countless hours with the group and they were better trained than most, but seriously lacked experience.

They were to escort both tanks to spots where they'd sit beside roadblocks so they could check any vehicles coming or going. The tanks were leading the way, and he'd instructed the point man and everyone else to step in the wide tracks left in the dirt by the heavy machines. That, in his opinion, was the only way to avoid a mine or booby trap.

The morning passed uneventfully. They'd just dropped off the last tank and he knew it would now turn more suspenseful for his troops. They'd have no foot wide tracks to step in, and were on their own.

Taking the radio handset from his radioman, he said, "Base Ops, Rugby One, over."

"Copy, Rugby One, is the last tank in place?"

"In place, and we are on our own."

"You are to proceed on your normal mission, but understand, we are currently working a cat and mouse game with the resistance. It is now very probable that you will become involved at some point. Do you copy?"

"Uh, copy, Base. Let me know when and if you need us."

"Copy, and Base out."

Walking to his Senior Sergeant, Georgiy said, "Sergeant Starikov, we may become part of a mission against the partisans, so keep everyone on their toes. I want the noise kept down, no joking or loud noises, and watch the sky-lining, okay?"

"I hear you, sir, and I am on it now."

Georgiy pulled out his map and said, "Senya, move forward and tell Pugin to take a compass heading of 126 degrees and maintain it until I tell her otherwise. Tell her to cut right across the fields and trees. Also, remind her to stay off of trails or paths of any kind."

"Yes, sir, 126 degrees." Private Senya almost yelled, and it was loud enough the Senior Sergeant rolled his eyes.

"Patience, Senior Sergeant, because they have no real experience. It will come to them after a few of their comrades are killed and injured."

Pugin was good on point, excellent as a matter of fact, and within seconds of stepping from the dirt road, she spotted a booby trap and less than an hour later she'd found another trap along with a ring of toe poppers around it. She'd marked each one with a stick stuck in the ground.

A number of times the Senior Sergeant had jumped some ass because the troops would bunch up and were not watching their distances. He was concerned about spending the night with them, because out of 100 people, 96 of them were cherries and only two others besides himself and the commander had ever been in combat before.

They stopped an hour before dusk, and Georgiy wanted fox-holes dug and security in place. He positioned the machine guns and riflemen as the Senior Sergeant put a quick stop to the bitching about how tired they were. In his mind, the Sergeant knew the troops were in for a rough four days because so far this had been a walk in the sun, too easy.

"I have sores on my shoulders from my pack. It must weigh a good 25 kilos. My back hurts and I am tired. Now the Senior Sergeant tells me I have to dig a hole. I never should have joined the army. I should have stayed a farmer." Private Teterev complained as his shovel struck dirt for the first time since it had been issued to him.

Suddenly, Senior Sergeant Starikov was behind him and, bent over like he was, the Sergeant kicked him hard in the ass. The lad fell face first to the grasses and for a minute or two it looked like he'd cry.

"W . . . why kick me?"

"Why kick me *Senior Sergeant*!" the Senior Sergeant exploded. "Private Teterev, you are a crybaby. Now, dig the hole because if you die tonight, you will already be in your grave. All we will have to do at sunup is push your body down and fill the hole in. Quit bitching and do what you have been told to do. Do you understand me, Private?"

Scrambling to his feet the Private was scared, and when he stood at attention out of respect for the Sergeant's rank, the Senior Sergeant punched him in the nose and dropped him to the ground again.

Standing over the Private, he screamed, "Do you want me to be killed? Never ever stand at attention for anyone in the field, no matter if a General nears. We never stand at attention or salute out here. I think your mother must have dropped you on your head. You are about a dumb-ass, Teterev!"

"Sergeant, watch the noise discipline." Georgiy said, and then grinned. He thought the troops were doing well for their first time in the field.

"Here, Teterev, let me assist you." a woman named Lytkina said as she began digging in his hole. The Senior Sergeant turned and walked away, angry that the young man could have gotten him killed.

"Sergeant," the Captain said, "come here for a minute or two."

The Senior Sergeant had just sat down when he gave a loud grunt and was knocked back to the ground, but not before a long finger of blood and gore shot from his back. Once on the ground he began to scream.

The Commander yelled, "Take cover and now; sniper!"

Junior Sergeant Dusya ran to the injured Senior Sergeant and assisted the commander in pulling the wounded man into his foxhole. Dusya was one of the men with a previous tour in America and an experienced man.

"The shot came from the trees off our left and since the sniper didn't shoot at me, I suspect Starikov's injury is severe. He must have suspected he was an officer the way Teterev stood at attention. His behavior is most strange. Maybe he is with a group and they are waiting to down a helicopter. What do you think, sir?"

"I have no idea why he did not shoot much more, because it is very unusual. You can be sure he had a good reason. It will be getting dark soon, but that will not make us any safer. Tell the troops to prepare for the night and I will see if I can get a helicopter here for the Senior Sergeant."

"Will do." Dusya disappeared into the dim light.

"Radio, contact Base and tell them I have a seriously wounded Senior Sergeant and need a medical helicopter here as soon as possible. Let me know what they say."

"Yes, sir."

Three minutes later he said, "The helicopter is on the way. They also said for us to stay on 50% alert tonight, because some boxed in partisans may move our way."

"Listen up, 50% alert for everyone." Georgiy said, and that meant only half of his troops could sleep at a time, but experience showed many more would sleep. He prayed at least 25% would remain awake, or some of them would die before dawn if the partisans moved toward them.

CHAPTER 8

I was interested in what Intelligence was learning from the Russian, so I paid my Intel section a short visit. Dolly was with me, and she loved the Sergeant that worked there because he usually fed her something. My whole intelligence staff consisted of a Captain, a First Lieutenant, and a Sergeant. A small staff, but they were very effective. The Captain was fluent in Russian having been born there, then coming to the states at the age of ten. He'd returned again when he entered college as an exchange student. His name was Stanislav "Stas" Yevgenievich, and his Russian I'd heard was almost as good as Willy had been. He'd eventually immigrated here.

I entered their tent and said, "Remain seated, please." I didn't want them to stand at attention for me, but to see how things were going.

"Well, sir," Sergeant Grant said, "the last time you visited me was when Willy was still the boss."

I laughed and said, "Grant, I was just in here not a week ago and delivered a Russian Colonel to you, personally. Have y'all been able to get anything out of him?" I'd known the Sergeant for years, and even before the fall. He'd been a local cop until they stopped paying the force, then they'd all walked off the job. Grant was a normal man in many ways except he had a thick Mississippi accent you could cut with a knife. He wore his brown hair short and his beard trimmed. He was never without his 1911 .45 Colt or his Russian Bison. Both weapons were always within reach. I don't think I've ever seen him without the Colt on, even when he slept.

"He's said a little, but not much. Do you want to talk to him? I think he'll surprise you, sir, because his English is better than all of ours put together and he graduated from Harvard law school. We did learn he was a plant here and was waiting for the Russians to arrive one day."

"Interesting, because I'd never thought of them having folks here, but it makes good sense. Sure, fetch the man and let's talk a spell."

"Sergeant, get Colonel Mirogod "Dennis" Denisovich for us."

Standing, the Sergeant grabbed his hat and said, "Sure, sir. I'll be right back."

When the Colonel entered the room, he was in chains. His legs were hobbled so even walking was difficult, his hands were chained to his waist, and he was naked except for a pair of cut off American battle dress trousers. He wore a pair of old shower shoes. Sergeant Grant had a chain in his hand that ran to an old dog collar that was around his neck. The Sergeant also had his Colt out and the hammer back, safety off.

Dolly growled and her hackles came up. I held her leash and said, "Easy, girl."

"Sit." Grant said.

The prisoner remained standing.

Grant pushed him down on the wooden chair and said, *"Sit!"*

"I am an officer of senior rank, Sergeant, and you will treat me as such. The Geneva Convention says all prisoners of war will be rendered the respect due their rank."

Grant smiled and said, "We weren't at the convention when it was signed this last time because our country was dying. So, excuse me if we don't comply with the rules. We didn't sign shit at the meeting, Igor."

"My name is Colonel Mirogod Denisovich, which you know, and you will treat me with the respect due a Full Colonel, Sergeant."

"That's enough, Grant." I said, and disliked the Russian right off. For some reason, he reminded me of the Nazi Gestapo interrogators used in the old black and white war movies. I moved to the man, saw no signs of abuse, and he looked healthy enough.

"Who are you?" Denisovich asked.

"I am the man, Colonel, who holds your very life in the palm of my hand. I can release you or crush you, depending on what you tell us."

"Bullshit. You American's are weak, and nothing will happen to me."

"Are you sure enough of that statement to bet your life?"

He met my eyes and I stared him down.

"Piss me off and I'll see you hanged."

The man stopped talking.

"Captain Stas, what do we know of our Colonel here?" I asked, but I knew he was the chief of the chemical and biological section at Fort Leonard Wood. That alone assured him of a short rope, once we were done with him. While they had used no chemicals in Missouri yet, they had in many other states, including Mississippi. I figured it would happen sooner or later.

"He's the chief of the chemical biological units at Fort Wood, and so far they've not used anything against us, but it's only a matter of time. His home is in Moscow, he has a wife, two boys, and one daughter. He's been married 22 years and his PhD is in microbiology. He has lived in the states more years than he has Russia, got his law degree from Harvard, was an exchange student here, and then after graduation, he applied for citizenship. It was granted, but his family remained in Russia. He is what we call a sleeper, a spy who stays out of sight until his country needs him, then he comes forward. As he waited, besides the money Russia sent him, he grew wealthy as a law dog. He was living with a woman named, uh, Sara Taylor, before the fall. She was killed in the first year of the fall when a group of thugs broke into his home, robbed the place and raped her. The Colonel was not at home when she was killed. He made contact with the first Russians to enter Missouri."

"You realize as a spy we have every legal right to hang you, right?" I asked, wanting to scare him a little.

"You'll end up killing me anyway, so it matters little. I've been told you have no POW camps, so there is little else you can do."

"We can trade you or let you go, if an exchange could be arranged. Let's say 500 prisoners from a gulag for one old Colonel."

Dennis laughed and replied, "The Russian Bear will not give much for me or anyone. We have a standard rule of not dealing with terrorists."

"We are partisans or the resistance, but terrorists we are not. We do use terrorist methods if they allow us to hurt the Russians. You are uninvited here and this is our country. We'll not stop fighting until every Russian is gone or dead."

The Russian, Dennis, did not reply.

"You, of all people, must know of the American tenacity when we are threatened."

He laughed, met my eyes and said, "Americans were soft, fat, and lazy. Most went home from work to sit in front of their televisions and drink beer. They would eat junk food until time to go to bed, then they'd sleep as their central air and heat kept them comfortable. No, as a nation all of you were spoiled."

"Then, if we were so fat and lazy, why hasn't your country taken over control of my nation? You are here in the woods with us, and it's been three years since the Russians invaded. Three years, and still the mighty Russian Bear struggles to control the land. I think you forgot to consider one aspect of all Americans before you invaded."

Smiling, Dennis asked, "And, what is that?"

"We are extremely proud to be Americans. Most I know are willing to die as Americans rather than to live under the Russian yoke. This is a partisan war, Colonel, and no one in recent history has ever won a partisan war. Look at our failure in Vietnam, but our politicians lost that war, not the military, or your disgrace in Afghanistan. You let a bunch of camel jockeys run you out of their nation, so surely we can do as much. Sergeant Grant, return our guest to his suite and make sure his wine is chilled."

"Yes, sir." Grant said with a chuckle. "Stand and let's move, Ivan."

"I demand this man treat me with respect!" Dennis yelled.

His tone of voice and sudden movement caused Dolly to leap at the man. If I'd not had the leash around my wrist, I think she'd have tied into him. As it was, Dennis sat back in his chair and watched my dog closely.

Stas nodded at Grant, and the Sergeant slapped the Russian hard in the face.

"I'll kill you for striking me!" Dennis screamed, and he exploded from his chair.

I stood and yelled, "Sit down, Ivan, or I turn my dog loose! She loves to chew on Russians."

"I will sit, but I will report all of you and how poorly I was treated to the U.N. as soon as I can." he sat in his chair and kept his eyes on my German Shepherd.

"Colonel, have you ever seen the way prisoners, no matter their rank, are treated in gulags? You're lucky this man doesn't beat your ass half to death or execute you. If you anger me one more time, I will turn Dolly loose on you. You, sir, no longer have any rank. Now, go with Grant or I'll turn my dog loose on your ass."

Dennis left, but he was not a happy man, and kept threatening to report us to the U.N., which didn't worry us at all. What could the U.N. do, invade us?

After they left, Stas asked, "What will we do with him, once he comes clean with us?"

"I thought of hanging him, because of his status and job, but I think we'll render him permanently disabled and have the Chinese deliver him to the Russians. I don't think the Russians will ever trust him again, because they'll suspect he broke under interrogation, like most men and women do eventually. They think our methods are like theirs, brutal, but we're different."

"Ours can turn rough if they don't talk, so keep that in mind. Most interrogators around the world use hurting and blood to gain information. We'll never kill a man as we talk to him, but we might give him some pain and a great deal of discomfort to handle."

"I want the man cleaned of everything he knows. Men in his position killed hundreds of thousands of people in Mississippi."

"Well get the information. Right now he's in isolation and will remain so another week. By then he'll be happy to talk to any-one."

"I'll leave all of this in your hands. If and when he talks, I want a full briefing on what he says. I think it's just a matter of time before the Russians start chemical and biological attacks against us. You know they must be frustrated because they expected to just walk in here and take over. That hasn't worked, and the fact they consider most partisans cowboys, rednecks, farmers, or peasants must make it harder for them. The easy control they expected hasn't happened."

Standing, Stas said, "I'll keep you informed, sir."

"Good. Now, I need to return to my office and see what Headquarters wants us to do next. I suspect we'll hit a convoy or train, but who is to say what they may be thinking?" I returned his salute, shook his hand, and then left.

When I returned I had four letters from Carol, and that filled my heart with joy. We had limited mail service, which was much better now with the Chinese providing choppers to deliver for us before they went on their missions. I sat down at my desk, looked at the dates and read the oldest letter first. I noticed all four were written this month and the oldest about 10 days ago.

The first three letters contained a lot of love and promises to wait for me. I hoped the wait wasn't long but to be honest, I was more worried about survival than I was being unfaithful to her. My job was risky at best with most commanders lasting around six months.

The last letter she explained she was attempting to be assigned to my intelligence section and wanted me to put in a good word. I would be happy to do that, but not because I loved her. I would pull to get her because she was damned good at her job. She'd also not be shielded from any risk my other intelligence people faced. I could not show the woman I loved to death any favoritism or I'd lose all respect as a commander.

It was near dusk when the radio came alive in the communications center, which was close to my tent. I could hear noises and voices, but was unable to make the words out. Dolly was asleep with her head on my left foot.

Sergeant Parsons stuck her head in my walled off office and said, "Reports are coming in from a sniper team of a company size unit spending the night in a fairly open spot. They claim to have hurt one, wanting to kill him, and then stopped. The man shot appeared to be an officer because one of his men stood at attention as he spoke with him. If we can get there quickly, we can take a few Russians out of the picture."

"What makes them so sure this unit will be an easy kill?" I asked.

"The sniper team thinks they lack experience and didn't operate like a well oiled unit would do. The man they shot was giving orders all the time."

"How far away are they?"

"Eight miles southwest, sir."

"Form our people; we're going to see if this unit is experienced or not. I want to be ready to leave in thirty minutes."

"Yes sir, I figured you'd say that so it's been done already. I've contacted all four squad leaders and they're gathering up folks as we speak."

"Good."

Two hours later, I was on a slight hill in the Ozark Mountains looking down into a lush valley. I was wearing NVGs, and the company I was watching was either made up of very young troops or they were very inexperienced. I saw men and women sitting on the edges of foxholes, thinking they were safe in the darkness. I watched a Russian Chopper arrive, load up the injured man, and then they flew away. I'd ordered the chopper left alone because I had a different target in mind.

I arranged my men and women for an attack. I'd learned early in my career that when new troops came under fire, only about 10% will fight back by returning fire. Most were scared enough to wet their pants, and some did.

It was near three in the morning before I sent my scouts to look the place over closely. Where possible, I wanted the Russian equivalent to our claymore mine, the MON-50, turned around to face the Russians, who'd originally placed the mines. With an experienced group, the turning of the mines was extremely dangerous, but most of my Russian friends in the valley seemed to be sleeping. Thirty minutes later my scouts returned and all were smiling.

I picked up the headset to our radio and said, "When you see my flare in the air, attack and try to overrun them in the initial thrust. If we don't, I'm worried about Black Shark helicopters coming to their aid."

I then pulled my flare gun and load it with a cartridge. I raised it overhead, pulled the hammer back, and sent a parachute flare with a 40 second burn time high into the air. It was then I heard screaming and looking below, I saw my troops rushing the entrenched Russians. I heard very little fire from the Russians and suspected they were scared shitless.

My troops were near now, and some were already among the Russians and firing into fox holes. Then a Russian machine-gun opened fire. I was confused by the tat-tat-tat, because I saw none of my troops falling. One of our flamethrowers sent a long spurt of fire toward a Russian machine-gun and the crew was engulfed by flames. The gun stopped firing.

"Copperhead One, this is Copperhead three, and four Russians have fled north by east. Should we follow them?"

"Negative. Finish your work there and then pull out, but only after taking all gear and supplies we can use. Be sure to bring the machine-gun and all ammo for the weapon."

"Will do, Copperhead One. Copperhead three out."

I heard the screams of the dying and the victory yells of my troops. I handed my radio to my radioman and then walked toward the battle. I saw two Russians make a run, and they were immediately cut down by rifle fire. The battle had been fairly easy for my troops, but only because they were dealing with inexperienced Russian soldiers. Bodies were ripped apart, blood pooled all around the meadow, and the cries of the wounded were pitiful, regardless of the side they were on.

"Johnson," I yelled.

"Yo?"

"Get me a body count of the dead and wounded for both sides."

"Will do."

I then walked to a dead partisan and found myself looking into the eyes of Sergeant Banks. From what I could see, she'd taken a machine-gun bullet to her chest. Her eyes were open, but rolled up in her head, so only the whites showed. I squatted, closed her eyes and then rolled her over. The big bullet had taken a big chunk of her spine too. She'd died instantly, thank God, but I'd miss her. She was a good worker, and I suspect, a very lonely young woman. I wondered how many more young men and women would sacrifice their lives to gain the freedom of America? Was it worth the cost? I think so and so did those who died, or they'd not have been fighting.

"Sir, our big brother, the Chinese, report a flight of attack helicopters heading our way with an ETA of about fifteen minutes."

"I understand. Load it up and let's move, people! In fifteen minutes the Russians will be here, and they'll be pissed. Move! Private Taylor, you take point and Dobins, I want you on drag. Let's get out of here and now."

Suddenly out of nowhere a Black Shark chopper lined up on us, and we scattered to the four winds. The bird came in hot, Gatling guns spitting death, and as the guns fired, I saw clods of dirt thrown ten feet in the air.

"Move, people, before he can come back around on us! *Now!*"

CHAPTER 9

Captain Georgiy was as mad as a wet hen. There were only four left alive out of his company after the partisan attack. He was sure he'd be disgraced and sent home because most of his troops were killed in their fox holes as they huddled in fear. Ira, the medic, was with him, as were Privates Beshov and Enya. The last two had minor injuries, but they must have hurt. Ira had given both of the wounded codeine pills for pain, but no morphine. Morphine would make them sleepy and, right now, as the attack helicopters and fast movers worked the partisans over if they found them, they needed to be covering some distance.

"Have you stopped their bleeding?" he asked.

"Yes, I have, but it could start again with them moving like this." she replied.

"Once we stop, I need you to look at my left arm. I have a rag around it now and the bleeding is nothing to worry about. I will stop in a few minutes for a brief rest. I do not want to stop, but you can look all of us over, and we will need food this day."

"Do you need something for the pain?"

"No, the pain is nothing. I just need you to clean it and wrap me well. I do not need an infection."

It was getting close to daylight now, and the Captain took a short break as the four of them ate something. Once the cold meals were behind them, Ira cleaned his wound and insisted he take a pill for his pain, but he'd refused. The wound was from a small caliber pistol and was a flesh wound. Ilik carried two canteens; one contained water and the other vodka. If his pain grew to a difficult level, he'd drink some of his strong clear liquid.

Pulling the handset from the radio to his head, Georgiy said, "Base this is Rugby One, over."

"Go, Rugby One."

"My position was overrun by partisans. From the looks of things, our survivors can all load into one helicopter. I have four survivors, counting myself, and the rest are estimated to be dead. Warn all Russian aircraft that other survivors may be in the area."

"Uh, copy Rugby. The Colonel wants to see you as soon as you return."

"Can you send a helicopter to pick us up? Three of us are wounded."

"Wait one."

The Colonel will eat my ass for lunch, but there was nothing I could do. There were just too many partisans and they struck in the middle of the night, he thought as he said aloud, "He will not get a virgin when he chews on me."

"What is that, sir?" the medic asked.

"Nothing, just talking to myself."

"Rugby One, you will have a helicopter at your location within fifteen minutes. They have requested you move to a field large enough for them to sit down in. Do you copy?"

"Uh, roger that, and we will move north a little, maybe 100 meters. Send them and I will contact them by radio as soon as I hear them."

"Copy and ETA is fifteen minutes, out."

"Let us move, because our ride home is coming for us."

When the chopper landed, the four moved for the open doors from the front of the aircraft so the pilot could see them. They entered the doors and strapped down in the red passenger seats. The medic gave Privates Beshov and Enya shots of morphine, but Georgiy refused the powerful drug. He had a Colonel to face and didn't want to do the job while on a strong drug.

As the helicopter started to raise up, a long line of machine-gun bullets walked from the nose to the tail. The co-pilot screamed and collapsed, and one of the door gunners took a round to his helmet. The gunner fell on his back with his whole face missing, and he trembled and shook as his body shut down.

Smoke poured from the engines as the aircraft fought for height moving forward and up. There sounded a *pop-thunk, pop-thunk*, and two holes opened in the floor near the open door, the bullets missing everyone but rupturing some lines overhead. A hot oily substance began to leak.

After they'd gained a couple thousand feet, the other gunner handed a headset with microphone to the Captain. He quickly showed him how to use it.

"Captain, is there anything we can to do help you?" he asked the aircraft commander.

"Pray, Captain, just pray. I am busy up here, so we will talk later."

Georgiy heard a jet pilot say "Where did you take the ground fire, Save One? This is Mongoose One and my wing-man, Mongoose Two, over."

"All around the field where I picked up the survivors. But, most from the west."

"Roger that, so I am rolling in hot with napalm and missiles."

"Good luck."

They heard nothing and then a few minutes later, the jet pilot said, "This is Mongoose Two, I caught about forty of them out in the open. What a day! I dropped napalm on them. Uh, I am going back around, because I see more of them."

"Watch your ass, Mongoose."

A couple of minutes passed and then the radio came alive. "Mayday, mayday, mayday, this is Mongoose One and I am punching out, now!"

"Base, Mongoose Two, and he has a good chute and he is well away from the fire from the napalm. I suspect we will need another helicopter to pick him up. I have enough fuel to remain on station and assist as needed."

The helicopter pilot changed frequencies and said, "Tower, I am claiming an in-flight emergency and I am coming straight in. I will land once over the fence. Almost every light on my console is red or not working, so I expect to fall out of the sky any second. I need emergency vehicles moving now, and we will meet off the nose of my aircraft approximately 100 meters, out."

They barely cleared the base fence and it sounded like the rear of the aircraft, near the tail, actually struck the fence. The nose came up and as the aircraft was landing, all power was lost. The bird fell to earth like a heavy rock. The pilot immediately switched all electrical power off before they touched the ground. They hit hard, with the impact jarring everyone inside. Georgiy, with a bad back, could hardly move as the pilot screamed for everyone to leave the helicopter. A quick check of the gunner showed him dead, and the copilot as well. Blood was streaked through the aircraft by the wind, and it now looked as if someone had painted the red lines.

When the ambulances arrived Georgiy tried to avoid the hospital, but he was given an IV and then morphine. Everyone from the helicopter was taken for a physical exam. At some point before the hospital, he fell asleep.

Three days later Georgiy was well enough to have visitors. His bullet wound had become infected and he'd slept more than usual. He'd been awake most of the time, only the painkillers really messed up his thinking and talking. He noticed every minute she had away from work, Lena would sit by his bed in a chair and talk with him. Even when working, she'd come by at least once a day to check on his progress.

On the third day a Full Colonel walked into his room, and moving to the side of his bed asked, "Captain Georgiy, what happened to your unit?"

"We were hit by a very experienced company size force and they chewed us up and spat us out, is what happened. 96% of my troops had never been in combat before, and then once the battle started they were killed in their fox holes as they cried for their mommas. You and I killed those troops, Colonel, as sure as if we had pulled the trigger."

"Well, I hardly think —"

"Colonel, he is on painkillers and morphine, so he can hardly be held accountable for what he says to you, sir. I personally do not think you will get much useful intelligence from him. I suggest you come back in a few days." the doctor said.

"I guess, but if he should come around before then, please call this number." as he handed the doctor a business card, "so we can speak with him. He lost almost 100 people and we need to know how that happened."

"Sir, no disrespect intended, but he just told you what happened. His exact words to you were 'We were hit by a very experienced company size force and they chewed us up and spat us out, is what happened.' I seriously doubt he can add much to that."

"Lieutenant, I think you should go back to your job of plugging holes as we fight the war. There was much more to it than that, I assure you. Good day."

The doctor nodded, but didn't reply.

The next morning Georgiy wanted to speak with the intelligence folks. A Major soon arrived with a Senior Sergeant. He explained what had happened, how his troops were terrified of the fight and how most were killed in their fox holes.

When it was all said and done, the Major asked, "Captain, you are a highly decorated war hero and we know you are no coward, so how did this happen? In your opinion, what can we do to prevent this from happening again?"

"Mix people up in units so you have more than two or three experienced troops in a company. If I had had twenty more experienced soldiers, I would still be fighting those partisans. Teach them more and better before they leave Russia. I do not feel so much as a company commander as I do a babysitter most of the time. Send me tougher men and women. Now, you need to leave; I am feeling tired."

The Major appeared shocked by the Captain telling him to leave, but the doctor had warned both of them that the man was on some strong drugs and might say anything.

Finally, the man nodded and said, "Come Senior Sergeant, we will learn nothing more from this man."

As the two left, Georgiy smiled, and thought, *Why is it so easy for men and women who sit in a chair all day to judge those of us who fight for a living? A million things can go wrong in combat and some you cannot control. But, until they train our troops better and mix them with our experienced combat troops the deaths will continue.*

A month later, Lena came by to visit and said, "Seems like I see you more often in a hospital than I do out of one." She then gave a little girl giggle.

"I am being released tomorrow and will convalesce in my quarters, again. Feel like visiting me a while?"

She laughed and replied, "I have been living there, just so I can smell you in the room with me. Sure, I will visit you, and even help you leave here in the morning. I have a girlfriend who is a driver for a Colonel, and she will come by the hospital and drive us to your place. I do not think you need to wait for the bus, and you for sure cannot walk home."

"L . . . Lena, we need to talk when we are alone."

"Uh-oh, is this a *we* need to talk as in I have done something wrong or a *we* need to talk about something good?" Her eyes met his.

"I love you, so you decide if that is good or bad." He knew it was the drugs talking, but he did love her.

"Oh, is that all? I have known that for months, but this is the first time you have said it to me. I happen to love you too, even if you are a bullet magnet."

A nurse walked in, nodded at Lena and asked, "How is your pain level, Captain?"

"Low, so about a two out of ten."

She nodded and said, "Good, I will not give you any more morphine because you have been in the vodka for your pain. Now, do not deny it, because I can see the bottle under your pillow."

Master Sergeant Romanovich entered the room, smiled and said, "Wow, you have two beautiful women looking after you, so maybe I need to leave, huh? You always were the lucky one, Ilik."

Everyone laughed and Georgiy said, "Come into my room and tell me the latest rumors about the war."

"This is no rumor, but truth; the director of our chemical/biological sections, a Full Colonel Denisovich, was taken prisoner by the partisans. They have offered to trade him for 200 prisoners from the gulag."

"Surely we will not trade with them, right?"

"I have no idea, but the Colonel is supposed to be an expert in chemicals and such. I heard he could make poison gases if need be because of his university education. Enough of that talk." Romanovich said, smiled, and then pulling a pint of vodka from his pocket, he tossed it to Georgiy, and added, "Painkiller, and it will do you more good than morphine will."

Lena laughed and said, "I cannot believe you gave him alcohol with two nurses in the room."

"He gets out in the morning, so he is off the heavy drugs already. Besides, what would the army do to a Master Sergeant? I have more power than many Generals and everyone knows it, too."

Laughing, the nurse said, "I must continue my rounds. If you need anything, Captain, use the call button."

"I cannot stay long, my friend, because I am leaving for a couple of days on a mission. When I return, we will meet and share a few drinks. Bring Lena too, so we will have some good food."

"You watch your ass out there, Boris, because the partisans are fighting smarter these days. I think it may come from the Chinese supplying them and supporting them in the field. One thing I can tell you, it did not take them but a few minutes to kill all but four of my troops. Take no risks, and you may come back alive."

"I hear you, my friend, but most of my troops are veterans of one or more previous tours in the United States. Some have served in other states, so some of the methods used by the resistance may be different, only not by much. I am an old war dog, and I will be back."

Early the next morning, right as the sun started to rise into the sky, Russian helicopters were landing in a large field near Licking, Missouri, a small one horse town. They were a good mile from the town's post office, but shielded by a thick forest of mixed walnut and oak trees. It was a company size mission, so the helicopters would be making more than one trip.

Romanovich was in the first group of helicopters and as they began their descent, the pilot was heard saying over the radio, "Uh, base, Eagle Six here, and I am taking ground fire. I repeat, the landing zone is hot."

The Master Sergeant had been given a headset to listen to the radio communications.

There sounded a loud bang, and a large piece of aluminum was seen passing the open door on the right side. The helicopter began to smoke.

"Abort, Eagle Six, this is Eagle One."

"I do not have that option, Colonel, because I have to put this baby on the ground, and now! Mayday, mayday, mayday, this is Eagle Six and I am going down."

Romanovich heard a loud series of *ping-klunks*, and when he glanced around, bullets were punching holes in the aircraft's skin. Suddenly, the man sitting across from him went rigid, his eyes grew huge, and then a bullet exited his chest to strike some aluminum lines above him. Blood was running down his chest from a large exit hole and when he opened his mouth to scream, blood poured from his lips and ran down his chin to drip onto his chest. Not a sound came from the injured Private, but his body jerked and twitched.

What a rough way to die. I think he was shot in the butt, and the bullet traveled most of the length of his body to exit his chest, the Master Sergeant thought as he shivered.

"Pilot to crew, we are going to hit hard, so brace yourselves."

The helicopter seemed to fall the last four feet and landed on its wheels, leaned hard to the right shattering the spinning blades overhead, and then righted itself. It came to a stop upright, but with the rotating blades slowing because all power to the aircraft was cut to avoid fires.

With the engines quiet, the pilot yelled, "Everyone to the infantry, and move! I suspect this aircraft will soon draw a lot of ground fire." There was a lot of ground fire taking place already, in Romanovich's view.

"I have a dead man back here." one of the door gunners yelled.

"Leave him, now go!" the pilot said as he opened the door to leave.

The co-pilot screamed as he left the helicopter, a partisan machine-gun almost cutting him in half as the bullets punched holes through his body. Then, one of the door gunners, who was running slightly ahead of Romanovich, must have stepped on a mine because he disappeared in a narrow flash of fire and hell. In an instant his body was dismembered and thrown in all directions. All that remained of the man was one smoking shoe.

Crawling beside a long log, the Master Sergeant heard mortars fired off in the distance. The loud *thumps* could be heard at great distances. He glanced up to see the other helicopters veer off and gain altitude. It was then the mortar shells began landing, and they walked the rounds right to the downed aircraft.   Then three rounds struck the damaged helicopter.

The fireball from the fuel was huge, with balls of bright red flames and dense black smoke rolling into each other. Then the compressed gases and munitions began to explode and cook off, the noise so loud it made it hard for the Master Sergeant to think.

He crawled up to a radioman, only to discover the man dead, so he took the headset and yelled, "Hello any station! I am call sign Cobra Three, on the ground and we are taking hard ground fire from the trees to our north and mortars from our east. We need assistance immediately!"

"Uh, Cobra Three, this is Wart Hog One and I am a fast burner out of Saint Louis. Get your heads down as my wing man and I make a run. Wart Hog Two, I will use my Gatling gun while you use your napalm. I am rolling in hot now. Get your heads down, Cobra Three."

There was a sound like a gigantic zipper was pulled down and tree limbs and huge sections of bark were seen flying through the air. Screams were heard as the first jet pulled up and the second began his run. What resembled fuel tanks dropped from the diving aircraft as it suddenly nosed up. The tanks rolled end over end until they struck the trees, and then a huge fireball moved toward the sky. Master Sergeant Romanovich knew when the tanks hit the ground the fire would keep moving from the forward momentum, and it would soon be a large burning wave that killed all under the flames. More screams were heard.

"Cobra Three, this is Wart Hog One, and we are going for your mortars next. Two, use your Gatling guns as I use my napalm. I am coming in low and hot. I will use the remainder of my Gatling gun ammunition before I use napalm."

The aircraft was seen just barely above the trees. The zipper was pulled once more, but before the jet could pull up, there was an explosion near the tail and the aircraft struck the trees and then disappeared, replaced by a huge red fireball and dense black smoke.

Wart Hog Two continued his run, fired his Gatling gun and then said, "War Hog Two to Cobra Three, I have taken heavy ground fire, have my console well lit with warning lights so I am returning to base."

"Copy Wart Hog Two, sorry about One, over."

"Understand about One. I have a flight of Black Sharks inbound in about ten minutes. This is Wart Hog Two, out." The aircraft gained altitude and soon disappeared.

Troops were moving now toward the trees away from the fire of the napalm. Other helicopters were starting to land and more soldiers were unloading. Once in the woods, they'd break into squads and try to find the Americans. Already the troops were complaining about the sixty to seventy pound packs they had to carry all day, but the complaining was typical. For some of the smaller men and most of the women, it was half their body weight.

As Romanovich always said, "No person in the infantry has trouble sleeping all night after carrying a pack all day."

The Master Sergeant gathered his squad around him, including a new Junior Lieutenant named Slavavich. "Okay, all is well right now. We are going to move on a heading of 220 and we stay on that heading until nightfall. Tonight we will sleep back to back. Vasilievna, you are my point and Isaak, you are my drag. No talking, and keep the noise down unless you want to die. Now, let us move."

The rest of the day was slow and the heavy packs became heavier after an hour. Every hour on the hour a ten minute break was taken, but loads were almost too much for some of the smaller troops.

Near dusk, the Master Sergeant had the squad move into thicker trees and place four NON-50 mines out and also some buried mines. They then sat back to back in a circle as they consumed their rations.

No sooner had they finished than a voice was heard in English, "Hey Sarge, do you think this trail might be mined?"

"Assume it is, dumb-ass and keep moving. Don't speak again unless I ask you a question. Move, Jones."

When Romanovich looked around, the eyes of his men and women were huge, but the Lieutenant looked like he wanted to crap his pants. He looked absolutely terrified. It was good the Americans were heard, because now his people knew the enemy was around, and they'd stay alert.

The enemy avoided the mines and it was obvious they were off the trail. Minutes later the group was gone, but the fear of hearing and seeing them remained.

It was near midnight when helicopters were heard flying in the local area and the Master Sergeant whispered to the Lieutenant, "Sir, did you call in our night position?"

"Uh, no, I thought you did."

The Sergeant shook his head and thought, *New Lieutenants are about useless*, and then he picked up the handset for the radio and said, "Base this is Cobra Three."

He'd no sooner than spoke when the ground around them was being torn to bits by machine-gun fire from one of the infrared equipped helicopters. Corporal Isaak stood, probably to run, and in an instant was knocked to his knees as machine-gun rounds passed through his body. Even in the dark, his body could be seen flying apart.

"Attacking helicopter, you are killing friendly troops! Break, break, break, this is Cobra Three and you are firing on my position!" Boris Romanovich screamed into the radio.

CHAPTER 10

I was tired, and fully understood I was no longer 18 years old. My back hurt, my legs felt like they were made out of lead, and my lungs hurt from running. All of my people had gotten out of the area before the aircraft strikes, but some others were burned to death or blown to pieces. I'd get the report from intelligence at some point this morning. I was glad I'd left Dolly behind, too. She was a great dog, but at times I wanted to only worry about me. I loved her like a child, if that is humanly possible.

There was a dirt road we were to cross, but about a hundred feet north was an intersection which was now guarded by a machine-gun nest and a huge Russian T-14 Armata, a tank that weighed over fifty tons and had a crew of three. I'd seen very few T-14s, with the T-90 as the most common tank in the states. I decided right then to take this tank out of action.

The only problem was I'd never tackled a T-14 before. I had nothing that was able to take it out at any distance, which meant I'd have to get close enough to drop something down the forward hatches, which were open. The turret of the tank was not manned and the crew sat in a protective capsule which offered them some additional safety. I then moved back into the woods with my people to allow the day to pass. I would attack the tank near midnight.

The day passed slowly and rightfully so, because we stayed as still as possible to avoid detection. I was more worried about a chopper detecting me than ground troops. We wore camouflage uniforms, had face-paint on, and wore gloves or paint on our hands. We were deep in a blackberry patch and few could get anywhere near us without making noise.

Just before midnight, I gathered up all the PVV-5A Plastic Explosive and detonators we carried. We usually used PVV-5A for cutting through fences, locks or other metals. Tonight I'd use two blocks of the explosive, all we had, and each was approximately 2 inches by 1 and a half inches, by 11 inches long. My explosive total weight with two blocks was approximately 2.50 pounds. I wasn't sure if it would do the job, but if nothing else I'd damage some electronics and computer systems on the inside, and perhaps kill the crew, if they were in the tank. I'd ignite the fuse and then have five seconds to clear the area.

I wanted my group to move in closely from the front, then I'd approach the tank from behind. I'd climb on the tank, move to the front hatches and hope one was open. Usually at night hatches were open because there was always a man in every crew with gas problems. It's hard to sleep when one or two are passing gas all night.

Once my explosive was dropped, Dobins, who would be with me, would toss a grenade into the machine-gun nest. We'd then move at a 90 degree angle from the tank. It sounded good, but I expected something to go wrong. I just hoped I didn't mess things up and get a bunch of us killed.

As my folks slowly moved toward the machine-gun, crawling, I took Dobins and we began circling the tank. We were wearing NVGs, and weren't slowed down in the least by the dense brush. When I neared the tank and machine-gun nest, I was surprised to only see one man on guard.

He was leaning forward, his elbows resting on the sandbags and every few minutes he'd stand up straight and walk in circles in an attempt to stay awake. I pulled the .22 pistol I carried with a silencer and moved to the very rear of the tank. The second time he came near me, I'd put him down.

He stopped, pulled out a cigarette and lit it with a lighter. He took a deep drag and then moved for the rear of the tank again. As he moved, I watched him closely as he passed, and on the next pass, he was mine.

When he passed the next time, I stepped up behind him, threw my arm around his neck and fired the .22 pistol into the side of his head. When he didn't stop jerking and fighting, I fired twice more and one bullet entered his temple. Each squeeze of the trigger brought a low *phoot* sound. He collapsed to the grasses.

I climbed on the tank slowly and as quietly as I could. I made my way to the only open hatch and heard men snoring below. I ignited the fuse and dropped the explosives in the tank. Just to make sure I did maximum damage, I dropped a fragmentation grenade, too. Someone in the tank screamed as I jumped from the heavy beast. I heard an explosion, saw the machine-gun fly up high into the air, and heard the screams of men dying. I was running like hell, attempting to get away from the tank.

I heard a loud *ka-boom*, and looking over my shoulder saw the turret of the tank flipping end over end as it moved in and out of a large fireball filled with black smoke. Dobins was now running right beside me as my troops dropped back to the woods.

Once together, we all decided to wait a bit and then move toward the tank. At about that time the munitions and other flammables began to cook off, which caused minor explosions in the fireball.

"Do you think the machine-gun is still good or the ammo?" Taylor asked.

"Hard to say, and depends how hard the grenade was on them. I did see the gun fly into the air, so it may be damaged. Once in place, we go through the stuff quickly and then haul ass out of here. Let's give the tank a few more minutes and then let's move."

When we arrived at the tank, I could smell the burned bodies, and all those assigned to the machine-gun were dead. Most of the ammo was still good, but the gun was a mess. We salvaged what we could and just as we turned to leave, I heard a chopper!

"Split up, and everyone run in different directions!" I yelled, hoping we'd not just committed a fatal mistake of being out in the open.

They must have seen the flames from the tank burning, I thought as I ran like hell for the trees we'd just left minutes ago. A long line of bullets passed by, missing me by less than a foot, and clods of dirt were flying high into the air. I made it into the trees, and watched the chopper very systematically follow each of my people, one at a time. I laid in the grasses and had my poncho close to me, so I could cover up if need be.

About thirty minutes later the bird circled the burning tank, and then landed near. I watched a crew member run toward the machine-gun nest, and then start back for the chopper. I heard a shot and the man dropped. I then heard a series of single shots, but the aircraft left the downed man and slowly gained altitude. My shooter must have caused some damage, because once up high enough, the aircraft flew toward Fort Leonard Wood. I cautiously made my way to the downed Russian. As I moved toward him, so did other members of my group.

"The bird was smoking when he left us." Dobins said.

"Good shot, Brown." I said to my sniper.

"Where are Green and Wilson?" Paxton asked.

"I saw Green catch a line of machine-gun bullets, so I know he's dead." Davis said, and then scanned the countryside for any sign of Wilson.

"Check the dead Russian for arms and ammo. Then form on me; we'll make one quick walk around the area, and then we head home." I said as I squatted and went through the man's pockets for papers. I pulled a couple of patches from his flight suit and by then we were ready to leave. I crammed what I'd found in my pockets and off we went. I watched Dobins place the man's watch on her wrist.

Minutes later we were once more moving in the darkness of the forest and I relaxed a little. We spent the remainder of darkness walking. At daylight, I stopped for four hours to allow everyone to rest a little. We'd been all night with no sleep. I'd just opened a Russian ration when Dobins came to me, almost in tears. Her eyes were wet and when she sat across from me I asked, "Are you okay?"

"No, sir, I'm not okay. I thought I could handle my problem alone, but I can't. I'm pregnant."

I was shocked but not overly so, because we were human beings first, then partisans. I thought for a moment and then asked, "Why did you come on this mission then?"

"That's it? All you care about is this damned mission?" she asked, and she was livid.

"What did you expect from me? We are lonely people, and I think it's natural for each of us to need someone at times. I have a woman I'm seeing and it's part of life."

"Would you want a baby born now, the way this country is? I may not survive this war!"

"Well, your baby may not survive either. Look, anytime we have men and women living together, this will happen. The fact that it has happened is not surprising, but after this you'll go on no more missions. You'll have a baby to raise, but I'll put you to work in Intelligence with Stas and the rest. I'm sure even the Russians face this problem. We cannot put men and women in lonely jobs together and not expect this to occur. How is the father taking all of this?"

"Ledford is mad because he doesn't want a baby to be born right now."

"Well, it's not like you have a choice in the matter. Look, I'm happy for you, actually for both of you, but you both might have planned this a little better."

"It just happened the first time, but after that it happened often. I'm not a slut, sir, but we love each other and I'm pregnant." She broke down in tears again.

"It's not the end of the world. Look, you'll work Intel, but Ledford is one of my snipers and he'll stay in the field, because he's too good to let go. I hope for your sake and the baby's he lives, but that's out of my hands. Reassigning you to Intelligence is all I can do right now. Do you want me to talk to him?"

"Oh, no, sir! He'd think I put you up to all of this and get mad at me."

"I thought you said he was already mad."

"He is, but . . . you're confusing me. I don't think he'll stay mad if I talk to him about this, but if you speak to him, he'll think he's in trouble."

"Look, you're both adults and as long as you don't break any laws, I have no reason to speak to him or you about this. What happened was natural for two consenting adults who just happen to love each other."

She met my eyes and then asked, "You don't think it's wrong? We're not married and don't plan to be because we seem to die so quickly living as we do."

"It's not my place to judge anyone, so your question is best saved for a preacher and not a commander. I will say this though, if any one of us gets a chance to forget this war, even for a few moments, they'd better grab it. Our lives are filled with little joy as it is."

"Thank you, sir. I don't have a mother or father still alive, so you're all I have."

As she turned to walk to Ledford, I realized I was much more than just a commander to most of my troops. Many of my people were still in their late teens, like Dobins. Just the thought made my chest swell that she trusted me enough to speak with me about a personal issue. Now, if the three of them survived this war, all would end well.

Later that day we entered main camp, and I made my way to Intelligence to file a report of a machine-gun and tank destroyed by us on the way back. I was bone ass tired, sleepy, and hungry. I needed a shower, shave, and clean clothes. When I entered the room, Staff Sergeant Grant yelled, "Officer in the room!"

Everyone came to attention, and it took me a minute to realize he meant me.

"As you were." I said and then looking at the Captain, I said, "Stas, I need to file an after action report. I had three lightly injured and one killed. My dead man was Green and Wilson is missing. On the way back we knocked out a machine-gun nest and a new Russian T-14 Armata tank. The tank is a powerful and big bastard."

"Sit, Colonel, before you fall on your ass, sir." Stas said and reaching into his cabinet, pulled out a bottle of bourbon whiskey. He poured a half a glass and added, "You need a drink."

I took the drink from him and then asked, "Any progress with my favorite Russian POW, Dennis?"

"A little, and we know now he was sent here in preparation of a chemical attack. He has no dates, but he knows one is planned for the future."

"Anything else?"

"Some secret stuff that you don't need to know, boss. I sent it in code to headquarters."

"Good, I can live with that decision. Give me the forms so I can sip this bourbon as I fill out my after action report."

When I finished the report, Stas said, "Sir, you have a newly assigned woman waiting for you in your quarters. I gave her permission; I think she said her name was, oh, what was it, Grant? I'm not sure, but she was cute, had a nice figure, and now that I think on it, I think her name was Mary or Carol. Oh, it was June, I think."

I broke into a big smile as I realized Carol was in my tent. I turned to Stas and asked, "Why didn't you tell me this before?"

"I wanted a detailed after action report and not something you'd throw together so you could run to your tent. Actually, sir, the bottle is yours for the two of you to enjoy tonight. I'm very happy for you, as we all are."

"Thank you, Stas, and I appreciate the bottle. Uh, I have a Private Dobins that will start working for you in the morning. She's pregnant, and I can't use her in the field."

"Her lover still alive?" Stas asked.

"Yep and in my squad; why?"

"Just wondering. Many of us are here today and gone tomorrow. We can use the help, honestly."

"She'll show in the morning. Look, I'm tired, so let me grab some rations, head to my tent and meet my new Captain. Thanks, guys, all of you."

At my tent, I walked in and caught Carol sleeping on the bed. I stood for a few minutes, just looking at her and appreciating her beauty, but finally sat the whiskey bottle on the folding desk I had. I grabbed a towel, soap, and clean clothes, then moved for the shower.

When I returned, she was sitting on the edge of the bed giving me a coy look. I smiled and said, "I have something to drink if you want some. It's on the table beside the bed."

"Do you want one?"

"Sure, and the glasses are on the box on the other side of my bed. I live a very spartan life." I replied, and then laughed.

"I hope you don't mind me using your bed for a few hours. I could smell you on the sheets."

"You could have had a good whiff just a few minutes ago. I had been in the field for two days, so I was gamy to say the least. Did you have any trouble getting here?"

"Nope, I put a bikini on and stuck a stamp on my forehead, and here I am." she teased with a smile.

I walked to her, looked deeply into her eyes and kissed her. She moaned, whispered my name, and then said, "Sit and let's have our drinks. I'm beat, and I know you must be."

I knocked my drink back, met her eyes and said, "I'm done with mine."

She smiled and said, "You're still as crazy as ever, huh? We have time now, baby, because I'm assigned here."

"I had a young lady come to me today and tell me she was pregnant. I'm not sure why I just told you that, except it could happen to us."

"Not with me, because I'm on the pill. We get them from China now, did you know that? Years back when they tried to control the births and population of their nation, they became the leading authority on birth control and I mean all forms, too."

"Interesting. Good to know."

"Now, I've finished my drink, how about we get some sleep?"

I waited for her to lay back and then I leaned forward and began kissing her neck. I was thinking how lucky I was as my passion ignited.

Early the next morning I was awakened by loud shouts and gunfire. I grabbed my Russian Bison and stepped from my tent. I made my way to the command post and asked the Lieutenant on duty, "What in the hell is going on?"

"Russian POW escaped. It was reported he killed his guard and took his pistol. That's really all we know right now, sir."

"Who was his guard?"

Looking at a sheet of paper in his hand he said, "A Staff Sergeant Grant out of Intelligence."

"Tell the troops I want that sonofbitch captured or killed."

"They are well aware of that, sir."

"Let me know the minute you have word on him, okay?" I asked, but thought, *That Dennis is a sneaky bastard. I knew we should have shot him as soon as we knew his job.*

"I'll do that, Colonel."

"I want all troops not on detail or gearing for missions after that man."

"It's already been done, sir."

I could see the man wanted me to leave so they could do their jobs, so I did. Just as I entered my tent, I heard Dennis say, "Good morning, Colonel, and if you move too quickly with that Bison, I may just kill this pretty woman."

I saw the man standing beside my bed, holding Carol with his left arm.

I said, "Let her go, she isn't part of this."

"All Americans and Russians are a part of this! It's much bigger than just the three of us. Now hand me the weapon, slowly."

I saw he had Grant's 1911 Colt barrel pushed against Carol's neck. If he pulled the trigger, he'd blow her head off.

I handed the weapon to him slowly and once he had it, he pushed her roughly away from him. I was far from unarmed, though. I carried a pistol in the holster on my right side and a knife with a ten inch blade in a sheath on my left side, and a .38 in the small of my back. I just needed a distraction or for him to move the barrel of that .45 away from me. Carol was on the bed as he stood at the foot. He more or less had both of us covered.

We could easily hear the noises outside the tent and then someone called out, "Colonel, are you okay in there?"

The Russian's eyes moved to the tent flap expecting someone to enter, but I answered, "Just fine. I'll be out in a bit; getting dressed and loading my weapons."

Just then, Carol rolled off the bed and reached for her pistol on her left side. I saw her bringing her hand up filled with the cold iron as Dennis moved his Bison toward her. Her Ruger 9mm coughed once and the Russian spun around. His gun discharged, sending a line of bullet holes down the side of my tent.

"Dennis, stop!" I yelled.

I reached for my .38, brought it away from my back, aimed at center mass on Dennis and squeezed the trigger three times. The first two bullets struck him center chest, but the last struck his right arm and the Bison fell from his grasp. He screamed and fell to the grass carpet that lined my tent. Blood seeped from entrance holes, but from his back it flowed freely, pooling under him. His hand found the Bison, but he didn't raise it.

"Carol, get out of here, now!" I yelled, knowing being shot didn't make the Russian any less dangerous.

She took her knife and cut the back of my tent and then stepped outside. She was smart, because by leaving that way Dennis had no target when she moved. The dying man was looking at me and tried to raise his gun, but was unable to do so.

"Colonel, are you okay in there?" I heard one of my folks ask.

"Yes, I'm fine. Gather up three more men, come in here, and take the escaped Russian Colonel to the hospital. Hurry now, he's dying."

Four men entered, the Bison was kicked away from him and he was searched for weapons. Another pistol was found, a sheath knife in the small of his back, and a Chinese grenade.

"I'm glad he didn't use the grenade, because they are unstable and undependable at the best of times." I said as the explosive was removed from him.

"You . . . you . . . will soon . . . die . . . C . . . Colonel." Dennis managed to get out as he grimaced.

"So will you, and be sure to say hello to the Devil for me." I moved to the side to allow the men to take him away.

Corporal Brown, one of my snipers said, "He must really hate you, sir. He could have escaped, but wanted you dead more than anything."

"No, he doesn't hate me, he hates Americans and what we are as a people. He simply saw me as a symbol of this great nation."

"Great nation? We're hardly that."

"I disagree. Our society may be gone, but as a people, our strong American spirit lives on."

Brown nodded and said, "We always root for the underdog and right now, that's us."

CHAPTER 11

"**D**amn you, stop! You are killing us!" Boris Romanovich yelled into the handset. The Master Sergeant looked around and saw Isaak for sure dead, and he had a number of wounded. He'd not know the seriousness of their injuries until the medic looked them all over. The helicopter had been devastating when it struck.

"Cobra Three, this is Wolf One, and we were told we have no friendlies in this area, over."

"We forgot to call in our night position, Wolf One; I have mostly green troops with me."

"Roger that; what is the extent of your injuries, over?"

"Wait one."

Checking his troops quickly, the Sergeant replied a minute or so later. "Uh, one dead and three injured, over."

"Sorry about that, Cobra Three, but this area is suspected free of friendly troops."

"Our fault, Wolf One. Let me arrange a ride home for my injured, Cobra Three out."

The Lieutenant was almost falling apart now, so the Master Sergeant said, "Slava, as the medic, how badly injured are these three?"

"They need a hospital, beyond any doubt, and Dima's arm is only attached by a thin piece of skin. I have had to give all of them morphine. Isaak is as dead as he will ever be."

"Cobra Three, to Base, over."

"Base, Cobra Three, go."

The Master Sergeant explained what had happened and then requested a medical pickup of his wounded. He soon handed the handset to Private Olegovich and then said, "Ten minutes on the helicopter. They are bringing us four replacements, too, so we can stay out here."

"*Oh, joy.*" someone said sarcastically.

"Knock it off, and I mean now! Remember, you are all soldiers and each of you volunteered to be in the army."

Using a strobe with an infrared cover, they had no problems linking with the rescue helicopter. They had moved the wounded to near a fairly large field and when the helicopter landed, as soon as the replacements were off the aircraft the dead and injured were loaded aboard. It was then the first ground fire was heard.

The loud rat-tat-tat of a machine-gun was heard and holes suddenly appeared on the skin of the helicopter right above the door. "We are taking fire, I repeat, we are taking ground fire from our west side."

"Copy, Rescue One. This is Bull One and we are two Black Sharks looking for a fight."

"Bull One this is Cobra Three and I need you to hit the trees west of me."

"My infrared screen is full of red hot spots in those trees, Cobra Three. I am rolling in hot and will use missiles first."

"Copy, Bull." Romanovich said and then yelled, "Get your heads down, now!"

As his folks lowered to the ground seeking cover, the rescue chopper labored to gain altitude in the confusion. Smoke was pouring from the engines, but so far both were running smoothly. With his NVGs on, the Master Sergeant noticed the windshield was shattered on the copilot's side and the man appeared dead. He also noticed a door gunner dangling about six feet below the aircraft, hanging by a nylon strap. He looked, but could see little more of the occupants.

Soon the rescue bird was out of sight. The woods to their west exploded from the rocket attacks and the Sergeant knew partisans were dying. On the third go around, the two choppers used their Gatling guns and the noise was unbelievable.

"Uh, Cobra Three, we are returning to base to rearm and re-fuel. We will be back as soon as we can. In the meantime, there are two Su-34 fast movers nearing your position."

"Roger and copy, Bull One."

"Cobra Three this is Tiger One, and we are here when you need us."

"Copy, Tiger One." While Romanovich knew the jets were near, they must have been high because he didn't hear or see them.

Yakovic neared and said, "I have the new troops settled in, and all four are seasoned with at least one combat tour behind them."

"Good, let us hope the remainder of the night is quiet. I want a fifty percent alert the rest of the night."

Near four in the morning the last two jets contacted him to say they were returning to base.

Near dawn, the Master Sergeant went from soldier to soldier waking them and telling them to eat. The four replacements were already eating and alert. He informed Makarovich that he was on point and Timur was his drag man. The compass heading was 163 degrees and Petrovich would count the steps. Both his point and rear men were new to the unit but this was not their first circus, and both were combat veterans of previous tours in America.

By dawn they were on the trail with each soldier cursing the weight they carried, but each knew if a heavy fight started they would have what they needed to stay alive.

Romanovich had heard nothing from his Lieutenant all night. He moved to the officer and asked, "Are you doing okay, sir?"

"For my first mission, I am doing much better than I thought I would do. These packs are heavy."

"The missions get easier with experience, and yesterday was just another day on the job for a person in the infantry."

"I want to thank you for doing all the work, because I had no idea what to do. I froze, I guess."

"That is expected too, sir, which is why the Army sent me to be with you. You will learn over time, so keep your eyes open, head low, and you will do fine."

The Junior Lieutenant nodded and kept moving. Romanovich moved back to the center of the line so he could be at either end of the line quickly. The morning passed slowly with Makarovich marking booby traps and mines, but the going was difficult.

During the noon meal the Master Sergeant sat beside Makarovich and asked, "Why do you not have any rank? You must be the best point man I have ever seen."

The Private gave a light chuckle and said, "I have been in the Army over three years and each time I get promoted I get drunk and then start fighting and I lose my promotion."

"Do you win most of your fights?"

"Most, but not all. I am too short and light to win all of them."

The man was about five feet and four inches and maybe 120 pounds. His red hair was cropped short and his smile was genuine. His lack of promotions he fully understood, and had no complaints with the Army over the action they'd taken.

"So, you are small and mean like a badger, huh?"

"Pretty much, but I do like a good fist fight."

"As of this moment, you can consider yourself a Corporal. I will not take a stripe from you for fighting, but I think I can satisfy your need for violence."

"Seems most commanders are glad to have me in the field, but in garrison, no one wants me. I know I am no spit and polish soldier, but I know my job well."

"How do you feel about the partisans?"

"They are the enemy of Mother Russia, and that makes them my enemy too. But personally, I have nothing against any American. I have never met one, and the only ones I have seen were dead."

"Hurry and eat; we will be leaving in about seven minutes." The Master Sergeant stood and began checking his much younger troops.

Over the course of the day, he used each new man on point and all worked out fine, with nothing getting by them. At dusk, they prepared an L shaped ambush and moved to the bushes to see what they'd bag. Their intelligence section told the Master Sergeant and Lieutenant that the trail was heavily used.

Until midnight they'd be on 100% alert and then they'd go to 50%.

It was just after one in the morning when a man materialized from the mist and all that were awake let him walk through. Then minutes later the main formation appeared and it was near twenty men, so Junior Lieutenant Slavavich squeezed the clackers. Instantly, between 485 and 540 steel balls or short steel rods shot from each of the NON-50s into the mass of partisans. Horrific screams were heard, and one man was walking in a circle with both of his arms gone, blood running down what remained of his two limbs like a river. A prayer was heard, but none of the Russians realized what the words meant. Then, the Russian guns opened up, loud and deadly.

"Grenade!" someone yelled in English, and a few seconds later the explosion was heard.

Then it grew quiet with only the wounded making any noise, and all but one of them only moaned. The screaming wounded was a woman, and her pain must have been great. Wearing NVGs the Russians waded through the bodies to kill those still alive. The deep cough of rifle fire was heard along with the higher bang of the pistols.

When it grew quiet, the Line Sergeant Slavavich neared and said, "The woman screaming was disemboweled and had a long piece of wood in her left eye. I have silenced her forever."

There sounded a Bison on fully automatic, followed by a loud scream.

"I just killed their drag man." someone said.

"Strip them of any maps, patches, or papers." he said, and then used the radio to contact base headquarters.

"Roger, base, a confirmed KIA count of twenty-one, with only their point man escaping. About a third of the group, seven, were female and the rest male. We are gathering intelligence and papers at this time."

"Copy, and thanks for the heads up."

"Hurry, because we are to move about 6 kilometers and place another ambush." the Sergeant said as he looked around at his men and women.

A young Private neared and handed two patches to the Lieutenant, and neither was the same.

"We need to move, because Chinese attack helicopters have been spotted near here." the Master Sergeant said.

"Do they have infrared capabilities?"

"They do, and are as advanced as ours, Lieutenant."

"Sir, you have a call from Moscow on line three, the blinking line." Sergeant Glasha Yevgenievna spoke through the intercom connection with Colonel Elin Yanovich.

"Hello, Colonel Elin Yanovich, here."

"Elin, it is me, General Tima Aleskeevich. How are you, my old friend?"

"I am fine, General, so what can I do for you?"

"Nothing for me, but the Marshal of the Russian Federation wants to know how a group of farmers and peasants wiped out one of our companies. He is livid, and his rage was obvious at this afternoon's meeting. He wants the commander shot."

"Sir, Moscow presented the commander of that company with three very high medals and even promoted him from the enlisted ranks, and now you want me to shoot him? Not a month ago the Marshal of the Russian Federation was praising his name."

"The Marshal has no idea what we are fighting there, but I did give him a copy of the recommendations following the attack and I hope that works to sooth his anger. Your Captain Georgiy made some very important and accurate statements in that report."

"That he did. Moscow must stop sending us complete units made up of new Privates right out of school or off the farm. I am afraid the violence here shocks the hell out of them and if we can get a mix of new and experienced people, we will do much better. The fight has changed, especially since the Chinese are in the game."

"Have any of their troops been used yet, other than those flying aircraft?"

"Negative as far as we know. I would not be surprised to see a Chinese tank in the field these days, manned by partisans. The resistance is suddenly better armed, but I hear their grenades have faulty delays and can explode early or late, or not at all."

"Well, old friend, that is the second reason for my call. Satellite images show hundreds of Chinese Type 59-I tanks being shipped and we both know where they are headed. I suggest, very strongly, that you start issuing anti-tank weapons to your squads effective today. The image I saw was an old one from about six months back, but our intelligence thinks the resistance are now ready to use them."

"Sir, they cannot seriously use tanks until they get more air support, and each tank would need to have enough partisans around to defend it. Where would they refuel them or do maintenance on the vehicles? However, I will follow your advice about the anti-tank weapons, because it would be like them to send a few out just to raise hell. I can tell you our anti-aircraft efforts are moving along smoothly with guns and missiles being installed daily."

"Other than Captain Georgiy's loss of his company things in Moscow are quiet, and while the war is more or less a stalemate, no bad news is out either. I want the dates and times for the gas delivery moved up by a month. This is being done because of the capture of Colonel Denisovich and the fact that every POW talks eventually. A man can only take so much isolation and torture, Elin."

"We will be ready, sir."

"Goodbye, and if you need me, you know how to reach me. I think the Marshal has his eyes on you for a star. God knows I have tried to help you get promoted as much as I can. I will know in about a week when the promotions come out. Enjoy your day, Elin, because I have a staff meeting to attend."

The phone line went dead.

"Me, a General?" he said aloud, chuckled, and then thought, *I never thought I would make Colonel when I entered the Army, but this will please Tyoma a great deal. I think if I make General, she will be a very proud wife.*

Pushing the intercom button on the phone, he said, "Glasha, I want all company commanders at a meeting at 1300 today, and I want the names of all who fail to attend. Tell all of them it is mandatory, unless they are in a hospital bed or in the field, for the actual commanders to be here. Tell them I want to see no representatives at this meeting, but the actual commanders. And, when you finish contacting them, I, uh, need you to come in and take some dictation."

Glasha smiled, because dictation was the code word they used when the Colonel was interested in sex. She smiled, unknowingly, and then said, "Oh, yes, sir. I hope we have a long dictation session this morning. Some days my dictation is better than others."

"Your dictation is always excellent. Now, see to arranging the meeting and then come into my office."

Captain Ilik Georgiy was assigned a new unit, and the Russians began to blend the seasoned troops in with the new recruits as a result of him losing his company. While he still had nightmares of the slaughtering of his troops, they were less frequent than the first week. All his squad leaders and the Lieutenant were combat veterans with about half of them having served two or more tours in America. He turned the training of his company over to the Lieutenant and experienced line Sergeants.

Each morning and night he received a briefing on the progress of the unit, and they were putting in twelve hour days. The troops were looking better and seemed more confident, but Georgiy knew the ultimate test was combat. In three more weeks he'd lead them into the field and see what they were made of. Right now he was talking with the First Sergeant.

"Our numbers for sick call are the lowest for the battalion. We are averaging a soldier every 3 days, where some units have twice that many every single day. I think the training is being taken seriously by everyone. I have spotted no problems of any serious nature, and they all seem to be fast learners. I think in six months this will be one of the best conventional units in the Army."

"In three weeks we will see how good they are. Now, I was warned at a staff meeting last night that the partisans may start us- ing tanks, Type 59-I. How this will be done by the partisans I have no idea, but the Chinese are suspected of giving them a large number of the big beasts. I want us armed with four 9M133 Kornet missiles, one for each squad, and for two men to be trained to be our primary team, but make sure others are trained on the missile too. The more that know how to use the missiles the safer we will be if the primary users are wounded or killed."

"I agree. I will pass the word and then get training started, sir."

"Good, now go see this happens." Georgiy said, and then grinned.

Near noon, Romanovich and his people met with a Russian T-90 tank, along with two squads, out looking for partisans. So far, they'd seen no one and they even had a helicopter in the air to help them locate targets. Thinking the tank would provide them with not only increased security, but also some valuable training, they asked to come along. The tank commander was more than happy to say yes. As far as the tank crew was concerned, they never had too many foot soldiers around, which offered them a great deal of additional safety.

It was near dusk when the Russian troops stopped for the night. Foxholes were dug, machine-guns positioned and NON-50 mines were placed. Romanovich and his men mingled with the other troops as they discussed the coming darkness. The other smaller group was led by a Senior Sergeant. Between the Sergeant and Romanovich, they'd each been in the army longer than most of the soldiers had been alive.

"Hush!" the tank commander yelled, "I hear something."

"I hear the blades of a helicopter, but all the aircraft out here are Russian."

"Not true." Romanovich said, "There are some Chinese helicopters around, too. I have seen them."

Suddenly, the tank was struck by a missile and burst into flames. Cannon shells followed and the tank was torn to scrap iron as the soldiers moved to their holes. The explosion of the fuel was loud, and some of the flaming diesel splattered on some of the troops who'd dug in too close to the tank. The tu*rret* of the tank flew into the air, flipping end over end, until it ran out of momentum and then fell to earth a good 50 meters from the burning hull. Flames shot up higher inside the turret ring as the compressed gases and ammunition exploded. The three crewmen died instantly.

The Chinese attack helicopter, a CAIC Z-10, was a known tank buster, and it hovered near the burning wreckage firing the 30mm swivel gun in the nose. Then the grenade launcher, mounted on exterior pods, began to work the infantry over. Romanovich began to scream into his handset as he tried to get air cover.

"Uh, a pair of MiGs can be there in a few minutes, Cobra Three."

"Get something here or you will be flying bodies out! This CAIC Z-10 is turning us into hamburger, Base."

The MiGs will be there in a little over a minute."

"Uh, Cobra Three, this is Bear 19 and I understand you are having problems with a Chinese attack helicopter. I have your night position, so where is the aircraft located right now? I am showing him on my radar to your west."

"That is affirmative, Bear 19, to my west."

"Get your heads down, because I will be using my cannons on this run."

Romanovich, yelled, "Everyone down, and now!"

The Sergeant didn't hunker down in his hole because someone had to tell the fast movers how well they did. He was sure the body of the Chinese helicopter was mixed with ground clutter on the jet's radar, so he prayed this one pass would do the job.

The helicopter suddenly began to move away at a fast rate of speed and every gun on the ground fired. Tracers from the machine-guns were seen striking the aircraft, and then there was an explosion near the tail. Cannon shells began to walk the length of the chopper, and smoke began to pour from the engines. A man was suddenly thrown from his foxhole as a cannon shell struck him in the chest.

The helicopter wobbled a bit and then slowly moved for the ground.

"Cobra Three, looks like the sensors on the Chinese bird failed to alert them of our attack, or they were not paying attention. I see the aircraft going in for a crash landing."

"It is going down, but the crash will be controlled from what I can see."

"Base to Cobra Three."

"Go Base." Romanovich said.

"Try to capture the crew. The commander said you will be well rewarded if this capture takes place. Copy?"

"Copy, capture the crew." he replied and then thought, *That may be hard because those Chinese just killed some of our men. I am sure most of our people are not in the mood to take prisoners.*

"Cobra Three out. Listen to me, men, we need to take the two Chinese in the helicopter captive. If we do, the commander has promised to reward us well."

"We need to get nearer then, because it is slowly moving away from us." Private Nikitovich said, and pointed.

"Bear 19, thanks for the assistance and you can paint a Chinese kill on your jet. Now we will try to capture the crew. Cobra

Three, out." He handed the headset back to his radioman and yelled, "Let us move toward the helicopter, but do not approach it from the front."

As they ran, the helicopter was seen to land in a small open field and the canopies immediately popped open. Romanovich sent a line of Bison bullets just over the glass and saw the two crew members raise their hands.

CHAPTER 12

I was notified an hour later that "Dennis" had died, and his body would be dumped a few miles from Fort Leonard Wood on the highway. I washed my hands of the man, and I'd spent all the time since he'd been taken away confirming Carol was okay. It scared the hell out of me to walk into my tent and see him holding her with the pistol in his hand. Neither of us had a scratch, but it was by the grace of God alone.

"Colonel!" Sergeant Parsons walked into the first part of the tent and yelled, "You're wanted in the communications tent. Something about a Chinese Chopper going down."

"I'm coming. I need you to see Captain Stas and make sure Sergeant Grant gets a worthy funeral. He was a good man."

"I'll see to it, sir, but you'd better hurry to the tent, they're all going nuts."

When I entered the tent with Dolly at my side, Captain Eller said, "A CAIC Z-10 was just shot down by a MiG, oh, maybe 30 minutes ago, and the crew captured. The last communications we had with them was they were having problems with their electronic warfare (EW) system and knew a jet had a radar lock on them. Shortly after, there were three weak mayday calls and they disappeared. Right now the Russians should have them prisoner, unless they were pissed and shot them. Pilots who come down near men they've just shot at seem to always be killed instantly."

"What was their mission, and what were they doing when they went down?"

"They had just taken out a Russian Tank and were working over about a company of infantry when a MiG locked onto them.

They heard the warnings, but none of the EW systems were working properly."

"Send this information up channel to the top. It's a given that the Russians will use images of the downed chopper and the crew to throw in the face of the United Nations. This will perhaps get the Chinese to provide even more supplies to us. I'm not sure how they think about politics and world opinion."

"Yes, sir. I'll see they're notified in a couple of seconds."

I walked to the rear of the tent and waited.

Ten minutes later, the Captain neared and said, "The Chinese want us to take out the two prisoners, if in fact they're still alive. Headquarters said they can deny the helicopter was theirs, but not the two crew members. They also said all Chinese aircrews are warned to not be taken alive."

"We have no idea where they're being held or if they still live." I said, and wondered if Headquarters had any idea of how little we knew of the fort. Most of our attacks on the fort were done using old maps handed out to visitors to the base before the fall.

"Headquarters is working on that, and they said the Chinese will launch a huge air attack to cover the killings once we know where they are located if they survived. Since the Russians have Mongolians and some look Chinese, just having two dead Asians bodies will prove nothing."

"I don't like this at all. Those two men have done nothing to warrant their being taken out except be captured, and that could happen to any of us. Once we know where they're being held, why don't they just bomb the place?"

"Sir, take it to the General, because I was just talking to him. He, in turn, had a Chinese General sitting right beside him."

"Well, get the General on the horn and let me talk to him personally. What he's asking me to do is out and out murder, and I don't like it at all."

"Okay, but I told you all he said and now he'll have your ass for lunch."

I laughed and then replied, "Son, he'll get no virgin. I was being chewed on by Drill Instructors before you were even born. Now, get him on the radio."

I'd argued with the General, both Generals actually, and lost the fight. I was ordered to determine, if I could, where the two men were held. While I tried to gather that information, the Chinese would use their satellites to see if they could find the men. Once they were found, I'd have 48 hours to get in under the cover of an attack, kill the two men and then get out. I didn't care for the mission at all and knew it was almost suicidal, but the orders were legal. The Generals were afraid the two crew members would be shown all over Russia and the world as proof of direct Chinese involvement in our war. They had intercepted some Russian radio traffic that stated the two captured fliers would be sent to Russia in six days, thus my 48 hours window of operation. Right now the Chinese were still at the crash site with their Russian captors. They were already here fighting, so how long could the Chinese continue to deny that fact? Sooner or later other crews would be lost, so what were they really upset about and why did these two need killing? I could think of nothing.

I left the tent and walked to my intelligence section to speak with Stas about all of this and to check on the burial of Staff Sergeant Grant. Normally, I'd let the OIC handle it, but in this case, I'd really liked the Sergeant and I felt I owed a good funeral to his memory. He'd been a good man and an excellent soldier.

I walked in the door and said, "Remain where you are, I'll be in the area a while. Stas, can we talk in your office for a few minutes?"

"I've yet to say no to a Colonel all day." he said in an attempt to be funny, but I felt the grief in the tent the minute I entered. Even his smile was forced.

Once in his office, I asked, "Do you have any idea what happened to Grant and how he was killed?"

"Apparently as he escorted Dennis here, he slipped and fell. The Russian wrapped the chains around his neck and choked him to death. But, he wasn't satisfied with that, he had to cut Grant's throat too. The rest, as they say, is history."

"From now on, when escorting a prisoner, we use two guards."

"Already have that in place, but no prisoners."

"What do you know about Fort Leonard Wood and the Chinese supporting us? I was just ordered to find two captured Chinese fliers, who may have been take prisoner alive, and to kill them. I want to know all I can about the Chinese and the fort."

"Makes sense to me." He stood and said, "Let me pull some files and maps, but I'm sure headquarters will have more information. I was stationed on the fort prior to the fall, so I can help you a lot by using a map. As for the Chinese, I have very little information on any of them and suspect you know more than I do. However, I'll pull that file too."

A couple of hours later, I knew where the fort brig was, where headquarters for the Russians was, near the flagpole I remembered, and some areas to avoid in the event of an attack. I wanted to stay in the bushes most of the way in and out, and to avoid any fuel or oil storage areas. I didn't like the idea of going into the fort with a small group to kill two men and then trying to get away. I just didn't think it could be done. I'd do my best, but I didn't think anyone could pull this mission off and survive.

That night I tossed and turned in bed and finally got up and made my way to the communications tent to see if the night in the field was quiet too. Nothing was going on in the tent, but Major Eller was on duty and said we were having a package delivered to him in the morning. He was told in code via the radio that it contained all they knew about the two pilots and photos taken by satellite. Headquarters said the images showed the two being taken into the fort brig. All images were blown up as large as they could be and not turn grainy. We talked a bit and discussed the funeral of Staff Sergeant Grant, which would be held a few hours after the package was to be delivered. By noon, I would have all the information I needed, or at least all I was going to get from any source.

I finally fell asleep sitting in a chair in the communications tent, and Eller woke me at 0200 when he went off shift. I moved to my tent and was asleep in minutes.

I woke at my usual time, 0500, and showered and then shaved. We had no real dress code, not really, but most of us tried to keep our hair short to avoid fleas and lice. I wore my salt and pepper hair cut close on the sides and had about an inch on top. I had a full head of hair and I didn't think I'd lose any of it before I died, which could be in the next few days.

They must know the odds are against me to complete this mission, I thought and then wondered, *Surely they must know most, if not all of us, will die in the attempt. I could use one of my snipers to take them out if I knew the date and time of their movement to vehicles, but I don't. Too many loose ends to please me.* I was shaving, and I saw no way to pull this mission off as a success.

Stas was heard talking with Sergeant Parsons, so I stuck my head through the tent flap and said, "Come on in, and what brings you to my quarters so early? It's not even 0600 yet." I gave him a smile.

"Take a look at the package Headquarters sent us. Now, one of the prisoners is the son of the current President of China. In case you don't know, the position has little legal power and is mainly ceremonial, but the man is powerful. He has a lot of power within the communist political system and I know now why they want *him* taken out. If he talks or is made to look bad, it will make all of China look bad. I see the order to have them killed was signed by the President, Zhen Xinya, himself. That's the pilot's father." He handed a thick tan envelope to me.

"The crew looks like junior high school kids." I said as I pulled two 8X10 color photos from the envelope. They look well qualified, with both wearing jump wings and aircrew wings. "I'm a bit confused by the rank though."

"Both are Captains."

"Names? And, don't tell me to read them, because I can't pronounce them, and I see the English over the Chinese."

"The President's son is Qin Xinya, the man on the left, and his weapons system operator is Cheng Shui. I'm unsure about Shui, but HQ tells me his father is also in politics, but of a lower position than Xinya."

"I imagine in a communist nation almost everyone must be in politics to some degree, if they wish to live decently. I see the Chinese as having two income levels, the have and have-nots, with most not having much."

"I don't get involved in politics, because just staying alive around here is hard enough."

"Do we have anyone here that speaks Chinese? There must be an inch of papers in here, but not a word in English."

"Uh, the radio said an American born Chinese by the name of Yang Xue is due in here today or tomorrow."

"Where did they find him, I wonder?"

"The Chinese are all over, and in most towns and cities, but all of them I know live in larger places that have a China Town or neighborhood for them. They don't bother most folks, tend to mind their own business, and are rarely noticed, something they have perfected since they began coming to this country."

"Okay, but other than reading most of this stuff in the pouch, why is he being sent? Looks to me like they could've translated all of this stuff at Headquarters much easier."

"He's coming to read this is all I know, well, what I suspect. If he has a different mission, he'll let us know."

"Suspect? You mean you don't really know?"

"Colonel, we have papers in Chinese and have a Chinese speaking American coming, so I assumed they belong together. If he's here for a different reason, he'll let us know, I'm sure."

"The Army ain't changed since I was an E-1, do you realize this? Still mass confusion half the time and now that I'm a commander, I don't know much more than I did as a no striper. I'm still blindly following orders."

Eller laughed and then when he sobered he said, "Let's change the subject for a minute and talk about Tom Hensley."

"Sure, is there a problem?"

"The last three times he's gone out, the squad bypassed targets and did not engaged a single Russian. In one case it was a broken down Russian T-90 tank, in another he let a whole company walk through his ambush and in the last, he could have grabbed two Russians who were with two local women about a half a mile from the fort. He claimed in the last situation he was afraid the women would be injured or killed."

"I see, so we may have a coward on our hands. When you return, tell Captain Hensley he's going out tonight with me to attack a train. Let him know he'll be in charge, but I'll be along to evaluate how well his people do. I want the train attacked between Rolla and Newburg and before we attack the train, we'll blow the railroad bridge over the Little Piney River. Tell him it's crucial this attack happens and we're looking for Russian supplies, especially chemical/biological gear, and other material."

"Oh, he won't like this at all, but I'll enjoy telling him."

"Tell him we'll not blow the tracks, but we will pull the spikes on some of the rails and then pull them out of alignment, maybe about 6 inches, on each side. That will be enough to make the cars run off the track, especially the engine. To do that, he'll need a way to pull the spikes. The last report you gave me indicated the Russians are guarding trains with about a company of men, so we'll need grenades, C-4 explosives, and two machine-guns. In my previous train experience, the Russians usually mount machine-guns on flatbed cars."

"How will you move the gear back here? We have some horses he can use, or bicycles."

"Give him both and let's see how he handles this. A bicycle can carry as much as a horse if a man knows how to use one properly. My dad showed me images of the Viet Cong in the Vietnam War and they put hundreds of pounds on a bike, extended the handlebars with a limb and then pushed the damned thing from Hanoi to Saigon down the Ho Chi Min trail. I discovered that's *1,092 miles* if you're driving, and much more if you were on a twisting and turning jungle trail. I can safely add another 500 miles to the trip on the trail. So give that some thought."

"What will happen if Hensley blows this?"

"I will demote him down to Sergeant and he can work his way back up again. I have no use for leaders who fail to lead or won't fight."

Sergeant Parsons stuck her head in and said, "Sir, Top is taking a turn for the worse and wants to speak with you. The doctors don't think he'll survive the day."

"Take care of Hensley and tell him to meet me here at 1800 hours. If I determine he's unsuited to lead, I'll get rid of him. I have to leave, because Top and I go way back."

"I know Top, and tell him hello for me." Eller said as he left my tent.

I made my way to the hospital with Dolly at my side and found Top awake, but not looking good at all. His face and even his lips were pale. He looked weak, but he did smile when I walked in his room.

"How are you doin', Top?" I asked with a smile.

"Not . . . well. I . . . hurt and I'm . . . so tired. I'll . . . join my . . . wife . . . today."

"Oh, you have years left."

"No, I'll . . . not . . . last the . . . day."

"What can I do for you, Top?"

"Nothin' . . . listen to . . . me. I am . . . proud . . . of you. Willy . . . is proud . . . too."

"Thank you, sir."

"Come . . . closer so . . . I can hold . . . your hand."

"Sure." I moved to his side and saw on a machine that his heartbeat was very irregular. I took his left hand in mine.

"I always . . . thought of you . . . as a son."

"Thank you, because I'm honored."

"I want to tell you —"

Top gave a loud gasp, his eyes met mine and they grew huge. Dolly began to whine. His feet kicked a couple of times and the machine monitoring his heart went off and in rushed a team of men and women. I saw the line for his heart was straight and not moving. I was pushed out the door and took a seat in the waiting room. Dolly moved to my side and placed her head in my lap.

Thirty minutes later, a doctor came from the room, approached me and said, "Our Top Sergeant is dead. There was just too much internal trauma to keep him alive. I'm very sorry, Colonel, because he spoke of you often."

I nodded and left, my mind numb, because I'd loved that black man like a father.

Near noon, Captain Yang Xue arrived and was quickly pulled into the intelligence office. Then they sent for me. Xue was larger than the average Chinese, about double in size, and quickly informed us in excellent English his father was Chinese and his mother an American. That quickly explained his size difference, which I guessed guess was six feet and four inches. He gave us a quick bio, but what caught my ear was Xue had a PhD in microbiology and was here to lessen the impact of Russian poison gases, if used. He knew how to make a gas from scratch, and explained it was simple to do. He said from a scale of 1 to 5, with 5 being the highest likelihood of gases being used, the Russians were sitting on a 3.75 or 4. He felt if they suffered a few more major losses in battle, the gases would be used right after that.

"When I dealt with poison gases in Mississippi, they'd fly over and spray the chemicals out like they were watering a garden."

"The gases can be delivered in many ways, but spraying is great for large sections of land, like a county or city. That is an easy and cheap way to deliver the gases. If they want to gas just a field, they'll deliver a bomb or artillery shell filled with gas."

"Is there anything we can do to prepare for an attack?"

"Not a whole lot, not really, except issue and keep your chemical/biological gear near."

"I don't like that at all. That will just add weight to the men and women in the field."

"Colonel, we have no choice." Xue said.

CHAPTER 13

Once at the downed Chinese aircraft, the Master Sergeant had the two Asians step from the cockpit and lay on the ground. They were searched and a pistol was taken from each man, along with a twelve inch survival knife. Their hands were tied behind their backs and they were made to stand.

"Base, Cobra Three, inform the commander I have two crew members from the Chinese aircraft and an almost intact CAIC Z-10 on my hands. Do you want to wait to pick us up at dawn or do the job now?"

"Uh, wait one."

"Anyone seen the Lieutenant?"

"He is dead, Master Sergeant, and most of his head is missing." Private Slava said.

"I need for some of you to return and work on our wounded. Also prepare the dead for body bags. Remove all grenades and ammo, along with weapons, from the bodies. Do the job with respect too, because these are our comrades. Corporal Makarovich, I want your squad to guard our guests, but do not mistreat them."

"Yes, we will guard them. Move toward the burning tank." the Corporal said as he pushed one of the small men forward. The other man followed.

Romanovich was suddenly tired and hungry. He was getting too old to be out chasing bad guys, and every night he spent in the field was progressively getting harder on him. He wondered what kind of special treat the commander would give them. *Most likely a couple of bottles of vodka*, he thought.

Ten minutes later, the radio squawked.

"Flight of ten helicopters coming in, Master Sergeant, and overhead are four jets." my radioman said.

"Our guests are valuable fodder for the propaganda machines, do you not see? Now, the Russian Bear has not only a helicopter of Chinese manufacture, but a pilot and weapons system operator. We have hit the big time."

"The two little men looked scared to death to me, but what do I know? I am just a radioman in the Army."

Romanovich laughed and when he sobered he took the radio and said, "This is Cobra Three and what is your ETA?"

"Two minutes. I will need someone to pop smoke for us and I will turn my lights for a minute or so. The POWs are to come out on the first bird, which is mine."

"Private Petrovich, move to the end of the field and prepare to pop smoke for the first aircraft landing. He will transmit wind direction as he lands for the prisoners."

"I am moving there now, Master Sergeant."

"Corporal Makarovich, bring the two prisoners to me and once the helicopters are here, help me load them."

The Chinese moved forward and even in the darkness, Romanovich could see the fear in their eyes. Both were short, maybe five feet two inches, and they looked more like young men in high school than combat veterans. He would have guessed their ages at around fifteen or so. Both had black hair and narrow black eyes.

When the first aircraft landed, the orange smoke moving east, the two Chinese were loaded along with five men from Corporal Makarovich's squad and the helicopter immediately took to the air. Romanovich immediately saw two escort helicopters, both Black Sharks, drop down to fly on each side of the aircraft and a fast mover was flying slowly overhead. Headquarters wanted the POWs returned safely.

"Master Sergeant Romanovich, you have been ordered out on the next wave, first chopper. Then all of us will be removed." the radioman said.

Once back at Fort Leonard Wood, the Master Sergeant was ushered into the base commander's private car and driven to the man's office. He was quickly taken inside Headquarters and met with the commander in a private room.

"Master Sergeant, your actions tonight were outstanding and, as a result, you will be returning home, your assignment cut short, and will go on a tour across our great nation. You are the first man to capture evidence, solid evidence, that the Chinese are playing an active part in this war. I am able to offer you a promotion to Major, some very highly respected medals, and a 60 day leave in Russia."

"This is most generous of you, sir, but all I did was my job. Of course I will take what you are offering, because a Major makes more retirement money than a Master Sergeant. I have medals, but if you insist, I will take them too, and no man will ever turn down free leave. I want to thank you, sir."

"Good; this afternoon, at 1800 hours, I will do the promotion ceremony and present you with some medals. Then, you need to pack, because you and I will be leaving at first light if all goes well. Then the Chinese POWs will go out later. It is imperative that they be thoroughly interrogated here before they go to the Russia."

"I understand, sir. What about my people who were with me? Capturing them was a team effort."

"Give me a list of your Sergeants and Corporals and all will be promoted one rank. I will also give all of them a week off and some bottles of vodka."

"They will appreciate that, sir."

"Thanks to you, Major, I now have my first star."

Extending his hand, they shook, and Romanovich said, "Congratulations, sir. When do you pin it on?"

"This afternoon at 1800 hours. We will both be promoted at the same meeting."

"Will that be all, sir? I need to meet my troops as they return and then rest a little."

"Yes, of course, and I should have considered your fatigue. You do what is needed and then eat in the officers mess. If you have any problems, have them contact me."

At the 1800 meeting, Romanovich and Yanovich were both promoted. Romanovich was presented three medals, which meant little to him. He already had almost twenty, so three more were nothing. One positive aspect of being an officer now was he could spend more time with Georgiy than before. The new General said, "I am sorry, but the Major and I will be leaving for Moscow in the morning at 0600, and we will not have a promotion party nor be at the Officers Club. However, we have informed the Officers Club that all drinks from 1830 hours until 2030 are on the two of us. So, go by and have some drinks on us, gentlemen. Colonel Olegovich, good luck on your new position as the base commander."

As the new General walked from the room, an old Master Sergeant yelled, "Teeeen Huuuooooot!" from the very pit of his stomach. Everyone stood.

Romanovich made his way to see Georgiy and when he knocked on the door, he was met by Lena wearing only a robe.

"My God, Romanovich, is that you dressed as a Major? Come, come in, please. Ilik will be so happy to see this."

When he entered, Ilik was sitting on the sofa, so he stood, gave a big smile and asked, "How did that happen?"

"I got lucky and captured two Chinese aircrew members and their attack helicopter almost completely intact. Even the external pods were loaded up. Moscow was so happy they promoted Yanovich to General and me to Major. I took the promotion mainly for the money, because I will retire in a couple of years. My assignment here has been cut short, and I am to return home and then go on tour after 60 days of leave."

"Boris, that is simply great news. I do not think this could have happened to a better man than you. It calls for a celebration, so let me pull some top shelf vodka. You a Major, wow, and you still outrank me." Ilik said, and then laughed.

"I cannot stay long or drink much, because I head home first thing in the morning with the General. I want you to keep your eyes and ears open, Ilik, because we are getting ready to use chemical and biological weapons in this state for the first time. That shit can kill you, and all you have to do is make one small mistake."

"I have worked in it before on my first two tours here. I think it is overkill, but no one asked what I thought." He took Lena's hand and pulled her to his legs, and she sat in his lap. She leaned forward, her head resting on his shoulder. Ilik poured the drinks and, handing one to Boris, he smiled.

"Keep in touch with me and we will get together again in the future, but if we have to do the job, it will be after we retire." He knocked his vodka back, wiped his mouth off and said, "I need to go. I spent most of the afternoon packing and now I need to go by the Officers Club, eat, and then get ready for bed. I have to be at the airport at 0600 for my flight."

"Take care, Boris, and if you need me, just let me know." Ilik stood and embraced his friend.

"I am a little excited, because my wife does not know of my promotion. I will contact you if I need you, my friend. Stay safe." He walked to the door and Lena let him out, then closed and locked the door.

At 0600 Romanovich and the General walked down a long hall in the airport to board their aircraft. There was a long line of well wishers lining both sides of the hallway, clapping and shaking hands with the two men. Ilik and Lena stood in the background waving at their friend. Boris saw them and waved back.

They pushed through the crowd and when they entered the aircraft, the General was shown to first class, as was Romanovich. Minutes later, a small group of men returning home after completing their one year tour boarded and were shown to the coach section. Not long after that the engines started and they began to taxi. The fasten your seat-belt sign came on and a beautiful woman stood in front of both sections showing how to use the life preserver and oxygen mask. The aircraft was a commercial flight booked by the Russian government to transport troops to and from America. Then they turned from the taxiway to the runway.

Romanovich smiled; he was going home and his wife, if she'd waited for him, would be so surprised at his promotion and happy he would be home for a year or more. Perhaps they would be happier now, because they'd have much more money to live on. He heard power applied to the engines, felt the bird shudder as only the brakes held it in place, and then they began to move down the long slab of concrete. They gently lifted off, the wheels were heard when they bumped into the wheel well, and then a whirling sound was heard as the flaps were adjusted. The aircraft made a hard bank to the right and, looking out his window, Romanovich saw a small missile fly past them. The aircraft had leveled, but the nose went up and more power was given to the engines. It seemed to Boris as if the pilot was fighting for more altitude.

Where did that missile come from? he wondered.

Then, there was a loud boom sound on the right wing and, looking out, the Major could see the engine was gone and the wing was on fire. The pilot aborted his climb for altitude and turned gently to return to base. Just as they were about to touch down, the aircraft leaned hard to the right and the undamaged wing, heavier now, struck the runway. The aircraft then cartwheeled down the landing strip, throwing parts of people and the plane all over the place. Then, it exploded and the last thing Romanovich saw was a wall of hot orange flames moving toward him. A micro second later, life as he knew it ended.

As Georgiy watched, a body flew through the air from the airplane to land on the grasses between the taxiway and runway. Debris was flying in all directions. A long wet strip of fuel and oil was following the aircraft as it slid down the concrete. Dust and smoke filled the air making it hard to see the crash site.

"My God, Ilik, the plane crashed! I need to get to the hospital and now!"

"Go; I will stay here and help. They will surely have injured and dead."

As she ran toward the hospital, he noticed the aircraft was broken into three sections and he'd seen the two surface-to-air missiles fired. He'd even watched one strike the outboard engine on the right wing. He thought the aircraft would land safely, but then at the last second it had cartwheeled and exploded. He stood stunned as the emergency response teams moved for the wreckage.

I need to help if I can, he thought and then took out running for the crash site.

Soon, he was assisting in pulling the injured and bodies from the wreckage. Those near the explosion were all horribly burned and disfigured. More than once he gagged at the smell of charred bodies and the condition of some of the dead. He'd just placed a dead woman in uniform on the ground near a row of bodies when he spotted Boris.

He moved to his friend and half of his face was melted from the flames. Most of this clothing was burned off, but he still had his boots on and that fascinated Ilik. Just as he started to cover him, Boris opened his one good eye.

His voice cracking and body in horrible pain, Romanovich managed to say, "I . . . I hurt."

His good hand reached for his friend. When Ilik took his friend's hand in his, he didn't say anything about the burnt flesh that fell from the extremity, but it made him shiver. Boris' hand and whole arm shivered violently as his one good eye darted from spot to spot.

Georgiy turned and yelled, "Medic! I have a live one here!"

A team neared and started to work on the Major. They quickly had an IV inserted. The medic then stuck a morphine needle into a connection on the tube and Boris' pain grew much less. He remembered hearing someone scream before they struck the ground and looking around, he saw no sign of the General. He'd find out later because right now, he was getting sleepy. A minute later, he was asleep.

"What are his chances of living?" Georgiy asked the medic.

"Twenty percent might survive, because he has been severely burned and he is in for months of bad pain. Many develop pneumonia and breathing problems. If that happens, most die."

"Thank you; now I must assist others."

When Lena got home, she found Ilik drunk and quiet. She could tell he'd been crying, because his eyes were red, wet, and swollen. She walked to the sofa, sat beside him and pulled his head to her breasts.

"Cry if you must, but remember I am here for you."

He cried.

Finally, he said, "As I held his hand, his burnt flesh was falling from his fingers, and his whole body shivered in pain. His . . . his face on one side was melted, not burned black, but melted like a piece of plastic! God help me, but I wish the crash had killed him!"

"And the General?"

"Decapitated and burned badly. They will have to identify him by his dental records and DNA. I suspect he was alive one second and dead the next. The terrible smell, cries of the injured, and praying of the dying, I will never forget, never!"

"I can understand how you feel, because I work in the burn unit and see those things every single day. Not a week goes by without a soldier from a burned tank showing up, a man burned by napalm, or one that has walked in flames for some reason. The wounds are horrific; we will always remember them and the memories will last a lifetime."

"I . . . I have seen many men killed, but to be alive and in such condition is something I do not want to ever happen to me. Let them give me too much morphine or something."

"I can understand, my love. Now, you need a shower and something to eat. After we eat, we will go to bed early and try to sleep. I am sure you will sleep because you have had enough vodka to float a ship. Come, let us eat first, then shower."

They ate lightly, a little smoked fish, cheese and bread. Then they showered together and when Ilik laid down for less than a minute, the vodka in his system along with a full belly, knocked him out. Lena lightly rubbed his arm and knew how he felt. She'd treated many burn victims and could hardly stand the smell. And then to hear them scream as they were treated would be vivid in her mind forever. She fell asleep thinking of Major Romanovich and how he must look, but she avoided thinking of how he must feel.

She was dreaming her and Ilik were at the country home of her parents and he was chasing her around the barn with both of them laughing. In the dream, she'd tripped and he'd jumped on her. He'd just leaned over to kiss her when she heard a scream.

She awoke to Ilik sitting up in bed, his eyes huge, and sweat running down his face. She knew he was scared and he'd had a nightmare. She lightly touched his chest and could feel his heart beating insanely fast.

"It was a bad dream, my love. Lay back down."

"No, I cannot sleep now. I must get up. I think the crash bothered me more than I thought."

"I will get up with you and we can listen to the television and cuddle."

"But you work in the morning."

"My baby needs me tonight. I will be fine."

Hours passed and eventually they both fell asleep on the sofa. When the alarm went off, Lena stood, lowered his head to the sofa and grabbed a quick shower. She dressed, left him a quick note, and then went to work.

An hour later, Ilik was up and moving around when he found the note on the table.

> *Dear Ilik,*
>
> *You are a good caring man and I love you for the compassion that fills your heart. While you are a brave warrior, you fight for the right reasons, for your country. No one could have seen what you did yesterday and not have bad dreams, and it does not make*

you weak. We, all of us in this war, even those we call our enemies, are seeing, hearing, and remembering horrible things. We are all humans, doing the best we can to stay alive where many die.

No matter where you are or where you go, I carry you in my heart. I am a part of you, since our hearts, minds and souls have blended into one. Loving you is easy, leaving you, even just to go to work, is very hard. Know I love you, my teddy bear, and I always will.

I love and cherish you dearly, my Ilik, and remember, you are my one and only man.

Love,

Lena

Ilik smiled as he shaved. She'd understood his feelings all too well, and the note showed she knew he was a big soft teddy bear behind his rough military bearing. Dressing and then checking his uniform in the mirror, he still found it hard to believe he was a Captain. Twenty-five years ago he was a snotty-nosed kid on a farm mucking out stalls.

You have come a long way, Ilik, he thought as he put his cap on and left his quarters.

When he arrived at his unit, he saw everyone dressed and ready for their morning five kilometer run. By dressed, he meant they wore battle dress uniforms, cap, boots, weapons, and 50 pound packs. The Senior Sergeant had his gear waiting for him.

They could actually run now, but when they first started, they were hardly able to walk with the packs on their backs and boots didn't help any.

"Captain! Commander Colonel Olegovich on the phone for you." Private Slava yelled from his office door. Slava had twisted an ankle a week back and did not run in the mornings with them.

"Senior Sergeant, you take them for our morning run."

"Company, at my command, double time, hooooaaa!"

CHAPTER 14

I was deeply impressed after I got to know Captain Yang Xue over a couple of hours. Like I said before, he was not a small man like most Chinese, but closer to six feet than five. I noticed he pronounced his last name as 'Zoo.' His features were a mixture of white and Asian, and he had a healthy sense of humor, which I appreciated. However, his deep intelligence was immediately seen behind his dark brown eyes. He wore his black hair in a style that we in the military called high and tight. The sides were down to the scalp and the top had maybe a half inch on top.

After I'd offered him a seat in my office I asked the purpose of his visit.

"The Russians will strike us with poison gases within the month, and I'm here to assist you in preparing for the strike and to analyze what they drop. We know they have tons of various gases stored in Russia, but how much have they brought here? While the UN forbids the use of gas, the Russians don't give a rat's ass, and they've used it extensively in the deep south. By the way, I'm on permanent assignment here, sir, I'm not on loan."

"Most of my unit here, Captain, has been relocated *from* the deep south, Mississippi, actually. We have seen many poison gas attacks. They must have a large number of Chinese-Americans if they can afford to send me one on a permanent basis."

"Well," he smiled, "maybe I can learn something from you, then. Sir, no disrespect intended, but when the Russians invaded America, they invaded our country too. When the fall came, we experienced big problems with the Chinese mafia, who tried to take over. We eventually killed them or scared them off, and then we began looking for ways to assist in regaining our nation. We're as patriotic as anyone else, some of us even more so."

"I seriously doubt that you'll learn much from us, but maybe. If we get enough advanced warning and protective gear can be donned, we're in no danger. However, any and all civilians that are exposed will die. I didn't meant to sound like a bigot, but I had no idea we had a large number of Chinese-Americans to turn to in our time of need. I apologize if my statement came across wrong."

Xue said, "Colonel, no need to apologize. Most don't realize just how many Chinese live here, and we all consider this our country too. Now, we need to post fliers that chemical/biological attacks are possible for the coming month. Our civilians must be warned."

"I can have them posted tonight, but none can be posted during the day. The Russians own the daylight hours, Captain. From this moment on, no one goes into the field without their complete chemical suit and mask." I said, and wondered if this young man had any combat experience.

"I'm well aware of your daylight control problems, sir. Now, a little about me. Before the war I was a young First Lieutenant in Special Forces, the Green Beret actually, and when the fall came, I joined a para-military group and it eventually grew into the resistance we have now. While with the Special Forces, I served in both Iraq and Afghanistan, and saw combat on each tour. I am fluent in Chinese, English, French and speak Russian and Texan fairly well." He broke out laughing at his joke.

"I'm still working on Texan." I said with a laugh.

He nodded, and wore a big smile.

"This evening I'm going out with a group led by Captain Tom Hensley, and we'll be attacking a train carrying supplies. We'll transport the needed gear and material here by bicycle and horses. How'd you like to come along?" I said.

Eller said, "Hensley is suspected of being a weak link in the chain of battle against the Russian Bear, and tonight will be a test to see if he has what it takes to be an aggressive leader."

Xue scratched the side of his cheek, thought for a moment and then said, "I suspect your Captain has no idea he is being evaluated, right? But, yes, I'll enjoy going with you and getting some field time."

"No, he has no idea his position is on the line." I replied.

"Be ready at 2000 hours. Now, in a few minutes the Major will take you to your tent, which you'll find hot in the summer and cold in the winter. Our chow hall serves from 0500 to 0700 for breakfast, 1100 to 1300 for lunch, and 1600 to 1800 for supper. The American food is bland without the use of hot sauce, but each day you have a choice of Chinese or American chow. Sick call starts promptly at 0700 and continues until all patients are seen." I said.

"I can eat either and I've not been sick often. The last time I went to sick call, I had food poisoning. Good about my quarters, because I am a bit tired from walking here. Texas isn't close." Turning to me, he asked, "Will that be all, sir?"

I tossed him the package of the two captured Chinese fliers and said, "Read this and tell us the important things you read. We've been ordered on a mission that pertains to them, but that's all you need to know right now. When you have a need to know, you'll be told more."

"Yes, sir." Xue said, and then snapped to attention and gave me a sharp salute.

I returned his salute and said, "We don't salute out here at all so you can give that up, and we never address anyone by 'sir' in the field. Actually, we wear no rank in the field, but we know who is in charge. We don't want Russian snipers to know who our officers and senior NCOs are."

"I fully understand."

I said, "Major, show our newest Captain to his quarters and point out the dining hall, post office, and latrine with shower stalls. Oh, and stop by supply and get him armed with a Bison, pistol, knife, and a couple of grenades. Keep the pistol on you at all times, except when showering, and hang it on a hook in the shower room. Again, Captain Xue, I'm glad to have you with us."

After they left, I grew concerned about the use of chemicals in the air. I wondered about the deaths of civilians, or even my troops that wouldn't take the threat seriously. Once the alarm went off, we had less than a minute to get our masks on. Some wouldn't carry their gear around headquarters here, but they would if I caught them without it. I'd be all over their asses. I needed to have all squad leaders and platoon commanders check for atropine as well. All of us carried two of the self injecting drug pens.

While I'd had a chemical suit modified for Dolly, she'd not worn it much and didn't like it at all. As a matter of fact, I wasn't even sure it'd work. The mask was an oblong piece of plastic we'd molded and while it was clear, I didn't trust it to work properly. Hard to seal a mask on a dog. She even had two filters, but each time I'd put the suit and mask on her, she tried to pull the mask off. She was a smart animal, so I think when the air turns poisonous, she'll know I'm trying to help her. The last time she inhaled poison gases, I had to use atropine on her.

At 2100, Eller, myself, and Xue were in position beside the train tracks as a half dozen men moved the rails apart about six inches on each side. Eller had placed his men and women well, but I could tell he didn't like doing this job. The train ran at almost 2130 each night, so we would hit them hard and hopefully do some damage and steal some gear. Another team had been sent to blow up a bridge over the Little Piney River after our attack.

We all moved far enough away that the moving train presented no danger to us when it left the tracks. We had six claymore mines, a flamethrower, and two machine-guns along if they were needed. The six mines were already placed and ready to use. Our contacts in Rolla informed us that the train was usually manned and protected by a company or less of troops, depending on what was being transported.

Right on time, I heard the train whistle as it left the small town of Newburg, and knew it would soon be here. A few short minutes later, I saw a bright light moving toward us.

"Everyone, lower your NVGs." one of the Sergeants called out.

I looked at Captain Hensley, and he looked like he was about to crap his pants. I knew right then he was no leader.

The train neared traveling at maybe 40 MPH, and suddenly it ran off the track throwing dust and rocks high into the air as the wheels still rotated. It wobbled a few times and then fell to it's side, and I heard a horrible scream. I learned later the engineer had been crushed to death when the cab fell on him. Though on it's side, the drive wheels kept moving.

The next car left the tracks, striking the engine, and the rest piled up behind the second car. I looked at my Captain and he'd still not moved. I waited.

Finally, I looked at Hensley and said, "Captain, you are relieved of duty." and then in a loud voice, I screamed, "Blow the mines, now!"

When the mines blew the noise was loud, and guns began to pop and crack. I watched a flatcar with maybe forty men as my machine-gun began to fire, it's rat-tat-tat bringing instant death to many of the Russians. Screams were heard, with most coming from the train.

"Charge!" I screamed, as we all ran for the cars of goods protected by our enemies.

One car was resisting very well, and no one could get close enough to use a grenade. I moved to my flamethrower operator and asked, "Can you take the threat out?"

"Yes, sir." she replied, with a huge smile.

She shot high into the air and let the flames fall into the open boxcar door, and Russians began screaming as the burning liquid fell on them. They jumped from the car to avoid more flames and they were taken out by the machine-gun crew. Finally, Captain Xue neared the door and tossed a grenade inside. A second or two later it exploded, sending dust and wooden splinters in all directions. Blood ran to the edge of the door and began to drip to the gravel below. I could see one arm extended out the door, and it was riddled with shrapnel from the grenade.

I looked for Captain Hensley, but he was nowhere to be seen. I suspected he was still in the trees.

"Staff Sergeant Young, check all the cars for Russians. Have the lightly wounded doctored up but kill the seriously wounded. The ones you leave alive, make sure they are permanently disabled."

Corporal Ledford neared and said, "If you're looking for Captain Hensley, he's behind a log in the woods scared to death. I think he even peed his pants."

"Let's move, people, and unload this train. Major Eller!"

"Yo!"

"See what this train is carrying and let me know."

"Private Davis, give me a count of our wounded and dead. Also get the same information for the Russians. Let's move, people, they may have radioed for help."

Ten minutes later, my radioman neared and said, "Base for you, sir."

"Base, Copperhead One, over."

I heard pistol shots up and down the train tracks.

"Uh, Copperhead One, radar shows attack helicopters leaving the Fort now and moving in your direction. Their ETA is approximately 20 mikes, over."

"Roger, I understand. ETA in 20 minutes. Copperhead One, out." I handed the headset back to my radioman, and then yelled, "Let's move, folks. We have twenty minutes or less before Russian choppers get here!"

Eller neared and said, "I found cases of Chemical/Biological suits, gloves, booties, and masks, along with atropine. I'm having that taken first and then the battery operated portable decontamination shelters too. All medical supplies and food is being taken, along with any ammunition. I had the horses loaded with small drums of Russian foods, but since I don't speak Russian I have no idea what they contain." He laughed.

Staff Sergeant Young neared and said, "sixty dead Russians; six we put out of their misery and nine with permanent disabilities, one way or the other."

"Let's go, and now! Move it, people. Split into your small cells and move!" I pulled out a card, the ace of spades, and walking to a dead Russian Captain, I placed the card in his mouth. I wanted the Russian Bear to know the Aces were back and still in a killing mood.

Xue neared and said, "I had all the civilians on the train roughed up, to protect them. No reason to let them be killed because of us. Once the Russians see they were beaten, they'll be safe—maybe."

"Good thinking," I replied, and knew when I got back Captain Hensley would be formally charged.

I knew many of my folks would hide in caves in the 'mountains' and not be found by any aircraft with infrared radar. They could go back to a bend in the cave and never be found. Others, like those on the horses, were probably at our main camp already, or fairly close. Then the ones like us would move overland and take the risk of being caught. I'd discovered many of the Russian aircraft had IR capabilities, but they weren't always working properly. I'd guess on a given night, 60 out of a 100 wouldn't be operational.

"Keep Hensley with me, because he's informally under arrest for cowardice in the face of the enemy."

"I have him covered, sir." Ledford said and then added, "Sir, Private Dobins and I would like to have you give her away at our wedding next week. You're the closest thing she has to a father these days and she almost considers you her dad, too."

"I'd be honored, if I'm still alive next week."

"I might not be there myself, depending on how this next week goes. I've learned since I joined the resistance to never take life for granted."

"Enough talk, but I understand."

We heard choppers but they never came close to us and, surprisingly, I heard no explosions or cannon fire. It was so quiet it gave me an eerie feeling.

As we moved, I wondered about the engineer we'd killed when the engine fell on it's side. I could see now as long as Americans worked the trains, I'd pull no more tracks apart. I'd find some other way to get the thing to stop. Don't misunderstand me, because I'd kill any Russian in a minute and do it any way I could, but I felt we murdered that engineer and all for nothing, so it bothered me. I thought back to the time we were stopping trains in Mississippi. Civilians there were forced to sign an oath to the Russians and they stated they were in favor of Russian rule. As far as I was concerned, they were targets too. When we began to hit the trains regularly, they mounted a small rail car on the front of the train. Then, they chained prisoners from the local gulag on the platform. If we made the train run off the track, prisoners were usually crushed by the heavy engine. It had not, may God forgive us, stopped our attacks.

The next morning as we entered camp, I said to Ledford, "Captain Hensley is confined to his quarters and will be issued rations to eat. I want a guard on him around the clock."

"Yes, sir."

After dropping off the gear I carried and placing my Bison on my bed, I undressed to my shorts and made my way to the shower. I was surprised to see Major Eller drying off with his towel.

"Tomorrow morning we bring formal charges against Hensley. He never moved out of the woods, and still got so scared he peed his pants. He's unfit to be a commander of a troop of boy scouts."

"Not all men can lead, Colonel."

"You got that shit right, but looks to me like he would have been screened out years ago."

"I've no answer, except we're much more active now than we have ever been. I heard rumors that on many of his missions in the past he'd walk about a mile, spend a couple of days and then return."

"If I could prove that, I'd have the sonofabitch shot. I want you to nose around and talk to some of the men and women who've gone into the field with him. By rights, they should be charged too, but I'll let them go if they come clean."

"I'll try, but I can make no promises."

"That's all I asked. I need to shower, grab a bite to eat, and catch some sleep."

The Major laughed and said, "I'm heading to bed just as soon as I get in my tent. Good mission, sir."

I turned the water on and said, "I think it was, too."

At daybreak the next day, Captain Hensley stood in front of our table, his face stern and showing no emotion. Four of us made up the Board, and all of us were officers. He was standing at attention, so I gave a long sigh and said, "Please be seated. Captain Thomas Hensley, you're brought before this Court Martial Board charged with cowardice in the face of the enemy, conduct unbecoming an officer, and lying to your superior officers. How do you plead?"

His attorney, Lieutenant James Worth, a real civilian lawyer said, "The defendant pleads not guilty, sir."

"Not guilty will be entered into the official minutes of this trial." I said.

"Sir, I request this court martial be stopped and Captain Hensley's record be cleared of these charges. There hasn't even been an article 92 conducted and he wasn't read his rights." Worth said, and at first I thought he was joking.

"Lieutenant, your client is guilty as hell because I was there, and I am an eyewitness. Now, by partisan law, we do not need a court martial to execute your client, none at all, but I'm a fair man. However, there will be no article 92 hearing conducted in his case."

Worth was a smart man. "Then why, sir, are you on the board that will determine his guilt, if he's already guilty in your eyes? Do you dare call this a fair trial?"

"I can agree with that. Captain Xue, I want you to take my place. By law, there should be a Full Colonel on the board, but I'm the only one assigned here. Counsel, do you agree with us not having a Colonel on the board?"

"Uh, yes, sir, we agree."

Suddenly, the flap to the tent was pulled open and Sergeant Parsons said, "Colonel, something is drizzling from the skies, and it's not rain."

Xue, who'd stood, ran to the flap, looked out and screamed, "Chemical attack! Don your protective gear now!"

Parsons met my eyes, and began to shake and shiver severely. She fell to the floor and started twitching and jerking as if she were having an epileptic seizure. It scared the hell out of me, but Xue pulled an atropine pen from his pocket and pushed it against her left thigh.

"It's a nerve agent they're using, I suspect, sir."

All of us were donning our gear quickly, except Hensley.

"Get a suit and mask on your client, Worth, or he'll be dead before we can determine his guilt." Xue yelled at the Lieutenant.

My only armed guard, Sergeant Ledford, was putting his chemical warfare jacket on when Hensley exploded from his seat and made a mad dash out of our tent.

The Sergeant started to follow him when I said, "As you were, Sergeant Ledford. You're not dressed to go out and he'll be dead in a few minutes. Get your mask on, all of us, and this trial is over, due to a dead suspect."

A handmade siren was sounding, and everyone on the base knew we were under a chemical attack. I knew most would survive, but as I dressed Dolly I wondered how many people we'd lose. I slipped her mask on and as awkward as it was, she didn't complain. I think she knew it was to keep her alive.

When we left the tent later, even Sergeant Parsons was wearing her chemical suit, and she was carried out by a stretcher team. I saw Hensley laying in an unnatural position in the dirt. He was on his back, his mouth still foaming, and his eyes huge.

His death had been a hard one, much harder than a bullet to the head or even a hanging. Fool; he was a damned fool. We would have found him guilty though, beyond any doubt. He'd lied about previous missions and rarely moved more than a half a mile from the base. He'd stay there two days, call in bogus reports and then return. We even had a good dozen enlisted witnesses, and I have no use for a man like him, I thought.

CHAPTER 15

The troops began the slow jog controlled by the Senior Sergeant that most could do all day if need be, as Georgiy moved toward his office. He was ready to run when he was informed of a phone call from the base commander. Seemed lately, everyone wanted to talk to him first thing in the morning.

Entering and picking up the phone he said, "Captain Georgiy speaking, sir."

"Captain, I need to see you in my office, and shortly too, so I can brief you on a classified mission you have coming soon."

"How soon do you need me, sir?"

Laughing, the commander said, "Five minutes ago. Come over now, and I will fill you in on the job."

"Yes, sir, I am on my way."

Since Captains did not rate individual transportation, he walked to the base commander's office. When he entered, a very attractive Private met his eyes, smiled, gave him a wink, and said, "Go on in, sir, he is expecting you."

In the office, Colonel Olegovich offered him a vodka, which he turned down because it wasn't even dawn yet, but did accept coffee.

Lieutenant Colonel Zakhary Leonidovich, head of the anti-partisan center for the state, was in the room and stood before some maps on an easel near the far wall. The man spoke. "What you are about to hear is classified Top Secret and will not be discussed outside of this room."

"Yes, sir."

Olegovich said, "We are about to bring full chemical warfare down on the partisans."

"Sir, that was tried in the deep south and did not work, except it did kill a lot of innocent civilians." said Captain Georgiy.

"Civilians mean nothing to me, nothing at all. Our attack will start in the morning, right at 0500 hours."

"What is the role of my troops in this effort, sir?"

"I want you and a number of other units out looking for results of our poison gas. Since your group is an airborne group, you will be dropped from around 182 meters, so reserve chutes will not be issued. I do not think you will have time to fix any malfunctions or use a reserve parachute prior to ground impact."

"When do we jump?"

"At 0600 the day after tomorrow. Tomorrow morning at 0300 the gases will start being dropped using a spraying system mounted on Transport aircraft. The area to be sprayed will be surrounding this fort and much of Phelps county, as well. This first gassing is a test only, to see if it produces enough successful results to make it cost effective. Now, we did drop some east and south this morning, just to make sure our equipment would work, and it is fine."

"How many of my troops are to go on this jump?"

"Your whole company."

Ilik nodded in understanding.

"Of course, any partisans you meet will be eliminated, clear?"

"Of course it is clear, sir, and it is normal routine."

Colonel Leonidovich said, "In a few days the nerve agent will start to dissipate, but it will still remain in low areas for some days to come. Try to avoid low lying areas and keep your masks and gear on through the entire mission. I know the gear is hot, but it beats death all to hell."

"Will that be all, sir?"

"Not exactly. See, we have a Russian missing that is both a scientist and a Colonel. He is an expert on Chemical Biological warfare, and we know the partisans have him. If he is seen, you are to spare no cost in rescuing or killing him." He handed a photo of "Dennis" Denisovich to Captain Georgiy.

"Am I to keep this photograph, sir?"

"No, we do not want the partisans to know we are looking for him."

If they have him as a POW, they must know you are looking for him, Georgiy thought.

"Now, return to your unit and prepare for your parachute drop."

Georgiy's Master Sergeant was pissed as he said, "Captain, some of our troops have not jumped in over a year, and a few have never jumped. We have not jumped in so long we no longer get jump pay, but we are to jump the day after tomorrow?" The man was speaking in a meeting with all the sections assigned to the company in attendance.

"Yes, and we *will* jump. We will each be carrying two equipment bags, and we must drop them as soon as the chute opens. If the bags are not dropped, we will have some people hurt. We will be jumping with Chemical Warfare (CW) gear on, so stress that as well."

"I will take care of the training and briefings, sir, but this is a real mess in my opinion."

"Go, start the training right now and tell them it is a combat jump, so they will be paid for this one. I want everyone in the first aircraft hanger at 0400 the day after tomorrow and ready to go. The only acceptable excuse to not be there is if they are in the hospital."

The Master Sergeant left the room.

Georgiy turned to his weatherman and asked, "What kind of weather can we expect on the day of the jump?"

"Very light winds from the north, clear skies in the morning with rain clouds moving in after dusk. Temperature in the low fifties near jump time, and our high will be around 59 degrees or so. We see rain coming the day after your jump, so the poison gases will dissipate with the rain rather quickly."

"Lieutenant, it is not just my jump but all of us in the company, including you and your personnel. Every man and woman in this unit will jump with me. Once on the ground, we will break into small five man cells and start looking for evidence the chemical spraying did any good."

"Sir, I thought the mission was only for operational combat troops."

"Well, you thought wrong. Return to your unit and see how many have been to the parachute training given by the Master Sergeant. I want all of you to attend before morning. Once we leave the aircraft is not the time to realize you need to be trained."

That night in bed, Lena asked, "Does it scare you to jump out of an airplane? I do not know if I could do it, because high places scare me."

"I am not really scared, but my senses are tuned much higher than normal and I expect something to go wrong, so I am really at my best when I leave the aircraft. Many men and women enter into jump status for the extra pay, which is substantial, especially if you are of low rank. In the morning, jumping into combat will earn each of us a large paycheck next month."

"If you survive."

Taking her head in his hands, he gazed into her eyes and said, "I have been jumping since before you were born and I am still here. I feel it is safer than driving a car in Moscow. We will jump, complete our mission and return home, simple." He then kissed the very tip of her nose.

She nodded, but didn't think it was all as simple as he claimed. She'd spent the last two days placing patients in CW tents and carrying her CW gear. Right now the winds were from the north, but they could change direction at any time, and then they'd need to don their protective suits and masks. The patients were already protected and breathing oxygen from compressed tanks.

"Come, Ilik, let us play a bit and then get some sleep. You will be up at 0400 and it is close to 2100 now. I love you and need to love you one more time before you leave me in the morning."

Ilik turned the light off, climbed into bed beside her and said, "I was lucky when I met you.."

I was the lucky one, she thought as she rolled over on top of him.

At 0500 Georgiy's company was loading on a Russian UAC/HAL Il-214 aircraft, and they would be using three of the big birds to make the drops. The commander and vice-commander, Olegovich, would be on different aircraft. This was in the event one aircraft was lost, a commander would still be able to lead the remaining troops. Three T-90 tanks would also be dropped using a low-altitude parachute-extraction system (LAPES), once the troops were on the ground. The tanks and additional ammunition would be dropped to better equip the troops for their mission and, like the commanders, one tank and pallet was on each aircraft.

Soon the aircraft zoomed down the runway, nosed up into the air, and then began a combat assault take off. The aircraft was nosed up as high as it could safely go and the angle was steep. The wheels and flaps made noises as they both moved. Once the aircraft was above small arms fire, they flew in a circle waiting for the second and third birds. A few minutes later, they joined up and moved east, flying side by side.

About ten minutes after take off the Jump Master, who wore a headset, stood. Holding his hands out palms up and flat, he raised them to about chest high, and as he moved them up and down, he shouted, "Stand up!"

The troops on both sides of the aircraft stood.

He then bent his right finger into a crook, held it over his head and moved it up and down. To be heard over the aircraft noises he yelled, "Hook up!"

All hooked up.

"Sound off for equipment check!"

"Number one, okay! Number two, okay!" and on down the row it went, until it passed over to the other side, "Number twenty-six, okay!"

The Jump Master nodded to the Load Master, who began to lower the rear ramp. The men would jump two at a time or one on each side of the aircraft. Now they held their static lines as they moved toward the open ramp. The jump light remained red. They were low, and the tree tops were clearly seen as the aircraft zoomed over them.

Georgiy found his mask uncomfortable and hot. He was first on the right side, so he watched the light. The Load Master held up one finger to show they had one minute left.

Exactly one minute later, the green light came on and the Jump Master yelled, "Go, go, go!"

He stepped off into space, bent slightly at the waist, legs together, and he was looking at the toes on his protective boots when the chute opened. He quickly released both equipment bags hanging at his sides and watched them drop below him. He then looked up and saw he had a good chute. Three swings and he was on the ground. The minute his feet touched he did a PLF, rolled, and then pulled the releases to his parachute canopy. When he stood, he noticed his folks were scattered all over a large field. Some were still landing. He watched one jumper's parachute fail to open and he struck the ground, hard.

Then the three large birds lined up for another approach, and Ilik knew the pallets were coming out next. The aircraft flew just feet off the ground, large parachutes deployed behind each aircraft, and at the same time they released their loads. The pallets rolled from the rear of the big planes and struck the ground hard, with a cloud of dust behind them as they scooted forward. When they came to a stop, the soldiers ran to unload them. A little further down the field the T-90 tanks were resting on pallets, as well. Their crews ran for the armor.

Less then 30 minutes after they'd jumped, the people were splitting up. Georgiy kept a squad with each tank and sent the others out in four man teams to look for partisans. The Master Sergeant, Danovich, went out with a five man squad, counting him. As a result, Ilik stayed with the two tanks and later, when they split up, he went with one of them.

Moving was rough wearing the chemical gear, and the men in the tanks must have been really hot, buttoned up like they were. Intelligence had reports of some Chinese Type 59-I tanks in the area, and all wondered how the two would do in combat against each other. Ilik prayed they'd not meet one on this mission, because it would turn bloody for both sides.

What he disliked immensely about the tanks was they were so loud. Of course, there might be some confusion by the partisans if they thought the tanks were theirs. Throughout the morning they saw absolutely nothing; then at around 1400 they shut the tank's engines off, camouflaged the big beast and dug in. They'd wait for their prey to come to them. There was a high traffic trail in front of them, so they knew it was just a matter of time. It was also raining lightly, so they'd checked the air and found the chemical gone. The masks were removed, but the suits stayed on. If they entered a low area later, after daylight, the gas might still be there.

The T-90s were fitted with thermal gear and he ordered the crew to man it at all times at night. It was then he learned the tanks had air conditioning too, so they would be comfortable enough.

His experienced troops helped the new men and women settle in for the night. They more or less ringed the tank, but not too close in case it came under attack. After darkness, Ilik had the crew climb in their tank and button up, meaning he wanted all hatches closed and locked shut. If they spotted movement on their IR screen they were to contact him by radio.

All passed well until around midnight, when the radioman woke him and whispered, "Partisans moving down the trail. I had everyone put on NVGs, and thought you'd want me to wake you."

"Did the tank confirm that?"

"Yes sir, they reported seeing them on their IR screen. I spotted a company sized unit moving toward us with my NVGs. Do we let them pass or use the NON-50s? It is still sprinkling rain."

"Wait for the main group to get in the kill zone, then set them off. Better yet, set yours off when I explode mine."

"Yes, sir." Yakovic said.

They moved to Yakovic's foxhole and Georgiy laid in the grass beside him. Just when the main force was in front of his mine, he set squeezed the clacker. A loud explosion, followed instantly by another. and earsplitting screams filled the air. The survivors tried to rush them, which is what most armies of the world are trained to do, but the NSV 12.7mm heavy machine-gun on the tank opened up. The big gun stitched the whole column of partisans up and down numerous times. The Russians actually saw body parts flying through the air.

"Everyone stay awake; we have gone to a 100% watch, and now we wait for dawn. Do not get out of your foxholes, but be ready to fight in case some of those partisans are not dead yet. At dawn we will check them." Suddenly, an American jumped to his feet and moved toward the trees. Ilik heard a gun shot, followed a split second later by an explosion, then a horrible scream. The big machine-gun on the tank fired again and it hit everything but the runner. A few seconds later he was safely in the trees.

"What is going on?" Ilik yelled.

"Beshov fired his gun and the barrel exploded. I need a medic here, and now!" a voice that sounded like Ioanna replied.

Ira, the medic, yelled, "I am coming."

Long minutes passed and then the medic said, "We need to report this to Headquarters because the breech of his weapon exploded, not the barrel. When I saw this type of injury before, it was due to the powder in the bullet being replaced with C-4. Beshov is not dead, but he soon will be if we do not get a helicopter here. His face is an absolute bloody mess. He is on morphine."

Georgiy turned to his radioman, who shared a foxhole with him and said, "Pass that on to base."

A few minutes later he said, "Helicopter on the way, and they suspect the bullet was picked up years ago after a battle with partisans. Somehow it made it back into our supply system and was issued. We no longer collect unspent bullets or grenades to use later. It seems when we first came here, they would sabotage bullets and change the timers on grenades to zero."

"Nasty tricks." someone said from the darkness.

Fifteen minutes later the Russians heard the whop-whop-whop of the helicopter's blades and Georgiy made contact with the crew. "Cobra One to unknown rescue aircraft."

"Cobra One, this is Angel One, over."

"Uh, what is your ETA?"

"Three minutes. I will remain in the air and lower a litter for your injured troop. Strap him in well, we will raise him, and then return to base. Understand he has facial injuries, correct?"

"Yes, along with some severe injuries to his throat and eyes."

"Copy. Use your IR strobe light, Cobra."

Ilik pulled the strobe from his vest, slipped the IR cover over the face of the bulb and then pushed the on/off button. It immediately began to flash, but it was not seen by the naked eye.

"It is starting to rain harder, so keep the strobe light on and tell me when I am right over your position."

"Overhead —now!"

The aircraft came to a stop and a whirling sound was heard. Ilik looked up at the noise and saw the litter coming down. The noise was from the winch.

Private Beshov was placed on the metal litter and strapped in tightly. Ilik said, "All clear down here, and you can raise our man now."

At that point, two tracers crossed in front of the helicopter and the aircraft commander said in a calm voice, "Taking fire, I say again, I am taking ground fire from the east and west sides of the injured man."

The machine-guns on both sides of the aircraft began throwing bullets in the general direction of the ground fire. By now, Beshov was at the door and seconds later, he was inside.

"We have the injured man and are returning to base. Good hunting, Angel One, over."

"Thank you, Angel One, and stay safe. Cobra One, out."

"Okay folks, from the shots fired at the helicopter we know the partisans are in the area, so stay alert. It will be daylight in a few hours but in the meantime, they may come for us."

The commander's hatch opened and the man stuck his head out and said, "IR is picking up a group of maybe 50 partisans moving this way. They are right in front of us, maybe 200 meters. Want me to fire a couple of cannon rounds to disperse them?"

"Sure, this might be interesting."

The hatch closed, Ilik heard it lock, and a minute later the radio said, "Heavy One to Cobra One, two shots will be fired close together. The first shot is going—now."

A loud boom was heard and, looking in the direction of the partisans, he saw the round land and explode but due to trees and brush, he saw no casualties. A minute later, the second shot was fired, and again he saw light from the explosion. The machine-gun opened up next and fired a few rounds.

"Cobra, they have dispersed in all directions. I am also showing only two faint IR glows in the group you ambushed, one near the front of the group and the other in the middle, over. The heat from the group died after they were shot."

"Copy, Cobra One, out."

All was quiet the remainder of the night, and at daylight they were out checking the dead from the ambush. One man near the front of the ambush was still alive with bullets through his chest, so he was killed on the spot. Then all heard two shots and a loud explosion.

Ilik Georgiy had five people down as he ran to the spot of the explosion.

"Senyavich shot a wounded American in the back twice and when he turned him over, a grenade spoon flew into the air."

The medic was looking his wounded over. Senyavich had some small fragments in his legs, but could walk. The others seemed to have minor injuries. It was then the tank started it's loud motor to charge their batteries and systems.

"Place the wounded on the rear of the tank, along with their gear and weapons. Yakovic, call in the dead partisans, and we are moving to check the others the tank fired at in a few minutes. Tell base we will update the body count after we move to the new location. Get your packs and gear on, people, we are leaving in five minutes."

They found five more bodies where the tank's cannon had struck and death had to be instantaneous, or so Ilik thought. Huge portions of their bodies were missing, and it was obvious they'd died quickly.

"Yakovic?"

"Yes, sir?"

"Call in our body count."

CHAPTER 16

I was tired. It had been three days since the gas attack and while most of the poison had dissipated, we still wore the awkward suits and kept our masks nearby. The first two nights were rough when we attempted to sleep in the masks. The rains were now carrying the nerve agent away, and the water would dilute it or completely break it down over time. The initial attack had killed over a hundred of us in the four counties that were sprayed. It taught us to always have our chemical gear nearby and ready.

We'd also had over 60 killed not far from my camp when a joint team of armor and troops caught some partisans going down a well used trail. They died while forming up for an attack against the tank. It was my opinion that Russian tanks had heat-detection capability. I suspected they were able to use it in the air as well, because the T-90 tanks were known to be armed with rockets and missiles externally, too.

Captain Hensley had been buried in an unmarked grave and as far as I was concerned, his death had been too fast, but I was glad he was gone and he'd died in pain. I hated the man for how he'd made all officers look bad. Our jobs as leaders was to do just that, lead or get the hell out of the way.

Parsons, who was back at work but was supposed to be on bed rest, stuck her head in the door and said, "Intelligence reports two Russian T-90 tanks and about a company of men out beating the bushes for us. They're suspected of being the same group that killed our folks last night. The tanks have separated, and they want to know how you'll handle them."

"Have Intel contact Headquarters and see if they want to send a Chinese attack helicopter or a Chinese tank against one of them. Let them know we'll take one of the tanks out and the men with it, as well."

"Will do."

It was then I realized if I could hit Fort Leonard Wood with Chinese armor and aircraft, I'd have a better chance of getting to the two Chinese prisoners. I'd give that some thought after this mission. Due to the poison gas dropped on us, the date for the original attack on the fort had been placed on hold. I'd heard nothing else of the mission since.

Minutes later, Major Eller stuck his head in the door and said, "One of the tanks and about twenty-five men are less that three miles from here. Headquarters said the Chinese will have one of their tanks tackle the other brute. They'll also get photos of the battle, so I think those will be interesting to see."

"Yep; listen, I want you to remain in charge here while I lead the group after the nearest tank. It's not that I think you can't do the job, because I know you can; it's just that I like to go on missions at times to keep my senses finely tuned. I want to satisfy some questions I have about Russian tanks, too."

"I figure you're the boss and can go when you wish."

I laughed and called out, "Sergeant Parsons, see my squad and two others are alerted we're going into the field in 30 minutes. You will not be going. Have them remove their Chemical gear, but carry it with them."

"Will do, sir."

I began checking my weapons as Eller said, "I'll be in the communications tent if you need me at any time."

I nodded, but didn't say anything, because my mind was on the mission against a tank.

One good thing about tracking a tank, anyone can do the job. Since the rains, the treads dug in deep into the mud and a blind person could have followed them. I was very interested in how the Chinese HJ-12 anti-tank guided missile would do up against the big tank. It was the latest in Chinese technology and would automatically track the target without any additional operator input. Just aim, fire and forget, or so they claimed. The missile supposedly attacked the top of the tank in a downward dive in the last minute. By hitting the top of the turret, that's where armor is usually the thinnest and weakest. The Chinese claim 1,100mm of steel armor could be penetrated in the direct mode, which is a lot. I had two of them with me and would field test both, if I could, and I was sure the weapon system had never been used in combat before.

It was raining slightly and everyone was wearing a poncho. I had a woman on point and a woman bringing up the rear. I'd gone even further on this mission and sent Ledford forward to scout the area. It was then I had a strange feeling about the tank tracks. At almost the same time, I heard an explosion off in the distance in front of us, and suspected the Russians had planted mines behind the tank as it moved, just in case we walked in the big vehicles tracks. Most troops did just that, walk in the tracks, because tanks would detonate any mines it ran over without any damage to the tank. The thought had never entered my mind until the explosion.

Three of us, along with Dolly, moved toward Davis and as we ran, I said, "Stay off the tank tracks, I suspect they're mined."

We spotted Davis laying in the middle of the tracks, and her left leg was missing at the knee. She was trying to stop the bleeding when we arrived.

Sergeant Light, my medic for this mission, immediately went to work. A tourniquet was applied above the damaged leg, morphine was given and she checked her over well. Finally, she wrote "Morphine 0900 Tuesday" on Davis' forehead in black water resistant ink.

Davis tried to talk but she made little sense, so I told her to rest and be quiet. I called two big men from the group and said, "Return to base with her and once there, stay. I'm not as worried about the infantry we'll find as I am the T-90. I need to see if this missile works as designed. Place her on a litter and get out of here. She's losing blood."

They were gone in seconds and then Ledford arrived.

"Colonel, I saw the T-90 tank and about two dozen dog-faces protecting the thing. They'd just pulled up and started fixing lunch. If we rush, we can attack the tank as they eat."

We double timed through the woods and I felt sorry for the people carrying the missiles, because they were heavy. Twenty minutes later we were within a hundred yards of the Russians and I could see them eating and had to admit, they were quiet. I saw my HJ-12 anti-tank guided missile was up and ready in no time. I then nodded to the man aiming and he pulled the trigger.

Just then the tank commander stood in his open hatch and was saying something. I had my binoculars out and was watching the tank. Sure enough, it flew higher than the tank and at the last second it nosed down and struck the T-90 hard not a foot away from the commander. I watched the explosion rip the commander to shreds and his head, arms and hands flew from his body. The tank exploded into a huge ball of reddish black oily smoke and the flames moved for the sky. The noise was loud. Russian troops were hauling ass away from the big brute, knowing it was prime to blow.

Suddenly, the turret flew into the air and fuel ignited, increasing the size of the flames, and now they were rolling inside of each other as they rose in the air. The turret came to rest about fifty feet from the tank and landed on its side. Then compressed gases, ammo, and other flammables began to cook off. My machine-guns opened fire with a steady rat-tat-tat. All of us had a mad minute as we emptied a magazine toward the Russians and then we retreated, after setting some mines.

We had tested the weapon system, which was mainly my reason to be there, so we moved toward our base camp. As we returned to camp, I wondered how many Russians we'd killed. I left Ledford behind, high in the trees, to see how much damage we'd done. I doubted we killed many soldiers, but an expensive tank had been destroyed and each one we took out of action hurt the Russians.

When I returned, I discovered the other T-90 was destroyed as well, but it cost the Chinese two attack helicopters and one crew. The second chopper destroyed the tank but had limped home damaged, and to the extent it was cheaper to replace the aircraft than repair it. I reported the HJ-12 missile system worked very well and completely as advertised. What I love about it was we could now attack tanks at longer distances and didn't have to move in close, which increased our risks of being killed or injured. I also liked the fact, once locked on a target, you could fire it and then forget about it, because it would stay on the target.

Ledford returned later in the day and reported four dead Russians and a good dozen injured. Now, we had no idea how they were injured and some, I suspected, were injured when the tank blew.

I didn't think it mattered how they were injured, as long as we took some Russians out of the field for a while.

Two nights later, we were to hit a small, poorly guarded warehouse on a remote section of the fort. I selected two squads to do the mission, along with all the bicycles and horses we had to carry the loads we would take. My squad would kill the guards and steal the contents, as Eller's squad provided us security. There was one guard tower with a powerful search light, two guards on the ground, and the doors were locked with padlocks. My man, Corporal Jones, was deadly with a bow, and quiet, too. I'd have him take out all three guards if he could do so. The man in the tower might be a problem, so I'd have my .22 with silencer, if needed.

It was near three in the morning as we moved in close to the chain linked fence that ran around the fort. We were wearing NVGs and I noticed the guards on the ground were wearing them as well. I watched the guard using the light for about ten minutes and noticed his routine. He'd always start with a long look at the fence checking, I suppose, to see if it had been cut or breached in some way. Then, he'd look around the bunker that held the supplies, then he'd scan the woods near the fence. Usually, he stopped at that point, and I saw he was a smoker. He'd smoke for a minute or two, then started moving the light all over again.

I took the bolt-cutters we had, removed a wide section of the fence, and then sent my folks in one-by-one. I then moved to the base of the tower and made my way up the ladder. At the hatch that was installed in the floor, I tapped the wood. The guard immediately opened the door.

I aimed for his face and fired four shots, each making a low sound as the cartridge fired. The man fell back and blood began to drip from the open hatch. I climbed inside the tower, waved to my people on the ground and saw Jones prepare an arrow. When one of the guards rounded the corner, the arrow was released and the guard dropped without a sound. The four slicing blades on the arrowhead stuck deep in the middle of his chest and continued out his back. I watched the bloody arrow stick in a tree. The next guard must have suspected something because he stopped, pulled his AK-47 and called out something in Russian. I had continued to move the light, so he had no reason to suspect I was an American. I moved the light near the body of the dead man and the guard moved to the downed form. I hadn't pointed my spotlight at the body or the live guard previously, but I did now, knowing the bright light would be hard on his eyes and the NVGs.

It was then Jones released another arrow, and it took the last guard low and in the belly. When he screamed, two more arrows struck him dead center of his chest. He dropped to the ground without a sound, but the tips of two arrows were sticking from his back. I climbed from the tower, glad to be away from the coppery smell of blood, and knew I was covered in red from the ladder. It seemed every rung was wet and sticky.

The lock on the bunker was quickly removed by the bolt-cutters and tossed to the side. The door was opened and inside we discovered a mountain of rations, chemical warfare gear, heavy and light machine-guns, six flamethrowers, ammunition, grenades, and a good hundred or more winter parkas with gloves and mittens. Green walked to the fence and removed a large section so our horses and bicycles could move to the door and be loaded.

Near the back of the room I found a dozen cases of mines, which I'd put to good use. After everything was stripped from the bunker and the dead guards, I mined each body, the trap door on the tower, and the entrance walkway to the supply bunker and the bunker door. I removed all of the mines, but left the boxes against the wall and booby-trapped them as well. Removing the lock on a small storage shed marked "flammables", I removed two five gallon cans of gas and placed them next to the mine boxes. If the mines went, they'd explode the gas cans too.

Now, all we had to do was leave and move back a few yards. I hoped the guard didn't have to report in each hour or I was screwed, but I expected all to go well until the changing of the guards at daylight. Usually an NCO and three replacement guards would show. I'd pulled enough guard duty in the army to know how the detail was done. If we worked this properly, we'd kill the four of them too. The first squad was gone with all the supplies, so all I was doing now was inflicting injuries on the Russians. If we killed these men, we'd booby-trap their bodies too.

Right at sunup an old American Jeep with a huge Russian flag painted on the hood neared with four occupants. I spotted the Senior Sergeant right off, because he was driving. His passengers were all privates and they looked bored.

It was then I realized I should have dressed my folks as Russians and given him a hell of a surprise, but it was too late now. The two guards had been killed behind the bunker, so they were not seen, and the door was closed with the padlock hanging on the hasp. You'd have to get close to see the lock had been cut.

The Sergeant turned the Jeep off, stepped from the vehicle and slipped the safety off his Bison. He then called out, "Сообщение охранников! Ваши замены - здесь! Охранники?"

Xue whispered to me, "He's telling the guards we killed their replacements are here."

The Sergeant motioned for the men in the Jeep to come with him. I watched all safeties switch off on all the weapons they held. One man went around the bunker on one side while another went around the other way. They must have discovered the bodies and checked them, because I heard a loud explosion minutes later.

The explosion was followed by piercing screams as dust and smoke rose toward the sky. The Sergeant and the last man ran to the rear of the bunker. Minutes later they returned with one man dripping blood from where his left arm used to be. The other man who'd walked behind the building returned with what appeared to be a minor injury to his cheek.

The Sergeant picked up a small radio from the Jeep; it looked like a military walkie-talkie, and I watched him, I guess calling base to report the breach in the fence and the three, maybe four, dead men. I saw him shaking his head, nodding it, and then he said something and threw the radio to the passengers front seat in the Jeep.

He then walked to the door, saw the lock was cut and removed it from the hasp. Now, obviously angry about something, he kicked the door open, which was the wrong thing to do. The door, booby-trapped, exploded, killing the Sergeant and a private instantly in a loud explosion of fire and dust. The remaining man, still by the jeep, picked up the radio. I pointed at the man, tapped my sniper on the shoulder and moved so he'd get a clear shot. Ledford fired once and the young Russian collapsed; the heavy slug struck him in the chest and penetrated his body, taking part of his spine with the bullet when it left. I heard the bullet strike the Jeep and then zing off into space.

We then began to move home, but only after I neared the man at the Jeep. I found him dead and then dropped a grenade, with the pin pulled and with a rubber band around the spoon, in the gas tank. At some point in the future the gas would eat through the rubber band and the grenade would explode. As I was leaving I stuck an ace of spades card in the mouth of the dead Private. I wanted them to know we were back.

We hadn't covered much distance when I heard a powerful explosion, I'd guess ten minutes after we'd left the bunker. When I looked over my shoulder, I saw smoke moving toward the sky so I knew someone had moved the empty boxes marked "mines." Ledford had remained behind in a tree maybe a 100 yards from the Jeep. I'm sure he'd fill me in, and I looked forward to his report.

Once back at main camp I did an after action report, praised the bravery of my troops, and then returned to my office. Sergeant Parsons said all was well and that Carol had been by to see me earlier. I detected a bit of jealousy, but let it go.

The week earlier I'd caught Parsons removing her shirt and wearing only a vee neck tee. I only had to glance at her to see her cleavage. I knew what she was trying to do, only it wouldn't work because I loved Carol. I'd simply told her that I was the Commander, so I didn't want her running around in a tee shirt half naked. I felt she should be fully dressed at all times because we lived by example. While she was well endowed in the breast area, I didn't want my visitors drooling in my office. She'd complied, but didn't like it much and told me so. I simply told her it was an order and not open for discussion.

Ledford returned after dark, and he'd seen a lot from his tree.

"The first to arrive were the security cops and they surrounded the place, then about a company or so of grunts arrived. The security police entered the bunker and one of them must have moved the boxes marked mines, because the roof blew off the bunker and the flames shot out the door as the roof disappeared. I know that blast killed all ten men inside, because I watched it happen. Then, when they tried to move the bodies of the guards we'd killed, three more troops were seriously injured by booby traps. Finally, where you mined near the hole cut in the fence, a dog team went up in flames, along with a Captain, so we had a good day."

It was near two in the morning when I awoke hearing tank engines and there was more than one. I grabbed my weapons and ran to the communications tent.

"Relax, sir. We have ten Chinese Type 79 tanks being assigned to us. According to the Chinese, you'd know how to use them on your mission against the fort."

"Contact Headquarters and ask if my mission to put down Xinya and Shui is still a go. Send the request in code, of course. Let me know immediately when they reply."

I took Sergeant Warren with me to meet the tank commander and discovered the tanks were driven by Americans. I honestly expected to see Chinese troops. The Non-Commissioned Officer in Charge (NOIC) was an Army Master Sergeant Alfred Brown and I liked him right off. He informed me they were to be used for a mission that involved entering Fort Wood, but that was all he knew. Each tank had a large white star on the side, and stenciled under the star were the words, United States of America. I grew proud just reading the words.

I met his smile and said, "Come to my tent, Sergeant, and I'll give you an idea what our mission is to be."

Once in my tent, I poured both of us a double whiskey, handed a glass to him, and asked, "Drink?"

"Just this one. I ain't much of a drinking man. Strong drink has ruined more than one black man." he said, his white and even teeth bright against his dark skin.

I gave a low chuckle and said, "It's ruined more than one white man too, so I don't think it's a problem that either race can ignore. Now, I don't think just one will hurt either of us, nor a second, if you want one. How much were you told about your mission and Fort Leonard Wood?"

"Just that we were to go where you wanted us to go and we were being permanently assigned to your headquarters." He took the glass of whiskey, drank about half of it, and then smiled.

"I'm waiting confirmation and a date for the mission as we speak. I imagine the mission will be at night, so do your tanks have Night Vision installed in them?"

"Yes, sir, and infrared too, along with a fully computerized system. Each Type 79 tank has a range finder, the hatches will automatically lower and lock when we enter a chemical biological area, and I can track aircraft in the air on my radar. My primary armament consists of 105 mm rifled gun and my secondary armament is a 7.62 mm coaxial and bow machine guns, along with a 12.7 mm antiaircraft machine gun. This tank is armed for bear, and I think you'll find us a valuable asset to your team, sir."

"How big are the crews?"

"Four men per tank, sir. Each tank has a commander, driver, loader and gunner."

"Did you bring anything with you? I ask because we lack tents for forty men."

"We brought tents, individual weapons, chemical warfare gear, ammunition, grenades, some clothing, and enough rations for a week." The Sergeant finished his drink.

"Sergeant Parsons?"

"Yes, sir?"

"Take Master Sergeant Brown to the supply tent and wake up Manny. Tell him to give Sergeant Brown what he needs now and in the future. I'll have to radio Headquarters later this morning and increase my food supply, because feeding forty more men will take a lot of food."

"Yes, sir. Sergeant, if you'll follow me." Parsons said, and away they went.

No sooner than had they left than Eller stuck his head in the door and said, "Classified mission order in the communications tent for you, sir."

CHAPTER 17

Captain Ilik Georgiy was eating with his troops when the tank commander opened his hatch and the top half of his body came out. He called out, "Thermal imager shows partisans about a hundred yards away and they are to our —"

A huge explosion occurred that no one understood. The commander instantly ceased to exist, blown into minute pieces, and the tank was gone, covered in a twisting and turning ball of hot red flames. Then the turret went high into the air and the ammo started cooking off. In a matter of seconds, the three members of the tank crew were gone, instantaneously blown to bits.

Intense small arms fire came on them from the west and it was devastating to the Russian infantry troops. Then machine-guns opened up on them. Their radioman was caught in the open, bullets stitching him down the middle of his body from the front and exiting the radio on his back. Plastic and rubber blew out behind him, all covered in ruddy blood and gore. Yakovic danced an almost comical dance as the many bullets struck him. He then fell to the ground, dead before he knew he was falling.

The gunfire didn't last long, so when it stopped, Ilik positioned his people in better spots and caught no more fire from the resistance. From what he could remember of the tank, he'd seen a brief view of a rocket or missile before it struck beside the tank commander. Now he had to get his folks home without a radio or tank support, and he'd have to worry about Chinese helicopter gunships too.

Finally, about an hour later, he said, "Let us get out of here. I want Pugin on point and Senya bringing up our rear. Pugin, move on a compass heading of 065 and it will take us right to the fort. Keep your eyes open for mines, of course, and I will rotate the point person every two hours."

The weather was cooperating, and not a cloud was seen in the sky. As they moved, Ilik kept seeing the tank commander flying apart. In his over twenty years in the Army, he'd never seen a tank destroyed so easily, and never by the resistance. He needed to get back to report what he'd seen to intelligence. *I suspect the weapon is from the Chinese, because the Americans do not have the capability to make such a thing,* he thought. Partisans are usually crude and while what they make usually works, to destroy a tank is not an easy task.

It was middle afternoon when the sound of a helicopter was heard and looking up, his stomach knotted with fear—he saw it was a Russian aircraft. He waved his arms and jumped up and down. The aircraft landed and a crew member ran to him. Captain Georgiy explained about his radio and the pilot said the helicopter would return to base and get one for him. In the mean time, the crewman left his survival radio so he could at least communicate if he needed help.

They remained in their spot and an hour later he had a replacement radio and gave the crewman his radio back.

By dusk they were nearing Fort Leonard Wood, but knew they'd have to spend the night.

"Base, Cobra One, over.

"Go, Cobra One."

"I am calling in my night position at this time." Georgiy gave his position.

"Understand; Black Sharks have seen a number of partisan groups moving in the area. These groups vary in size from five soldiers to almost a company. If you run into trouble, we have both attack helicopters and artillery available to assist you, over."

"Copy, and Cobra One out."

Ilik opened his 'green frog' ration and discovered he had a portion of stewed beef, two meat-with-vegetables dishes, two spreads, one was a sausage stuffing, the other was a processed cheese. There was much more in the frog, but that was all he wanted right now. The box was nicknamed 'green frog' by Russian troops, because it came in a sturdy olive drab plastic blister pack. It provided enough food for one soldier for a whole day. The Captain only ate once a day usually, so his evening meal was big. He'd nibble on the crackers and breads later, along with the jellies.

Just after eating he was handed the radio by Junior Sergeant Timur and he said, "Base for you, sir."

"Uh, Cobra One, go Base."

"Be advised of a large company size group of partisans headed your way. Attack helicopters just chased them from the woods and they scattered, but we expect them to join again and continue in a westerly direction. If that happens, you will encounter them."

"Copy base, understand, and do you want me to engage this group, if possible?"

"Correct, but only if favorable for you to do so. If you do not have the upper hand, let them go by you."

"Copy, Base. Cobra One out."

"Junior Sergeant Timur, get some NON-50 mines around us, we are expecting visitors tonight. I also want mines on the trail and two NON-50 mines in the trees, up high, pointing down toward the trail."

A Corporal took to the trees with the mines in a small pouch. Once up high enough, he wired them in place and then fed the wires for the clackers down between the tree branches, across the trail and then in the bushes where Ilik was.

In less than an hour, they were ringed with mines and their two flamethrowers were ready to go too, but it could end up being a long night.

"One hundred percent awake this night. If I catch you sleeping, I will either kill you or take a stripe, depending what happens during the attack. I want no sleeping, and I mean this. No talking and do not get up and walk around under any circumstances or you may get your ass shot off. If you have to pee or crap, do it in your position and in your helmet, if you have to go badly enough. Do not give us away to the enemy."

Ilik's men and women knew him as a fair man so his threats were taken seriously, which was good, because he meant them. If one of his troops caused the enemy to be alerted, he'd send them to a gulag in Sibera, if he didn't shoot them first.

The early evening was quiet; the only sound heard was a few helicopters off to their north, but they didn't know which side they belonged to, so they remained still. Of course the mosquitoes came out and started feeding. They seemed to absolutely love the Russian insect repellent. Each slap to kill one of the flying pests brought a whispered, "Stop," from a Corporal, Sergeant, or the Captain.

It was near 0230 when Junior Sergeant Timur tapped the Captain on the shoulder and pointed. All were wearing their NVGs, so he spotted the movement of the point man for a group of partisans. They were moving down the trail and the point man was good. He marked two mines and continued walking until he was out of the kill zone. The main body followed and it looked to be close to 40 or 50 men and women. When they were all in the kill zone, Ilik squeezed the clackers and at that point, hell visited the resistance. Screams were heard and three more NON-50 mines exploded, each in itself an individual form of hell.

Bodies were shredded, limbs blown off, and heads disappeared. The air was replaced with a light red mist that hung over the trail. Then the Captain squeezed the clackers for the mines in the trees. Some victims had been screaming, some obviously praying, and others yelling for their mothers or wives. With the explosion of the NON-50s in the trees, it grew quiet. But the coppery smell of blood filled the air, along with the disgusting scent of human feces from released bowels and ripped intestines. One young troop beside the Captain began to puke. She puked until she had dry heaves.

"Sergeant Timur and Corporal Snetkov, move to the trail and fire your Bisons up and down the bodies. Then, stitch the side of the trail on both sides, in case some crawled away from us."

"Move, and now!" Master Sergeant Danovich said. "Each second gives them a chance to get away from us."

The two men moved to the trail and fired into the bodies and along the sides of the trail. Timur was surprised to hear a scream as he fired into the brush beside the trail. After firing two magazines of ammunition, they both moved back to the others.

"Now, we wait until sunrise."

The rest of the night passed slowly, and Ilik wished he had a cup of tea or coffee. He grew very sleepy between four and five, but was able to fight it off. As he looked around with his NVGs, his people were awake, so he had to set an example.

Once the sun was full up, he sent two troops to check the ambushed. They found where two seriously wounded had crawled away, leaving trails of blood, but they counted 49 bodies. All weapons, munitions and ammunition was taken and would leave by helicopter.

"Base, Cobra One, over."

"Go Cobra."

"Our dance last night was attended by 49 people and I need a helicopter to come for the weapons and other gear."

"Wait one."

"Will do."

"Cobra, was a search done for patches, papers or maps?"

"Affirmative, but only one unmarked map was found."

"Understand only one unmarked map was found. Be ready to load the helicopter with any of your people who may need medical attention and the gear from the partisans shortly. A helicopter, call sign Gopher, will make contact with you."

"Copy and out."

The loading of the helicopter was quickly completed and the unit once more began it's walk back to base. All went well in the morning, but just after noon the point man suddenly screamed and stood jerking and shivering.

Master Sergeant Danovich ran forward and yelled, "Medic!"

Private Teterev must have turned right when his foot stepped on a fulcrum and it pivoted up, a steel spike struck his left arm, went through the soft flesh, and then entered his rib cage.

Danovich knew most barbs on the booby-traps were smearing with human waste, so he said, "He needs an antibiotic in his IV, because the Americans cover the barbs with excrement. That is to insure the wound gets infected."

"How are we going to get him off the barb?" Ira asked; she was the second medic assigned to the group.

"We are not. Let me move a bit and I will untie the part that holds the barbs in place from the wood below it. It is a separate piece. They can remove the barb in him easier at the hospital."

The second he moved, Danovich knew he'd just made a mistake.

"What is wrong?" the medic asked.

"I am standing on a mine. When I remove my foot, it will explode. Let me untie him, because there is no reason for all of us to die."

Once the injured man was untied from the wooden beam, he was assisted to the main group by the medic. The Master Sergeant remained in place, gave long thought to his wife and family, prayed a while, crossed himself, and then jumped to the side.

There was no explosion, nothing happened. Looking at the mine closely, he saw it was made in China, so he marked it and moved back to the group. He pulled out his canteen, took a long swig and then enjoyed the burning the vodka did all the way to his stomach. It was the closest he'd come to death so far in twenty-eight years of service.

"Why did it not explode?" the medic asked.

At that instant the mine detonated and the blast was loud. Dust, flames and smoke filled the air. After it grew quiet again, the Master Sergeant said, "Thank God the Chinese make poor munitions, and their grenades are just as bad. Nothing they make with a timer is worth a damn. Then again, it may have had a delayed timer. All that matters is that I am still alive."

"Let us move; someone may have heard that blast. Master Sergeant, I think you need another drink of water, because only the good Lord alone kept you alive today." Captain Georgiy said and then winked at the old NCO. He knew what most carried in their canteens, because he used to do the same and he didn't care. He didn't care as long as the Master Sergeant could still do his job.

The Sergeant took a longer drink this time and then shook his head. He'd come so close to dying and very well could have. He should have probed for mines with his bayonet, but got in a rush, and being in a hurry had killed many a soldier. *I will never do that again*, he thought as he screwed the cap back on his canteen and placed it back on his belt.

Just before dark, they entered the front gate at the fort and made their way toward their quarters. All were exhausted and wanting a real meal and not something out of a "green frog" for a change. The Master Sergeant saw his troops squared away and then showered and shaved. He slipped on a clean battle dress uniform and moved to the club where he had a few drinks. He didn't go there to drink so much as to socialize with other senior NCOs and to eat. He had supper and by 2000 hours he was back in his quarters listening to the radio as he sprawled out on his single bunk bed. Within minutes he was asleep.

Colonel Zakhary Leonidovich was livid. As the head of the Anti-Partisan Unit, they'd interrogated the two Chinese, using a Chinese speaking Mongolian, and had gotten nowhere. The two kept repeating that China was a signer of the Geneva Convention, as were the Russians, and they expected to be treated with the full respect due to their rank as officers. So far, the Russians had not used torture, but it was next. Captain Xinya was of special interest because of his father's position in the Chinese Government. The man was worth his weight in gold if they could get him to talk, and torture almost always made a man or woman talk. There was a limit to just how much pain any person could take.

Of the two, Captain Shui was the most expendable of the two and they might have to kill him in some horrible fashion as Xinya watched. They'd once burned a partisan alive as an American Colonel watched, and then he talked quickly after that.

The two men were being kept in the fort's old brig and each cell was crude at best, with an open toilet, concrete bed with one blanket, and a light in each cell that burned 24 hours a day, seven days a week. They had nothing to read, except a Holy Bible printed in English. They were fed twice a day. Breakfast was bread, jam, and tea. Supper was what the Russian soldiers ate, but as men raised eating rice and fish, the meals were not to their liking. As a result the two men were losing weight. Russian music was played around the clock in the jail, and neither man liked the music either. They'd taken the flight suits from both men, so they were wearing underwear and yellow shower shoes they'd given them.

Captain Xinya heard the keys the guard carried jingling way before he saw the man. Soon his cell door was opened and the guard motioned for him to come with him. He suspected another interrogation was in his near future. So far the Russians had not mistreated them, but as the son a high political figure in the Chinese Government, he knew torture would come at some point. The Captain was well aware that his father's status made him a valuable propaganda tool for the Russians. It was karma, and he'd deal with the pain when it came.

The big burly Chinese-speaking Mongolian was in the room this time, and he held a steel pipe in his right hand. The guard placed Xinya in a wooden chair and, using cuffs, secured his ankles and wrists. It was then he knew they'd torture him on this visit. He'd spotted blood on the chair before he'd sat down and suspected Shui had been interrogated earlier.

A Russian Full Colonel entered the room and said, "Well, Captain Xinya, I trust you are enjoying your stay as a guest of my people. However, today you must pay for your room and food, so you will answer a few questions."

The Mongolian translated the words for the Colonel.

Xinya kept his head up, maintaining his dignity and asked, "What kind of questions?"

The Russian spoke and then the Mongolian asked, "How many Chinese are in this country assisting the Americans?"

"I am a Captain, not a General, so I am not told such things. Surely something like that would not be told a Captain in your army either. I have no idea how many of us are here."

The Mongolian translated and the Colonel suddenly slapped Xinya in the mouth. The small Chinese raised his head and ignored the slap.

"How many aircraft are in your squadron?" the Mongolian asked.

Silence.

"Answer me, or the game will turn rougher and much more painful for you, my friend." the big man said.

Silence.

The Russian said something and the steel pipe in the big man's hand slammed down on Xinya's left arm. He screamed from pain and glancing at his arm he saw broken bone sticking from his skin. The pain was rough and he had to grit his teeth to keep from passing out.

"How many aircraft are in your squadron?" the Mongolian asked, and then added, "Tell me, or I will break a leg next."

"There were fifteen assigned, but I am sure we have had some losses since my aircraft went down."

"And, your Commanders name?"

"I do not remember."

"You lie. Answer the question or I will break a leg."

Xinya spat in the big man's face when he leaned over to threaten him. He hoped the man would get mad enough to kill him with the pipe. However, the pipe moved in the air, impact was hard, and deep pain shot up his leg and he knew his shin was broken.

"He is stubborn, but he will break. Everyone breaks at some point. Now, ask him if he will pose with the wreckage of his helicopter."

"He says no, and for us to go to hell."

"Twist his broken arm a few times, but only until he passes out. Then take him to his cell and let him think about what is in store for him in future interrogations with you."

By the second twist of his broken arm, Xinya passed out while screaming from pain. He next woke up in his cell. He crawled to the wall to Shui's cell and tapped on it with the metal spoon he ate with. Their cells were side-by-side. The tapping they'd learned before they'd been assigned to a combat squadron.

Shui immediately responded by tapping code on his wall in return.

"Are you well?" Xinya tapped.

"No, I have a broken arm, broken leg, and all of my fingernails on my left hand were pulled off. I am in great pain."

"I have the same, except my nails are fine. Do not give up, comrade, because I suspect we will either be rescued or killed by our own forces. They must know exactly what building we are in, and I am sure a guided bomb will take this place out."

"I hope so, because I cannot take much more of this. Two days ago they tied my arms behind my back, then they tied another rope to my hands. The Mongolian then pulled a rope routed through a pulley, so I was lifted off the ground. I was pulled two feet off the floor and left like that for hours. I know both of my shoulders are dislocated, too. I am in much pain."

"Have courage my friend." He tapped as he thought, *It will be much more painful in the future, and we will leave here permanently maimed.*

"I am trying, Qin, I really am trying, and I have prayed much."

"Good. Can you rest now?"

"No, I have a headache. I have struck the corner of my concrete bed many times with my head, trying to die, but it does not kill me."

"You must stop that and if we are to die, die like real men, not cowards. As your aircraft commander, I order you to remain alive as long as you can. You must not attempt to kill yourself."

"I will obey."

"A guard comes."

The tapping stopped.

The guard slipped a tray of covered dishes into the cell. The dishes were all hard metal and could not be broken like glass or china. The man then took a tray to Shui.

Xinya uncovered his bowls and to his surprise found white rice, sticky rice, and some traditional Chinese foods. He used the provided chopsticks to eat his meal and then placed his tray with the empty dishes in the hallway through a wide slot in the bars of his door.

He moved to the wall and tapped, *"How was your meal?"*

"Good for a change, but I think that means things are about to turn really rough."

"They have already twisted my broken arm, so how much rougher can it get?"

He was to soon discover it could turn a hell of a lot more rough.

CHAPTER 18

I was angry as hell. I'd just gotten off the radio with Headquarters and the General said our raid on the Fort would be this evening. I was expected to attack the place now, and I'd actually thought the mission was more or less dead. I'd heard nothing over the past weeks and then I'm to do the job tonight? I looked at the map of the fort on the wall and selected the spot I'd use the tanks to break through the fences. It was the shortest distance to the brig. Hopefully, with help from the Chinese, I'd be able to get in and get out quickly, because I'd lose in a long drawn out fight.

I immediately called a meeting with the tank commander and all my officers and Sergeants. Slowly they began to filter in and they arrived in ones and twos.

Once all were in place, I said, "Gentlemen, this meeting is classified Top Secret and anything you see or hear here will not be discussed outside of this tent. Tonight at 0001 hours, we're to hit Fort Leonard Wood in a joint operation with Chinese air support and our tanks. We are to rescue, if we can, and kill if we cannot, two Chinese POWs currently held by the Russians."

Eller asked, "How much air support and how long will they be on target?"

"They'll start with bombers and as they bomb, we'll breech the fence. Then, if all goes as planned, a squadron of fast movers will strafe and use napalm on known hard targets. The jets will use all their munitions and then return to base."

"Any Chinese choppers in on this?"

"We'll have a squadron of attack choppers and two teams of rescue choppers to assist in getting the POWs out if we can. Each rescue team is made up of two Z-8 Search and Rescue choppers. No Chinese military personnel will be used in this ground attack on the Fort. Once we are in the area of the brig, I want the tanks to surround us and protect us as we storm the jail."

"How much time do we spend in the fort?"

"As little as possible. My people will try to rescue the two men, but if that proves to be impossible, I'll call an air strike in on the brig. We either get them out or kill them. Any questions?"

Silence filled the tent.

"Spend the rest of today cleaning weapons, packing gear, and selecting the mines we'll take with us. I want the Fort heavily mined when we leave. Gentlemen, please see to your troops."

As the senior enlisted man, Master Sergeant Brown started to call the room to attention as I left, but I said, "Please don't come to attention this morning. We have a lot to do and not much time to do it in."

About thirty minutes later, as I walked into the tent that I shared with Sgt Parsons as our offices, she said, "The supply Sergeant just left, and he's got more requests for stuff than he has on hand."

"Okay, have him issue what he does have, even if it cleans him out, and then he can radio Headquarters and speak with his supply counterpart there. Most are gearing up for tonight's mission, which is priority number one. If he or anyone else from supply comes in bitchin', tell 'em I said to give the troops what they need or they can see me. If they see me, they'll end up issuing what they have and, plus, he'll get a free ass chewing."

"Okay, I'll do that. Carol was by, but asked me to tell you she's busy in the Intel section doing photo intelligence, photos from a Chinese satellite, and it has something to do with tonight's mission."

"I need to go over there then, and see what they've come up with. I have no idea what changes the Russians have made."

"Yes, sir."

I'd not taken my hat off, so I turned and walked from the tent, moving for the Intel section.

Carol was working on a stack of 8X10 black and white images. I saw circles drawn on some building and other areas, but didn't ask any questions.

"This is the last one, Major." she said, noticed me and smiled.

"Why don't you tell the Colonel and me what you found?"

"Sure. Many of these images show little or nothing of importance, but there are four that I think both of you need to see. In this first one, the Russians have two chemical decontamination buildings newly constructed, and both are close to the brig. I suggest you blow them up while you're there; not that it will stop them, but it will take them a few days to replace them. In this other image, you can clearly see an anti-aircraft gun placed on the roof of your target. I suspect the Chinese will try to take it out with machine-gun fire, which would not be hard to do, but there are about twenty troops on the roof at all times too."

"Make sure the Chinese know I want both the gun and soldiers on the roof taken out. I don't expect all the soldiers to be killed, but if they can knock out most of them, it will make it much easier for us to enter and leave the building." I said.

Picking up another image, Eller asked, "What is this you have circled in red near the fence?"

"Like other sections of the fence line, there are pillboxes constructed at different intervals. Most are armed with heavy machine-guns, but some may have anti-tank missiles or rockets. I suspect, from the thin shadows on the ground from the barrels, most are machine-guns. Your best weapon against them will be your flamethrowers. I'd suggest you place them behind the turrets of your tanks."

"Anything else?" I asked, and just didn't see much until I looked at a circled object, and then it stood out clearly.

"There are trenches that connect to all the pillboxes, most likely dug by a backhoe, and that is so if attacked, survivors can retreat to another pillbox, or it will allow more ammunition to be safely brought to the fighting positions. The Japanese did the same thing on many of the islands we invaded during World War Two."

Eller looked the images over in his hands and then said, "I think you'll have one hell of a fight just to reach the brig, so I'm very uncertain if you can remove those two men safely. If the Russians suspect any rescue attempt, they could rig the facility with explosives. The explosive could be either a time delay and explode if you don't punch in the proper code, command detonated, or maybe both."

"It goes down tonight, so I don't have time to play the "what if "game. If it blows, it may just keep us from having to kill them."

"I see. Best of luck to all of you then, because there must be 10,000 Russians on the Fort, and only a company of us. One hundred to one is not good odds."

I laughed and replied, "It's what we in the infantry call a target rich environment."

Carol gave me a kiss on the cheek and said, "Don't try to be brave and pull a John Wayne stunt tonight. Do what needs done then get the hell out of there."

"I feel it's sort of like the Alamo, but in reverse." I said, and then laughed.

Sergeant Parsons entered, glared at Carol standing close to me, and I know she saw her arm around my waist. I didn't care, honestly. I loved the woman standing beside me.

"Sir, Headquarters called on the radio, and will fake two other attacks on the fort while you will be the only serious attempt. They will attack at 0001 on the dot."

"I'm glad to hear that, because it'll take some pressure off me and my people."

"Good, let me walk you back to the office." Carol said to me.

"Sure." I said, and then kissed her cheek.

When I gave Carol the kiss, Parsons turned red and the glare returned. I knew she was jealous, but I loved the woman I was kissing.

At 2350, my group was as close to the wire as we could get. The tanks were still a half a mile back, motors running, and ready to strike the fences. They'd move for the fences at 2356 and just drive right over them. They'd knock out any pillboxes we encountered and we'd follow the tanks to the brig.
Minutes later the big brutes came out of the trees, moving at the fences at about thirty miles an hour. The fences didn't even slow the big tanks down.

At that point, Chinese bombers, unseen by us, began bombing the fort. I suspect thousands of bombs were falling and most were 500 pound bombs too, from the explosions I saw. Suddenly, a fast moving jet, at less than 500 feet up, zoomed over us with his machine-gun bullets striking the roof of the brig. As he pulled up, a missile fired from the ground, taking the aircraft in a wing. The jet wobbled a bit, but was able to move to a higher altitude where he began smoking. I knew the pilot needed to eject, but I also knew he didn't want to come down in the Fort. He'd have a better chance of survival for every minute he moved away from his target. The last I saw of the airplane, he was in flames moving fast at about 2,000 feet.

We moved in behind the tanks, walking in the treads to avoid mines. The tank destroyed a pillbox, but when cannon fire failed to take the next bunker out, my flamethrower man, squatting behind the turret, squeezed a long stream of oily flames at the structure. I saw the burning jell pass into the gun slit and seconds later two men, both burning, jumped from the trench behind the pillbox and ran for safety. The machine-gun on the tank cut them both down. Now the smell of burning bodies joined the hundreds of other battlefield smells.

Bullets flew over our heads, knocked clumps of dirt ten or more feet into the air and my people began to die. Tracers laced the air, with all colors seen. If they'd not been so deadly, they would have been beautiful. I was impressed with the tanks as they stood their ground and knocked out problem area after problem area. Suddenly, there was a loud *ka-klang* and I saw the tank commander's vehicle take a missile or rocket.

The hatches opened, the commander jumped out and when the driver was half out, the tank exploded. The driver joined the turret as they both flew into the air. I knew the gunner and loader were both dead as hell. Then I saw a man with a flamethrower on his back laying behind the tank in the grasses. I assumed the blast of the explosion had knocked him off the vehicle.

A squad of Russians, obviously sent to fight us, rounded the corner of the brig and one of our tanks took most of them out with a single cannon shot. Then the machine-gun on the lower front of the tank opened fire. The Russians died in a river of blood. Dolly suddenly leaped at a figure on the ground and when I glanced at her, she had a Russian female soldier by the throat. The woman fought back hard, finally remembered her pistol and as she pulled it from her holster, I shot her in the chest. She fell back limply.

Now Chinese jets were all over the base and I heard explosions off in the distance, so Headquarters did have other assaults taking place. The main buildings on the post, at least on this side, were bombed to hell and back and many were burning. I heard a bullet miss me, strike the side of a big tank, and then zing off into space. I was getting concerned because bullets were flying in all directions. We finally reached the brig only to have a tank go up in flames, and I have no idea what happened. I could still see my man with a flamethrower behind the turret, but the whole tank, including him, was on fire. I never saw him move an inch, so maybe he'd been killed when the tank was hit.

Ledford and I shot and killed two guards near the door, blew it open with a grenade, then entered shooting. There were only two Russians inside, but one was an officer and he pulled a pistol. My Bison stitched the whole wall from left to right and the Colonel fell, two bullets taking him in the middle of the chest. Ledford shot the other man with a Russian pistol. I searched the Russian quickly, taking his pistol and ammo, as well as his brig identification card. He had no other papers.

We moved in to where the prisoners were kept and half way down the hall, I spotted two prisoners that looked Asian to me, so I shot the lock off the first door.

Entering, I asked, "Xinya? Shui?"

The man gave me a weak smile and said, "Shui!" and then pointed to himself.

I heard another shot and knew the other man had been found too. Shui had two broken limbs, his face had been beaten to hell and back, and his nails had been ripped out. Something had taken his left eye because all that remained was an ugly empty socket. I dropped my pack to the floor of the cell, picked the small man up and carried him outside, where Ledford stood packing Xinya. The attack helicopters were raising hell with the Russians and missiles filled the air.

I looked around and saw three of my tanks in flames, and I guessed I'd lost about ¾ of my men and women. This rescue had been costly to me and the resistance.

I saw one chopper hit, burst into flames, and the remains falling on Russians below. When it struck the ground it exploded, and a burning fuel splattered on people and buildings, bringing fire to a nice neat row of Russian buildings. People were screaming on both sides, so I blew my whistle four times, indicating we needed to leave, and now!

Both injured POWs were placed on stretchers; two men per stretcher could easily pack them, because I don't think either weighed over 90 pounds. We were soon pulling back, withdrawing to the woods outside the fort as I called the tanks. "This is Copperhead One to Iron Mike, we are pulling out of here. I repeat, retreat, and we'll see you back at camp."

Now the aircraft on the flight-line were being worked over by Chinese aircraft. By mistake, someone must have bombed or sent a missile into the fuel storage area, because a huge explosion was heard and a rolling ball of fire resembling a nuclear shaped blast developed over where fuel tanks used to stand. Most of Fort Leonard Wood was lit up as if it were full daylight.

"Copperhead, this is Base, do you read me, over."

"Go, base."

"Did you get your new car?"

"I couldn't make up my mind, base, so I bought both of them. The outsides of both are in very poor condition, but the bodies can be fixed, and one has lost a headlight."

"They can be repaired."

"Yep, and they run well."

"Let us know when you are ready to use the garage."

"Will do. Heading home now." I replied and knew, being coded, it was safe enough. If the code was broken, it was still unlikely the Russians would understand the double talk.

I hung around the downed fence long enough to see the seven surviving tanks move toward the trees and Chinese aircraft leave. As one tank backed up, it was struck by a missile and impact was low, near the treads. I watched the long treads roll from the wheels and lay on the ground behind and in front of the big beast. Hatches flew open and three of the four men made it to safety. The last man had just dropped a grenade down the hatch of his tank when the heavy vehicle was struck once again by a missile, but this time it struck the turret.

The explosion was loud, and the man on the tank disappeared in a blinding flash of light and fire. The turret lifted about three feet as flames shot out from the carriage of the tank and then the top fell back in place. It looked slightly lop-sided from before, but the tank was destroyed. Everyone ran from the fire knowing the fuel and munitions would soon blow too.

Then, out of nowhere a Russian Black Shark appeared and most of the remaining tanks fired turret mounted missiles. The ECM on the chopper was working just fine, and I was awed when the fiery chaff dispensed, spurting in all directions. The missiles all exploded and some close enough that the helicopter took some damage, but not to the weapon systems. A missile mounted on an external pod fired and another tank went up in flames. As the bird lined up to attack another tank, a Russian Rocket Propelled Grenade struck the Black Shark in the engine housing.

The aluminum cover on the engine was blown off, and the main rotor blades began to give a high pitched sound. I watched the pilot struggling with his control stick. Smoke began to come from the exhaust system, light gray at first, but then almost black. Abruptly the chopper leaned hard to the left, and the main overhead rotating blades stuck the ground. The aircraft threw pieces of the blades in all directions and every man or woman near ducked for cover. The pilot was seen still fighting the stick as the aircraft struck the ground hard, not fifty feet from the last tank destroyed. I saw the pilot reach overhead just before the crash and I suspected he was turning the power switch off to prevent a fire.

While I deeply respected this pilot and his weapons system operator (WSO), they were extremely dangerous to me and the resistance. I raised my Bison and placed the bullets from one magazine into both in the cockpits. Some would call what I did murder, but as far as I was concerned, I was killing two very skilled and dangerous enemies who'd invaded my home.

I shook my head as five out of my ten tanks disengaged the enemy and moved into the trees.

I hope these Chinese men live, because we got them at a great cost in men and material, I thought as I stood looking the battlefield over.

This attack had cost me five hard to replace tanks and the lives of twenty men that crewed them. However, the Fort was in flames as far as my eyes could see, and I knew they'd lost a much larger number of men and women. I hoped most of their aircraft were gone, along with their tanks, but had no real idea how much damage had been done to the Bear.

I quickly moved into the trees and soon passed our woman on drag. I moved to the main group and found a spot in the middle, beside Parsons.

Since I no longer had my pack or a POW to carry, my return to camp was an easy one. About halfway back I took over the end of one litter and helped carry Xinya to our camp. I was worried about both men because they'd been worked over hard, and I'd not be surprised to see one or both die on us before we made it home, or shortly after.

We were about an hour from home when I saw a bright flash of light move across the horizon, and it was followed a few seconds later by a loud *crack* of thunder. I felt a slight warm breeze and then the rain came, gentle at first, but slowly increasing in force. I realized the tanks were already home and I was sure the rain would soon wash most of their deep tracks away. Unlike scenes I'd seen in old war movies, I didn't load my troops onto the back of a tank to get a ride home. The main reason was if the Russians took out the tank, I'd lose both my people and a valuable piece of armor.

We were soon back at camp. The rains came hard, with so much force I began to worry about a tornado or damage to some of our gear and equipment due to high winds. My weather guesser told me the winds were in excess of 60 MPH. I was also worried about the two men we'd rescued, because they looked no better now than when removed from their cells. I'd had them taken to our medical section and turned over to them.

After a cold shower—we never had hot water—and a shave, I changed my clothes. I walked to a tent we called the hospital. The second I entered, a Doctor Peters stood and walked to me.

"Both will live and, while they look like hell, the only serious injuries they sustained are the open compound fractures. According to what Xue told me, he was doing the translating, the Russians beat them both with a steel pipe."

"Are they taking the pain okay?"

"You could say that, since both were given morphine. They are malnourished and dehydrated, which is normal for any prisoner of war."

"Sir," Sergeant Parsons stuck her head in the tent and said, "Headquarters on the radio for you. According to them, it's an emergency call."

"We'll talk later, doc! Thanks." I said, as I ran for the communications tent.

CHAPTER 19

Romanovich was in pain as he pushed the call button for a nurse. A thin and short Captain entered and asked, "What are your needs, sir?"

"Something for my pain."

"It is too soon to give you morphine, so I can give you two pills."

"Get me a bottle of vodka, by God, and pills I will not need."

She laughed and said, "Sure, I will bring you a bottle after my lunch."

"Really? Please do not be joking with me. If you give me the drink, you can keep your morphine too. I am hurting like a sono-fabitch right now. I thought that whirlpool bath this morning would kill me as it washed away dead skin."

"If I gave you alcohol, I could lose my job."

"How many of us survived the crash?"

"I told you yesterday and the day before that, and the number is still seven."

"It is a bad way to die, but one dies quickly. I do not think I will ever trust an airplane again in this lifetime."

When the nurse left a few minutes later, Boris gave her some thought. She was a pretty woman, but not beautiful, with a well shaped and toned body. He liked the way she wore her blond hair, and the curve of her rump. He'd always had a weakness for blonde women with blue eyes, and he found all he'd ever met sexy. Maybe, just maybe, if he took the time he could get to know the Captain.

It was near noon when Georgiy showed up and was escorted into Romanovich's room by the nurse. As an officer, he was entitled to his privacy.

"Oh, Boris, you must be in bad pain. You have suffered some bad burns, my friend."

"I am alive. Did you bring me any vodka? My pain is rough at times, between shots of morphine."

Pulling his thin coat open, he pulled a new pint of vodka from an inside pocket. He handed it to his friend and said, "Take a long drink, because she was doing paperwork when I interrupted her, so she's busy."

Romanovich must have downed about half the bottle before he pulled it from his lips and said, "See if you can get me another bottle in here later this evening. I will stay drunk and worry about the hangover later."

"I heard you had been burned over 60% of your body."

"I have minor burns over all of me, but the serious burns are to the side of my face and my right leg. I have lost an eye, but at first I thought I had lost them both. I have no idea how that happened. They had spoken of taking the burned leg off and I told them, 'hell no, I'll keep it and live, or I die with it.' I have to admit, when I sit in the whirlpool and watch the dead flesh wash away from my leg, the pain is so severe at times, I wish they had cut it off."

"Lena told me you were going to live, and I just did not see how that could be."

"The devil is scared of me, and God wants me to change a great deal before he will take me." Boris laughed, but it brought him pain.

Out of nowhere, the two officers heard a series of explosions.

"I hope they did not have a plane blow up while they were working on it, because those were loud." Boris said.

The window in the hospital room suddenly exploded as a line of machine-gun bullets walked down the length of the room. The nurse ran in, only to collapse as bullets struck her in the chest and head. She was dead before she struck the floor.

A siren began to wail, and both of the men in the room knew they were under attack. Pulling Boris from the bed, ripping the monitors from his chest, and bringing his IV, Ilik moved to the basement. Boris had a fresh IV, so he could leave him because he had a battle to fight. He noticed the Major still held his bottle of vodka firmly in hand. A minute later nurses, doctors, and the wounded capable of walking were moving toward the basement as well.

"Who is this man blocking the stairs and what are the extent of his injuries?" a Colonel asked.

"He is a burn victim of the airliner crash a couple of days ago. I do not know the extent of his injuries, but his nurse is dead, and this may be the safest place for him and you. I have to go now, sir, but take good care of him, because he is my friend."

When he walked out of the hospital, Ilik was amazed by the number of fires and damage done to the Fort. For some reason, it reminded him of old footage he'd seen as a kid of the Japanese bombing of Pearl Harbor in 1941. Flames flickered and danced, and along with long columns of smoke and dust filled the air. Screams were heard, but it was difficult to tell which were screams of pain and which were screams of anger.

When he reached his unit they were all ready to go, so he led them to the area that had been breached by the tanks. He'd taken the time to grab his Bison and pack along with his belt and canteen. On his belt he had a knife, pistol, three grenade pouches and first aid kit.

Before they reached the broken fence, the radio came alive and they were ordered to a second area, this one on the western side of the base. It was completely opposite of where they were heading now.

Unexpectedly, a Chinese attack helicopter flew down low and sent a long burst of cannon fire toward them, but luckily only struck two men. One lost his head and a big part of his chest, and the other lost his left arm. The wounded man was quickly doctored up, dragged out of the way, and placed behind a huge oak log. Ilik then called in the man's position, and continued on his way.

When the fuel tanks exploded everyone dropped to the ground, some screaming that nuclear weapons were being used. A huge fireball rose in the sky from where the fuel used to be stored. Once on their feet again, Georgiy had them double time toward their assigned area.

They arrived just as the partisans came running through a gaping hole in the fence line.

Dispersing his troops, Ilik moved to the commander and reported his company had arrived to assist. The sounds of battle made it almost impossible for anyone to think clearly, because they were so loud. Bullets filled the air as screams were heard from those freshly hit, moans and yells from the injured wanting a medic, and prayers from the dying. Grenades exploded with loud booms, and overhead an air battle was taking place between the Chinese and Russians.

The Russians had less than a dozen aircraft in the air and one by one their resistance was shot down. Too quickly, the air belonged to the Red Chinese.

"Sir, if you look, you will see the aircraft are ignoring us and attacking with force on the eastern side of the Fort. This is not the main threat!" Georgiy yelled to be heard.

The Major in charge turned to speak when a stray round took him in the middle of his face and his skull exploded, splattering blood, brains and shards of skull out behind him.

The radioman handed Ilik the handset and said, "Base on the line for the commander, Captain."

"Base, Cobra One, the previous commander is dead. Be advised I am only facing infantry and no aircraft. I repeat, I am facing no aircraft." He screamed into the radio to be heard.

"You are to remain in place. We have other assets being sent east, over."

"Copy and out."

Like most battles, when it was all said and done they were bone tired, physically and mentally. The Americans pulled back slowly in a disciplined manner and were soon gone. Captain Georgiy stood, looked the area over, and realized he'd had about a dozen people in the two companies killed and maybe twice that many injured. Everyone was up and helping the wounded, and the dead were being placed together, lined up, so they'd be easier to load in the trucks that would come for them.

Some of the soldiers, not needed to treat the injured, stood and turned in complete circles seeing nothing but flames and smoke in the air. Most wore a tired expression, like someone who'd been awakened before they were fully rested. One woman stood and silently cried, while a man sat in a foxhole shaking his head from side to side, both reacting differently to being in combat.

Less than an hour later, a small convoy of six trucks brought members from the base civil engineers unit along with enough fencing to repair the broken stretch of wire. They'd brought two squads of men to provide security, and all combat troops were ordered to return to the operations center. Of course, they were to walk back.

Ilik gathered the two companies, and as a single mass of soldiers they began to move toward the more populated part of the base. Along the way they picked up the man who'd lost an arm to the helicopter and carried him on a stretcher. The other wounded in battle by the fence had been left for the civil engineers to take to the hospital. None of those left behind were critically hurt.

The walk gave them a chance to see all the damage done by the Chinese, and it was extensive. Crashed aircraft from both sides were seen near the flight-line, and the fire department was still fighting fires at a number of places. The fuel tanks were left to burn out on their own, while hospital patients were being taken to the base gymnasium and schools. All around him Ilik saw death, destruction, and fires still burning or smoking. He heard the pitiful cries of those dying and the deep soul cutting moans of the injured. With all his years in the military, he'd never experienced anything as devastating as this minute was for him. The viciousness and strength of the attack shocked him deeply, and he knew he'd relive this moment for as long as he lived. Never would his mind allow him to forget.

Back in the company area, the soldiers were dismissed, only to have Master Sergeant Danovich detail most of them to one part of the base or another helping those units in need of more people. The dead and injured had to be collected and cared for, the fires needed to be put out, and there were countless piles of brass from fired bullets as well as discarded weapons of all kinds. Georgiy knew thousands of things needed done, but his first task was to see if Lena and Boris were okay.

He had to walk by the brig on his way to the hospital, so seeing a lot of senior troops in the area, he walked near enough to hear them talking.

"Are you not the commander who brought the two Chinese in for us?" a Full Colonel asked.

"Yes, sir, I am."

"Did you know Colonel Zakhary Leonidovich was killed in this raid and both captives are gone?"

"No, sir, I was out in the field with my men and women. I am sorry to hear of his death."

"Both of the Chinese are gone too, so that was the purpose of their mission. The brig guards were murdered in cold blood, too."

This is war, and I doubt they were murdered in cold blood, Ilik thought, but said nothing to the Colonel.

"If you will excuse me, sir, I must see to my men and women receiving care at the hospital. I understand they were taken to the base gymnasium and schools after the hospital was bombed. Do you know if that is right, sir?"

"That is correct and you are dismissed, Captain."

When Georgiy saluted the Colonel, the man waved him off as if he were a fly. That irritated the Captain, but once again he kept his mouth shut. He turned and walked away, moving toward the gymnasium.

He saw Lena working and she looked like hell; he was sure she'd been through the pits this day. He approached her from behind and said, "Hello, my love, are you tired yet?"

She quickly turned, smiled and then flew into his arms. He heard her crying and wondered how much was relief and how much was fatigue. He knew she'd been working over 12 hours and probably closer to 16, but in war you worked as long as the job took.

"When do you get off?"

"In just a few minutes, but I cannot leave the building. All of us are stuck here until this emergency is over. I will be able to eat and sleep here though."

"Have you seen Boris?"

She broke eye contact with him and said, "Yes, I have seen him, but you will not find him in here or one of the schools. He was killed in the bombing, and most of those in the basement were crushed by falling concrete when the build collapsed. I am so sorry, Ilik, because I know you loved him like a brother."

"Boris, dead? But he was fine when I left him at the hospital. He cannot be dead!" The Captain's eyes blinked rapidly for a minute or so.

"Honey, he had to be dead when they pulled him from the rubble, because his chest and head were crushed. There was nothing we could do for him."

Georgiy was stunned and couldn't believe, after surviving the plane crash, Boris was killed during an air raid. *Why? What purpose would God have in saving him and then taking him?* It made no sense to him.

"Come with me, and I will get us a couple of green frogs and we can eat together. Then, if you want, we can curl up in a corner and grab some sleep." Lena said, hoping the death of Boris wouldn't change the man she loved.

"Yes," Ilik said with a forced smile, "let us do that."

Morning dawned with rain and thunder. Finally, the night before all medical personnel were released and told to report back at noon the next day. Ilik noticed just before he'd turned the light off it was 0200, so ten hours later she'd be back at work. He had to be at his job in another hour, and he'd already showered and shaved.

He was dressing in his camouflage battle dress uniform when he heard her ask, "Are you okay? I was worried about telling you of Boris, because you two were like brothers."

"I will have a drink in his memory tonight, and life goes on. If nothing else, combat has taught me about death, and while I do not fear dying, it hurts each time I lose someone special in my life. I feel like a big chunk of my heart is ripped off with each death."

"I can understand that."

"It has also taught me that each soldier lives inside their own little world and no one, except maybe a family member, lover, or wife, cares what happens in that world. By that I mean we are born alone, we live our lives alone, and we die alone. No matter how much we are loved by someone, they cannot enter our little world because there is a physical barrier. The closest we come to entering someone's world is when we make love to another, but it ends so quickly. But, I think, I really do, that during sexual orgasms, we briefly become one. We become one in body, mind, and soul. Life is pure loneliness. Often, while in a crowded room or surrounded by others laughing, they think they are having a good time, only it's the vodka talking."

"Oh, you *are* depressed this morning."

He kissed her on the tip of her nose and said, "No, not really, and I have felt this way for years. Death is as important in life as birth. How long we live, princess, is not important, but what *we do with those years* we have is very important. Take Boris; he was an excellent Sergeant, and beyond any doubt, there are many men and women alive today because he once lived. He trained his people hard, he gave them discipline, and he gave all of them pride in themselves. Now, since we all live alone inside, pride in ones self is important. We know no one better than ourselves, and just a little pride can make a big difference."

"You are talking too deep for me at this hour. I am going back to sleep."

"Sleep, baby, and I will be here when your shift finishes tonight."

Once in his office, he began to read the names of those injured and killed in the attack. When he'd walked to work this morning he'd seen many buildings, cars, trucks and aircraft smoldering and smoking. The damage was extensive. He wasn't surprised to find a four page, single spaced, typed report of the many injured and dead. He quickly found Major Boris Romanovich, and shook his head at the senselessness of this death.

We cannot win a partisan war, not if the people are on their side. Now, with the Chinese aiding them, we will never beat the Americans. I am fighting, but only to survive my tour so I can return to Russia and retire. I would love to marry Lena, but I am not sure what her parents would say about our age differences he thought as he sipped his morning tea and looked at the after action reports filed.

The tanks had been easy to follow, even from the air, but then rain washed most of the tracks away overnight. Headquarters was thinking of bringing Spetsnaz to find the main headquarters of the resistance and having them call in air strikes against the position. Then they would enter and kill everyone they found alive. The problem was, Spetsnaz was spread thin right now because they were needed everywhere.

What Lieutenant Colonel Jora Ruslanovich, Base Operations commander, wanted to do would be expensive but probably would work well, only it would be slow. He wanted to have the whole state flown over by special aircraft using infrared radar. He also insisted that more photography interpreters were needed to identify things in photos, and photos were low cost. The Russians had aircraft that could fly like a bat out of hell and take high quality photos all day long. He made the suggestions and then took a seat at a recent meeting.

Glancing at the calendar on his desk, at 1000 hours Ilik had to be at the base chapel for funeral services for Boris. He was also one of the officers that would pack his friend's coffin onto a super cargo plane to be transported home for burial.

At 0800, he went to the daily Commander's briefing called 'stand up.' If the Commander asked you a question, you stood up (thus the name) and gave him an answer. Lord help you if you did not know the answer to his questions, because an ass chewing would soon be delivered, and as you stood, too.

Most of the meeting was spent covering the damage done to the Fort, casualties, crash recovery of both Russian and Chinese aircraft, and discussing how badly the chemical attacks had done. No one would have thought that after the gas had been delivered to most of the counties around the state, thousands of partisans remained to attack the Fort. Future gas attacks were off and would not even be discussed.

Then, Olegovich asked the Fort military police, "How did the Americans gain not only access to the brig but to the prisoners as well?"

"Sir, I sent a majority of my people to assist against the attacks of which there were four attack points."

"How many men were left at the jail?"

"Five men, sir. One outside by the entrance door, one manning the desk, one mounted on a tower along the fence, one cleaning the inside of the jail cells, and a dog handler with a German shepherd walking between the two fences. Uh, but two squads remained on the roof, sir."

"Where are those men today, Major?"

"Uh, dead, sir."

"How was access gained to the building?"

"We *think* C-4 was used to enter the compound after the dog and handler were killed. Then the lone guard outside the entrance door was killed, and once inside the partisans killed the remainder of my guards and Colonel Leonidovich, head of our anti-partisan unit."

"You think? I seriously doubt you know the meaning of the word, think! *How did* they gain access to the jail, if the door was locked on the inside?"

"As I said before, sir, we do not really know. I think they used C-4 or a thermite grenade. We are currently running an analysis to see what kind of explosives were used, sir."

"No need, you fool, they got in anyway! And, if you cannot tell the difference in metal that was melted versus metal that exploded, you are useless to me. I want the jail replaced with windows and doors that cannot be blown open using traditional explosives."

"A thermite grenade can cut through steel and partisans have them, so I need to discuss the door designs with Moscow, as well as cost figures. I suspect it will not be cheap." the Commander of base supply said.

"In the meantime, I want the jail guarded 24/7 and by a platoon of your police officers."

"Sir, no one is locked up at this time."

"I did not asked you that question, did I? From now on, as long as you serve under me, the brig will be guarded well and around the clock, every day of the year. I cannot believe we lost two Chinese prisoners, and all because you sent all your folks off to fight somewhere else without orders. We have many infantry units on this Fort, Major, but only one Police Force. By rights I should fire you because I feel you are incompetent, but I honestly do not have a replacement. Sit down and think about what I have told you this morning. If I had a replacement, you would be on your way to Siberia right now." the Colonel's face was red, and it was clear to all that he was pissed.

"Yes, sir." The man quickly filled his seat.

"Now," the commander said, "we will be getting replacement aircraft, fuel, personnel and anti-aircraft systems from Moscow soon. Our priority will be in getting our aircraft in the air, then installing all the anti-aircraft systems. I want details formed from every unit on this base, except for the police, helping to get these systems installed properly. We will also have 530,000 sandbags coming, and guess what? I want them filled and placed six feet high around all buildings, every single one. When you get low on the bags contact me, and I will have another 500,000 sent to us."

The commander looked at his Master Sergeant and nodded.

"Teeeennn Huuuut!" the Sergeant yelled from the very pit of his stomach. A room full of officers sprung to attention as if shot from a cannon.

As the Colonel left, he said, "At ease, gentlemen."

"Wow, Turov, the Commander sure ate your ass alive."

"I learned in the future not to send my people to anyplace during an attack unless ordered to do so."

"Then," a thin Major said, "he will jump your ass for not thinking on your own and standing around with your thumb up your ass waiting for orders. There is no proper way to avoid an ass chewing when you are in a combat arms field and a base is destroyed like this one was."

"I have an opinion," another Major said, "but I will save it for my room over vodka. Too many brown noses in this room."

As the group started leaving the room, Ilik knew he had an hour to change into his dress uniform and get to base ops so they could pack Boris into the aircraft. Just the thought saddened him deeply.

CHAPTER 20

I was concerned about all the traffic leading to my base camp following the attack on the Fort. I realized most of the tank tracks were difficult to see from the air, but a child could follow them on the ground. All the Russians had to do was fly following the tracks and when they grew faint, put a few squads on the ground to search for us. I was considering selecting a new location and having our people split into small groups and meeting there. I'd have the tanks hold off moving for dry weather and just before a front moved in. If the ground was hard, they'd leave less of a track and if it rained shortly after they moved, the tracks would mostly be gone. I'd have them move away from this camp, and hopefully avoid the Russians until the weather cooperated with us.

"Sir, this area down by Cold Springs looks good with plenty of timber and brush. It also has clean spring fed drinking water." Sergeant Ledford said.

"Let's you and I check it out tomorrow morning, and I want to be up and walking by daylight. Take weapons, grenades, and a fanny pack with food and first aid items. I see no reason for us to hump sixty pound packs on a quick sneak and peek."

"Now, it's about a 25 mile hike overland one way and will take us some time, so we may be gone for two days and not just one."

"We'll carry a radio and rations for the two days. Now, make sure you're ready, because once I leave here, we'll not return. Remember the big three; beans, bullets, and medical supplies." I grinned.

"Yes, sir, and I'll be ready." He left the tent as Carol was walking in.

"Well, hello, this is a pleasant surprise, during duty hours too."

"I'm here for my lunch hour." She smiled and winked.

I took her into my arms, gazed deeply into her eyes, and asked, "Will you marry me? I love you, and can see no reason we can't have the Chaplain marry us." Why I did that, I have no idea, but now that I'd found her, I wanted to keep her mine.

She grinned, winked at me again, and replied, "Sure, I'll marry you, but I want the honeymoon to start now, on my lunch hour. I have some other good news too, or at least I'm excited about it."

"Oh, and what good news is that?"

"The medical folks told me I'm pregnant, so maybe getting married is a great idea, Colonel."

I was slapped with mixed emotions. I wanted a child, for sure, but what kind of life would my baby have growing up in the middle of a war? I smiled, kissed her and said, "Have you considered a name?"

"I just found out not ten minutes ago, and I'm so happy I had to rush over here to tell you the wonderful news." I saw she was crying tears of joy.

I kissed her deeply, felt her passion ignite and soon I was covered in the flames of desire as well. Soon, she was leading me to our bed.

Ledford and I were a good five miles from camp by the time the sun was in the trees. We were traveling light, with the absolute minimum for the field. He carried the radio and I carried a corpsman's first aid kit, which would allow us to treat almost any medical injury, wound, or illness. While I didn't expect to run into anyone you never knew what could happen, so it paid to be ready for anything. We each carried one NON-50 mine, grenades, and a bandoleer of bullets. If we couldn't take it out with what we had, we were in sad shape.

The area we moved over was high hills and deep valleys, made by glaciers moving over the land millions of years ago. Some of the valleys were over a mile long, and the hills were close to the same in length. Usually small rivers or streams ran at the bottom of the high cliffs and in a different time and situation I would have found the area beautiful, but now my senses were on guard. I was starting to get the feeling we were being watched, but I'd seen nothing to make me feel that way.

I suspected Ledford felt the same, because he kept turning in circles to look all around us. I too scanned the countryside, but I saw nothing out of place.

Back in the bushes, and I mean a good 15 miles from the nearest town or city, we spotted a farm house, and a farmer was up early caring for his animals and doing the countless other jobs a man had to do to survive in the country. I decided we'd Injun up on him and see if any Russians had been spotted in the last few days. Most country folks supported the resistance and I prayed this one did as well.

As he was feeding his hogs, I asked from the brush, "Seen any Russians?"

"Yep, big group passed on the back road in front of the house near daylight. I counted four deuce and half's in the bunch. Maybe 80 men, but I ain't sure. You boys hungry?"

"No, sir, we have food. Which way were they heading when you saw them?" I noticed the man was thin, like most Americans now, and he must have been in his middle or late sixties. His hair was white, eyes green, and he wore a constant smile. He was chewing tobacco, and every other minute he'd let a brown stream fly toward the grasses.

"Toward Fort Wood. See, this road will eventually lead to a back gate at the fort. Ain't many folks that know that unless they live around here, so I 'spect they have 'em a collaborator along."

"You being bothered much out here?"

"Nope, and I like it like things are. I wish you boys nothin' but the best, and iffen I were twenty years younger I'd be fightin' alongside of you. I love this country."

"Thank you for the information, sir, and may God bless you. We have to move on now."

"May He set aside a special place in heaven for our partisans that die in this awful war."

After he spoke he disappeared into the barn, and I knew he never saw either of us well. Besides, we were wearing face paint and I don't think our mothers would have recognized us. As a matter of fact, I don't remember his head turning toward us even once. Of course, as a hunter, and I was positive he was one, he'd be able to track us easily enough.

We moved back into the woods, crawled up under a huge cedar tree, and had a short talk. I could see no reason for Russians to be out here unless they were new troops coming in from Saint Louis, but why not use the main highway?

"Why are Russians on the back roads?" I asked in a whisper.

"Maybe the Russians are putting out small cells to try and sniff us out." He spoke in a very low tone, just above a whisper.

"That's always a possibility." I whispered and then added, "I have movement, listen."

We both heard the sound of material rubbing against material as someone walked near us. I knew from years of hunting and war it was their pant legs rubbing. I then heard voices in Russian and it was followed by a loud laugh. A deep commanding voice immediately stopped the laughter, and said something I didn't understand in Russian. I shivered at how close our enemies were to us.

Looking through the branches of the cedar tree, I spotted a camouflage uniform, and the soldier was wearing the blue and white striped tee of Spetsnaz and a blue beret as well. I knew then we'd been watched by Russian special forces, and they must have lost us temporarily and were looking for sign of where we went. I used hand sign to tell Ledford to remain still. Ten minutes later, they walked away.

I waited until almost dark before I left the relative safety of the tree. I slipped my NVGs on and then moved back toward the main group. I liked the area, and figured Spetsnaz was simply checking the area for partisans. Once they returned and reported this area was clean, we'd be safe enough. We'd have to keep the farmer at a distance and not move any closer than three miles from him. Since he was an older man, I didn't expect to discover him beating the bushes any time soon.

We kept our eyes open the whole trip back, moved slowly, and saw no one, but that didn't mean we weren't seen by the Russians. Spetsnaz were the very best of the excellent, and they were well trained for a variety of roles. Most spoke another language fluently, and could disassemble and reassemble just about any weapon in the world. They were fighters from way back.

We returned at about dusk, so I sent the tanks with their infrared radar out looking for our Russian friends. They were to stay out all night and be back early enough in the morning to move with the rest of us. They'd even carry the heaviest loads. My weather guesser said tomorrow during most of the day would be dry, and then heavy rains in the evening and overnight.

Carol and I shared our love and fell asleep early, knowing daylight came early. How long I'd been asleep I had no idea, but I awoke to explosions and screams.

I met Carol's eyes and said, "Spetsnaz must have reported our positions. That's artillery you hear, not bombs or missiles. Hear the loud scream as it falls to earth? Let's move, and now!"

As we ran from the tent just minutes later, I could see white phosphorus exploding in the night. The stuff was nasty, but so beautiful on a dark night, unless like in our cases it was being fired at us. We moved to the communications center where everyone was packing up to leave earlier, but now it was empty. I tossed a thermite grenade on the big radio and another on our one computer and then ran out of camp with a radio in my hands.

Others ran beside us and we scattered into the four winds. I'd given the location of our new camp to all the officers and senior Sergeants, so they'd know where we were to move. I just prayed I didn't lose most of my people overnight. After moving a mile, I turned the radio on and listened. We were wearing NVGs and everything was a normal pea green through them.

"Copperhead One, to any station." I said.

"Copperhead One, this is Bear four, over."

"Four, did anything get moved to the new location?"

"Uh, negative to my knowledge, One."

"Headquarters to Copperhead One, how do you read me, over?"

"Five by five. I may need a major resupply soon. White phosphorus was walking into my camp when I left. Artillery, and from the fort too."

"Understand, One, move to your new location and we'll LAPES some gear to you over the next few days. Headquarters, out."

I'd just taken a step on the trail when I heard a voice say, "That's far enough. Drop your guns and put your hands into the air."

"Who are you? It's me, the Colonel."

"I am glad to meet you, sir, I am Senior Sergeant Veselov Yefim Yegorovich, of Mother Russia's Spetsnaz. I am afraid you are my prisoner, Colonel. Now drop your weapons or my men will fire theirs. I assure you, this is no game."

Carol and I dropped our guns to the grass and then raised our arms over our heads.

A man moved from the brush, started checking Carol for other weapons and I heard her slap him when he checked her breasts. The man laughed and said, "Looks like the Colonel brought us some really nice entertainment for tonight, boys. We have a woman here, and she's firm too. I'll take her first, then we'll go by rank."

I shouldn't have been appalled but I was, as I asked, "You'll surely not rape her?"

I knew there were many others moving on this trail behind us, so I attempted to get a conversation going with the man to buy us time. I suspect he wanted to snatch us and be gone. However, finding Carol a woman gave him other ideas. They'd not searched me yet, and I had the .22 hush puppy in the small of my back.

"Why not? She is my prisoner and I can do with her as I please. Make too much noise, and I will have one of my men rape you too."

"Disgusting is what you are, you sonofabitch."

I heard him laugh and saw his mouth open as he did so. I pulled the .22 from my back and shot twice, not realizing one bullet struck him in the forehead and the other entered his mouth and exited near the nape of his neck. The bastard was dead before he hit the ground. Carol threw a grenade behind the Senior Sergeant and by the time it exploded we were on the ground. Bullets zipped by me and limbs fell as they were cut in two.

I grabbed my Bison and saw Carol moving for hers when the woods became a madhouse with tracers and bullets flying in all directions. Apparently some partisans had seen enough through their NVGs to get into position behind us as the Sergeant had been talking with me. Screams were heard on both sides and I'd learned years ago, screams meant nothing. Some folks screamed when they died, when wounded, when they killed an enemy, or at times just to hear their personalized war cry.

I heard the Russians moving away from us as they made an attempt to disengage my much larger group now. Finally it grew still.

"Colonel, it's me, Eller. Are you two okay?"

"I'm fine."

I heard nothing from Carol, and my heart began to race.

"Carol?" I asked.

"Green, you're the only medic we have. Move forward and check the lady." Eller said, and I knew by the tone of his voice, he suspected the worst too.

In the green light of my goggles, I watched the man move to Carol and roll her over. Her eyes were open, but they were rolled up in her head with only the whites showing. She had taken a round to the center of her chest and another to her neck. Beyond any doubt, my darling and my unborn baby were dead.

I felt my heart shatter as the medic said, "I can't help her Colonel, she's dead."

I fell to my knees on the trail, threw my head back, and screamed like a crazy man as tears ran down my cheeks. I had just lost my woman and baby in a heartbeat. I was alone again. Everyone I ever loved or even liked was dead. Would death follow me the rest of my life? I would never get to kiss Carol again, hold her, hear her laugh, see her love for me reflected in her beautiful eyes, and I'd never see my unborn child. I think I went insane for a while, and I know I put Eller in a difficult spot.

Somewhere in the back of my mind, I heard him say, "Green, give the Colonel some morphine and let's get out of here. Brown you and Ledford make a stretcher."

I took Carol's mangled and bloody head in my hands, kissed her blood stained lips and rocked back and forth as I tried to talk to her. I touched her cute little nose, ran my fingers up and down her badly soiled cheeks as Green moved to me. Eller held me still as he squatted and hugged me tight, and I felt the prick of the needle as it entered my body. Seconds later I felt the morphine entering my system. I held her in my lap and cried until my world faded into darkness.

TO BE CONTINUED IN

"AIRBORNE, BOOK 7"

OF THE

FALL OF AMERICA SERIES.

ABOUT THE AUTHOR

W.R. Benton was born on his grandfather's farm, delivered by his grandmother, near Vida, Missouri, down in the Ozark Mountains. He attended public schools in the local area and graduated from Rolla Senior High, Rolla, Missouri, in 1971. After graduation, he joined the United States Air Force and began a career that would span over 26 years. He has an Associate's Degree in Search and Rescue, Survival Operations, a Bachelors Degree in Occupational Safety and Health, and a Masters Degree in Clinical Psychology completed, except for his thesis. His first Book released was *"Silently Beats the Drum,"* and over 40 more books have followed, along with 9 Audio Editions of his work. Many of his stories are available in paperbacks as well. His book, *"War Paint,"* will soon be a feature movie.

W. R. Benton is popular among readers who love hard continuous action and adventure. As a young reader, he would often turn pages to find more excitement. So, when he turned to writing, he decided his readers should be entertained, made to think, and feel the emotions of his characters. Many readers say his work grasps them in the first paragraph and maintains their interest until the last paragraph, which is exactly what W. R. strives for when writing.

Mister Benton lives in Mississippi, with his wife, dogs, and cats, on an imaginary ranch with thousands of make-believe cows and horses.

www.wrbenton.net

www.facebook.com/wrbenton01

On a trip to the Lake Clark area of the Alaskan bush, a sudden arctic weather system forces down the small plane of Dr. Jim Wade, and his son David. Both have survived the crash, but not unscathed. Food, fire and shelter are all a priority. Following the death of his father, now it is up to David to figure out what to do next, and how to survive, on a remote Alaskan mountain—in winter!
This is a fictional story of survival, resilience and of the spirit to live. It is both authentic and accurate, having been written by a former Air Force life support survival instructor. For ages 10 and up

Both are available at Amazon and other online bookstores

Set adrift, a family of three are cast out to sea in a rubber raft, where they must find a way to conquer one terrifying tragedy after another or die in the process.

In this gripping story of survival everyone will be tested to their limits. Christian faith and hope are hallmarks of this tale that will touch your heart..